"So that's the way it's going to be."

Matt glanced at her. "Uh-huh. Unless you flip the script."

"And how would I do that?"

"Surprise me," he said, opening his arms wide. "Do something unexpected and surprise me."

Haley took the steps that put her in front of him, and stared him straight in the eye. This close, Haley could see that the shade of blue was more like a cloudless sky.

"Matt Brandon, I was truly blessed by the hymn you sang this morning. Thank you for that."

His eyes widened and darkened. And then, taking advantage of the opening she'd presented, he kissed her.

Books by Felicia Mason

Love Inspired

Sweet Accord #197

FELICIA MASON

is a motivational speaker and award-winning author. She's a two-time winner of the Waldenbooks Best-Selling Multicultural Title Award, has received awards from *Romantic Times, Affaire de Coeur,* and Midwest Fiction Writers and won the Emma Award in 2001 for her work in the bestselling anthology *Della's House of Style. Glamour* magazine readers named her first novel, *For the Love of You,* one of their all-time favorite love stories, and her novel *Rhapsody* was made into a television film.

Felicia has been a writer as long as she can remember, and loves creating characters who seem as real as your best friends. A former Sunday school teacher, she makes her home in Virginia, where she enjoys quilting, reading, traveling and listening to all types of music. She can be reached at P.O. Box 1438, Dept. LI, Yorktown, VA 23692.

SWEET ACCORD

FELICIA MASON

Published by Steeple Hill Books™

STEEPLE HILL BOOKS

Steeple
Hill™

ISBN 0-373-87204-6

SWEET ACCORD

Copyright © 2003 by Felicia L. Mason

Visit us at www.steeplehill.com

Printed in U.S.A.

Sing to the Lord a new song,
And His praise in the assembly of saints....
Let everything that has breath praise the Lord.
—*Psalms* 149:1, *Psalms* 150:6

Chapter One

Landing the job at Community Christian Church had been easy. Convincing some of the dyed-in-the-wool traditionalists that hand clapping and foot stomping wouldn't guarantee them a one-way ticket to hell was another matter entirely.

Matt knew he'd face resistance.

He just didn't expect it to come from a twenty-seven-year-old blond beauty. From across the table he watched Haley Cartwright shoot down every one of his ideas. Of course, she did it with such grace and sweetness he could almost forgive her the interference. Almost.

"When we lift our voices in song, particularly praise song," she said, "the melody should be one that would make angels weep."

Translation: That raucous noise you call music will be sung in here over my dead body. Matt had to smile. The lady had a way with words.

"I don't see anything funny about this impasse, Mr. Brandon."

"Call me Matt," he said. Again.

Everyone else had quickly done so. Well, everyone who supported him.

Tall and softly rounded, Haley Cartwright was what his grandmother would call a big-boned gal. Matt preferred to call her pretty. But right now, she was doing a fine job of frustrating him.

"And no, there's nothing funny about this." His gaze took in the other seven people at the table. "I've been hired to direct the choir. That's my job."

An arched eyebrow rose over big brown eyes. She'd apparently picked up the not at all subtle message that since he was doing his job, she should do hers.

"Many of the young people in this church are also in my Sunday school classes," she said. "To see them influenced—"

"Haley, I think Matt has a point."

All eyes turned toward the man at the head of the table who'd quietly taken in every point of the debate.

Haley's shoulders slumped at the pastor's words. Matt bit back a grin. Having an ally had its merits, especially when the ally was Cliff Baines, the shepherd of the Community Christian flock. Since Reverend Baines declared this round a draw, Matt couldn't really claim a personal victory. But he'd won and that meant an inch in his favor in the tug-of-war with Haley.

"However," Reverend Baines said.

"However?" Matt echoed.

Across the table, Haley folded her arms and glared at him, but a flare of triumph danced in her eyes.

The pastor nodded at them both. "I think a compromise is in order. Introducing some of Matt's ideas into the service will be good for us. He's right. That's why we hired him. Community Christian needs a good dose of fire every now and then."

Matt resisted the urge to poke out his tongue in a "so there" gesture at Haley.

"However, taking it slow will be better than turning the worship experience completely topsy-turvy."

"I think that's an excellent idea, Reverend Baines," piped in Mrs. Gallagher.

Eunice Gallagher, church clerk, pastor's secretary and all-around terrific lady, had been in Matt's corner from day one. If now though, after an hour's worth of wrangling, she advocated a compromise position, Matt knew enough to heed the warning.

It galled him to say it, but he offered a concession he knew would appease them. "I can jot down the lyrics of the compositions so you can review them if you'd like."

"Well, that's a terrific idea, but I don't think that—"

Reverend Baines held up a hand. "Deacon Worthington, we've been up and down this road already. And we do have other agenda items today. I don't think it's necessary to have lyrics approved by council. This is, after all, a church. And we're of one accord on the gospel."

Matt gave a huge internal sigh of relief. The last thing he wanted to do was write music by committee.

And with this committee, the church council, his chances of getting anything approved ranged from slim to none. The church council consisted of Reverend Baines, Eunice Gallagher, Haley who directed the Sunday school, the heads of the deacon and trustee boards and two at-large members of the church. As the newly hired choir director, Matt represented the newest blood on the staid council.

Not for the first time since he'd arrived in Wayside, Oregon, Matt wondered why God had led him here. He glanced at the woman across the table. Haley Cartwright couldn't be the reason. She'd been nothing but the proverbial thorn in his side from the moment he'd stepped in the door. She had apparently taken one look at him and decided she didn't like him. Granted, his look was a little on the wild side for Community Christian.

"Reverend Baines," Haley said. "If not by advance approval, how do you propose that we keep that..." She glanced at Matt and paused. "How can we ensure that the new *music* is appropriate for our services?"

"I'm glad you asked," the pastor said, a definite gleam in his eyes as he met the curious gazes of those at the table.

Matt suddenly got a really bad feeling in his stomach. He knew he wasn't going to like the plan or the proposal about to be hatched.

"A committee can do the deciding," the minister said.

Matt inwardly groaned.

Deacon Edward Worthington cleared his throat and raised his hand. "I'll volunteer."

"Thank you, Deacon," Reverend Baines said. "But I think since Matt's work with the choir and Haley's work with the young people overlap, that they should be our committee of two."

"But…" Haley sputtered.

Matt's head shot up. This was worse than he'd imagined. Couldn't Cliff see the woman had it in for him?

"What a wonderful idea," Eunice said with a clap of her hands. "You can come up with recommendations for us."

"Exactly," Reverend Baines said. "At next week's church council meeting, the two of you can make a presentation on how to best weave some new life into the service."

"But…" Haley squeaked.

"What about this Sunday?" Deacon Worthington said.

The minister rubbed his chin. He glanced between Matt and Haley. "Let's just let our new committee handle that. Now, Eunice, I understand there's a conflict between the Smith wedding and the senior citizen's monthly luncheon."

With the council onto other business, Matt took a moment to study his new partner. Scratch that; his fellow committee member. Thinking about Haley Cartwright as a partner, of any kind, would land him in nothing but trouble. She was too intense, too dedicated and too pretty by far. In other words, too much of a distraction.

Her steely dedication to her belief—that church music should sound like funeral dirges—nearly cost him the job as choir director at Community Christian. Backed by Edward Worthington and a group of traditionalists, she'd balked at every step of his interview process. Matt knew the vote to hire him had been close. And he had no doubt that Haley had led off the Nay column.

Not for a moment did Matt believe he was here by accident. The Lord had directed him to this small Oregon town for a reason. It was more than two thousand miles away from everything familiar to him. With its crisp clean air, green trees and Mayberry R.F.D. feel, Wayside was a world away from the sultry heat and humming intensity of his native New Orleans.

He didn't miss Louisiana, though. He'd left a lot of anger and disappointment in that part of the country and had no particular urge to return to it or to the person he'd been then. He knew he was exactly where he was supposed to be right now—in the will of God. But knowing he was where he was supposed to be and *liking* his current situation were two different things. Being on a committee with Haley meant he'd have to be near her, and if he'd learned nothing else in his life, he'd discovered through harsh experience that he didn't need to be that close to temptation.

"We're agreed then, Matt?"

He blinked. Seven sets of eyes stared at him. "Yes?"

"Then you do approve?" Haley said.

If Haley approved he probably didn't. His eyes narrowed. He'd been caught woolgathering. "Excuse me, I think I missed something."

Deacon Worthington harrumphed. Eunice filled in the gaps: The Wayside Revelers, a local social group, couldn't find a place to hold their annual fund-raiser and requested the use of Community Christian's big room.

Annabelle Lancaster, one of the at-large council members, twittered. "I know our small-town ways are different for you, Matt. But even you surely couldn't approve of a dance being held in the fellowship hall."

He didn't.

"It took five police officers to break up the melee at their event last year," Annabelle said. "They're banned from the VFW hall. Tore the place up, they did."

Matt quickly provided his perspective. The request was denied, then mercifully the meeting wrapped up.

As the other council members left the classroom they used for their meetings, Reverend Baines asked Haley and Matt to wait. They remained behind while the minister finished talking with Annabelle.

Haley shifted the file folders in her arms. Matt stayed in his seat. He leaned back, crossed his feet at the ankles and tucked his hands behind his head. He took a moment to study her. Her blond hair came to her shoulders; he couldn't tell if the crimped curls were a natural gift or the effect of a salon. Today it was pulled together with a clip and left hanging in the back. Her skin glowed with the health and vitality that only came from clean living. But her eyes, a deep chocolate brown, and her smile arrested him.

In the time since he'd been hired at Community Christian he'd had the opportunity to see her eyes flash with anger, frustration and mischief. The latter, of course, not directed his way. He just got the glares. But that, he knew, was a good thing. Though she sported no ring, she'd seemed the hearth-and-home type, all-American, apple pie and lots of kids at her feet. He'd already found out that she wasn't married, so a boyfriend or fiancé who'd give her all her heart desired had to be lurking somewhere. Matt just hadn't met the paragon yet.

"Didn't your mother teach you it's not polite to stare?"

A slow grin lifted the corners of his mouth. "As a matter of fact, she didn't. She died when I was two."

Haley's mouth dropped open, mortification filled the eyes he'd just been admiring. She came around the table and reached for his hand. "I'm so sorry," she said gently pressing her hand to his. "I didn't mean to be snippish or rude. I didn't know."

In the face of her genuine regret and concern, he was sorry he'd been so blunt. She truly looked contrite and sympathetic, as if she hurt for his loss, even though he'd been too young to understand it at the time.

"Matt, we've gotten off..."

"Ah, there you are," Cliff said. "Thanks for waiting."

Haley dropped her hand and clutched her folders. Matt wondered what she'd been about to say. It had almost sounded like the beginning of an apology, an olive branch offered. In a way, he was sorry the minister had intervened at that moment. Matt found it curious that mention of a deceased parent had triggered a turnaround in Haley's attitude toward him.

"I know you two don't get along very well," the minister said. "That's one of the reasons I put you together to come up with a compromise. You'll find common ground. I know you both have very strong opinions about this, and I know you also have the best interests of the church at heart."

"Thank you, Reverend. I won't betray that trust."

Matt cut a glance at her. "Neither will I. We'll work out our differences. One way or another," he added in a barely audible mutter.

Haley's quick intake of breath told him she'd heard though.

"Excellent." The minister patted Matt on the shoulder and did the same as he passed by Haley. "Have a good day."

Matt looked at Haley. The day had been just fine until he'd been tasked to spend time with her. As long as he remained focused on his ministry, though, everything would be fine. Just fine.

"I'm sorry about what I said," she told him. "I didn't know about your mother."

He shrugged, then gathered his own papers before standing. "Not a problem. Look, when's a good time for us to meet? The sooner we get this over with, the faster we'll be done with each other."

"Our task is very important, Mr. Brandon."

He sighed. "Call me Matt."

"You make light of it, but we can't have tambourines and guitars in service. I can understand if it were during some sort of special program, but not in the regular service.''

''Too much like having fun in church?''

''Yes!''

His eyes speared hers. ''Then we really have a ways to go before we reach a compromise on this committee,'' he said. ''The God I serve says make a joyful noise. Do you even know how?''

He walked out of the room before she sent a scathing reply his way.

Haley seethed.

''He's the most conceited, self-absorbed, egotistical lout I've ever had the misfortune of meeting.''

''Lout?'' Haley's cousin Amber grinned. ''Now that's a word you don't hear very often.''

''Whose side are you on?'' Haley said as she snatched a saucepan from a cabinet in Amber Montgomery's tiny but well-appointed kitchen and banged it on the counter.

Amber winced. ''I think I'm on the side of those very expensive pots and pans you're slamming all over the place. Those are my work instruments, you know.''

''Sorry,'' Haley said. Amber was such a terrific cook that she carved a living at it.

Amber put down the knife she'd been using to chop celery and took the saucepan from Haley's hands. ''Why don't you sit down? I'll finish this.'' She drew a bit of water, put the pan on a burner, then returned to a waiting pile of fresh broccoli and grated carrots.

Haley stomped through the small kitchen and

plopped into a chair at the drop-leaf table Amber used as both eating surface and desk in her studio apartment.

"He sounds like a dreamboat."

"You're taking his side again."

Amber adjusted the flame, then dumped all of the chopped veggies in the saucepan with the now boiling water. After a quick blanching they'd go into the salad.

"Well, from what I remember, the Bible does say something about making noise in church."

One of Haley's missions in life was to get her cousin back to church. She couldn't make the faith decision for Amber, but she could try to get her back to a place where she'd be exposed to the Word.

"Come with me Sunday, you'll see."

Amber glanced up. "Nice try. But I'm running in a 5K in Portland on Sunday. *You* should come with *me*. You hardly ever go into the city. We could have brunch and then stop at Powell's."

Haley considered for a moment, the bookstore a temptation. "No. This situation with Matt Brandon is tenuous enough. If I'm not there, Lord only knows what he'll do."

"So, when's your date with him?"

Haley leveled a heated look at her cousin. "It's not a date. It's a committee meeting."

"Yeah, whatever," Amber said as she nibbled around a leftover carrot. "I think you object too much. You haven't even heard any of his music."

"I heard what he played during his interview and believe me it's not at all church music."

Amber shrugged. "Maybe your definition of church music is too narrow."

That offhand comment stayed with Haley throughout the evening. As she readied for bed that night she wondered if she was being overly critical without giving Matt Brandon a fair hearing. It didn't sit well with her at all that she had to question herself. If nothing else, Haley had a reputation for being fair, scrupulously so.

So, she reasoned, her visceral objections sprang from elsewhere. Too bad her friend Kara Spencer was out of town. As a therapist, Kara would have some definite ideas about this. Most likely the attraction she'd felt when she'd touched his arm, the awareness she'd been trying to feign indifference toward from the moment she'd laid eyes on him. Not since Timothy had she been so aware of a man's presence.

"And look where *that* got you," she muttered.

Matt and Timothy were nothing at all alike. She and her ex-fiancé, both tall blondes, had been the golden couple in Wayside. Timothy, an up-and-comer at the town's branch of Portland's largest bank, was perfection and propriety—which made them a matched set. Matt on the other hand put her in mind of James Dean in his rebel without a cause persona. Where Timothy had been solicitous of her opinions and feelings, Matt's attitude in the church council meetings put her teeth on edge. She'd seen every one of the weary sighs and rolling eyes that he thought he'd hidden so well.

Of course, to have noticed those things, she had to have been studying him pretty intently. She told herself it was the welfare of the church and the integrity of the council's mission that had her watching his every move. The fact that he carried himself with an easy confidence that was both appealing and refreshing had nothing to do with it. Neither, she told herself, did the fact that when he smiled, tiny laugh lines at his eyes made her want to smile in return.

But watching him in a meeting and working with him on a committee of two were entirely different issues. In the meetings at church, she could hide her feelings behind the shield of the others present. In a one-on-one situation, she had no protection—not that she feared for her physical safety around him. Sparks seemed to fly whenever they were together, and those sparks could prove dangerous to her on a variety of levels.

"And so you're stuck," she muttered.

Reverend Baines was determined to have them together on this committee. Realizing it was futile to hope that the pastor might offer another solution to the music issue, her prayer that night was for tolerance and understanding. She ignored the other part of her problem, the awareness of Matt Brandon, an awareness that left her in a decidedly uncharitable mood.

The next afternoon, Haley struggled with a box jammed to overflowing with colorful cutouts and posters. As usual, she'd been the last teacher at Wayside Prep to clear out her room for the summer. Thank goodness, this was the last load. She'd store everything in her garage until she had time to sort through it all and figure out what she wanted to keep for the new group of fourth-graders she'd greet in the fall.

She fumbled for car keys that tangled somewhere under the box.

"Here, I'll lend you a hand."

Haley yelped and dropped the box—straight onto Matt's foot.

"Ow." He hopped out of the way, too late to protect his toes, though.

"What are you doing creeping up on me like that?"

Even as she said the words and her heartbeat slowed down, her mind registered running shoes, jeans, white T-shirt and a sport jacket, the same uniform she'd seen him in the day before. And the same objectionable thin gold hoop remained in his left ear. "And what are you doing here?"

"I came by so we can have our meeting."

She reached for fallen posterboard apples and egg crate lions, remnants of the bulletin boards she'd designed and created that year. Their hands met when both sought the same fruit cutout. Heat raced through Haley. Rather than maintain even that minimal physical contact, she surrendered the cutout to Matt.

While he appeared nonplussed, she found herself totally flushed and flustered. "H-How did you know where to find me?"

"Eunice told me you were probably here. I thought you'd be at the church so I went there first."

"Oh." She couldn't think of anything else to say. Jamming her key in the latch of her Honda, she unlocked the trunk and turned to get the box. She crashed into it and Matt instead. Again the box tumbled to the ground, this time most of its contents scattering.

"What are you doing?" she snapped at him.

"I thought I was helping you. Since that doesn't seem to be the case, why don't I just leave? Meet me at the church at six and we'll go over some things."

Haley lost her patience and her temper. "You're just going to walk away? You destroy my bulletin board material and you're leaving."

He turned to face her. "Look, lady. What do you want?"

At the tone and the words, she stood tall and proud, ready for battle. Her fierce positioning must have convinced him she didn't cower to anyone, least of all an upstart choir director. Without a word he bent down and started filling up the box.

Careful to put lots of space between them, they picked up the assorted decorations that during the school year illustrated the parts of speech and new vocabulary words.

"You just make me so...ugh!" She shook her head, apparently unable to think of a despicable enough word.

"The feeling's mutual."

They completed the rest of their task in silence, though Matt paused every now and then to read the words and descriptions on some of the illustrations. He handed her a piece of white construction paper with a blue sailboat drawn on it. "So, you're an English teacher."

"Language arts."

"Why don't you like me?"

She opened her mouth, but no words came. Haley swallowed, glanced away and then tried to meet his direct gaze. "Excuse me?"

He shoved his hands in his pockets. "You've hardly rolled out the red carpet to make me feel welcome here. Do I look like a boyfriend who dumped you or is it just the music you hate?"

Haley found herself flustered. She'd never met a man who was so straight to the point.

"I—I don't know what you're talking about. I don't hate anyone or anything."

"You've made no secret about what you think of me. I was just wondering why."

"Mr. Brandon."

"Call me Matt."

She ignored that. But she did decide to level with him. It was the right thing to do. She could be honest with him without revealing that it wasn't just the style of music he preferred that disturbed her.

"I joined Community Christian because it was a small conservative church with traditional values and services. If I had wanted to be affiliated with a congregation that had rock bands, hip-hop artists and jazz ensembles as part of the so-called worship experience, I would have joined one of the churches in town that feature that sort of…" She waved a hand as she floundered for an acceptable word. "Sound," she finally said.

"So if you expect me to turn cartwheels down the center aisle because you're here, I'm sorry. That's just not going to happen."

She lifted the box, placed it in the trunk next to several other boxes and closed the hatch with a hearty thwack.

He glanced at the trunk. "Something tells me you were wishing that was my head."

She ignored that, too, and resisted the smile that threatened.

"There's no way we're going to be able to work together."

He nodded. "Yeah. It's looking like that. But listen," he said, reaching for her arm when she would have walked away. "We can work this out."

His thumb grazed her skin, but whether deliberately or as a result of him simply touching her as she pulled away, Haley couldn't say. Frissons of something very like pleasure raced through her, causing her to catch her breath and feel even more wary of him.

"Let me go, please."

Instantly, he dropped his hand and stepped away from her. She saw something flash in his eyes, but it was gone before she could determine if it'd been anger or something else entirely.

He reached in his jacket pocket, pulled out an envelope and handed it to her. "When you decide to stop playing games and being Miss Holier Than Thou, call me," he said.

Haley watched him walk to a motorcycle parked not far away. He slipped a helmet on and a moment later the bike's engine revved and he peeled out of the school parking lot.

Instead of being angry, she found herself even more curious about him.

She tore open the envelope he'd given her and pulled out two sheets of paper. The first was the order of worship for the Sunday morning service with two songs penned in where traditional hymns were normally sung. The other held lyrics to a song labeled "Acceptable."

Standing in the parking lot, Haley read the words of the poem, a praise song about Jesus's love and sacrifice. By the time she finished reading, her eyes were filled with wonder and with moisture that she furiously blinked away.

Surely he hadn't written such an emotional song. But there, at the top of the page, under the title was "By Matt B."

"Where is Mr. Brandon?" Haley asked Eunice. She had to find him. She'd gotten her emotions in check by the time she arrived at the church. The pages, though, remained clutched in her hand.

"I thought he was with you. I sent him over to the school when he came here looking for you."

"He found me, but he left. Is there another way to reach him?"

"Sure, Haley," Eunice said as she reached for the Rolodex on her desk.

For a moment, Haley thought she detected the hint of a sly smile at Eunice's mouth. But in a flash it was gone.

Eunice plucked out a card. "He's staying in the Amends House over on Grove Street. You know, the one they rent out. Here's the phone number."

Haley glanced at the card and then at Mrs. Gallagher who *was* smiling this time. "No. Thank you, though. I'll just go over there." She held up the pages. "We, uh, need to go over this."

"Sure thing, Haley."

It wasn't until she stood on his front porch rapping with the brass knocker that she realized just what she was doing. The words to the song had touched her so deeply, moved her so completely that she wanted to hear the music, had to know if it sounded as emotionally gripping as the lyrics. For a moment, she wondered if Matt had really written the song. He'd claimed to be something of a songwriter when he'd interviewed. It just seemed so incongruous that a man who wore jeans and an earring and drove a motorcycle would or could compose such stirring lyrics.

No one answered her repeated raps on the door. Dejected, she turned away and went down the three wide steps. She sat on the middle one and opened the paper again to read the poem.

"So what did you think?"

She started and clutched her heart, the envelope and papers crumpled in her hands. Matt stood not six feet in front of her. She hadn't even heard him approach.

"Do you always sneak up on people?"

Two brown paper bags of groceries filled his arms. "Since I live here, I'd hardly sneak up on my own house. What are *you* doing here?"

It took a moment for her heart to stop its accelerated beat. Twice now he'd caught her unawares. It wouldn't happen again. "Is this one of the songs you plan for the choir to sing Sunday?"

"No," he said, stepping around her and going up the steps. "It's one I was going to sing. If, of course, it meets with your approval."

His sarcasm wasn't lost on her. Haley didn't quite know what came over her when he was around. Matt seemed to bring out the worst in her.

"It's a beautiful piece."

Not saying anything at all, he stared at her a moment. Then he murmured a quiet "Thank you" as he hoisted a bag on his hip and jostled for his keys. Haley wondered at his quiet intensity and then the soft-spoken words of thanks. What had he been thinking?

He managed to open the door.

"I'll get that," Haley said. She plucked the second bag from his arms and followed him inside.

"Thanks. The kitchen is this way." The Amends House, named so because old Mr. Anderson built it for his wife to make amends for running off to the war, had been a landmark in Wayside for many years. These days, Mr. Anderson's grandson used it for long-term rentals.

The sprawling house, twice the size of Haley's small rancher, seemed quite a lot for a single guy like Matt. Maybe it was all that had been available for rent. Or maybe he had a wife and lots of children somewhere who would soon fill the many rooms. Would they be joining him when he got settled?

Haley trailed behind him through a dimly lit living room and dining room into the kitchen. Here, late-afternoon light streamed in through windows at the sink and a sliding glass door that opened onto a large deck.

"I didn't know they'd built a deck."

"You know the Andersons?"

She nodded. "They go to First Baptist. I taught their oldest boy two years ago."

"So you've lived here all your life?"

Haley didn't particularly want to talk about her life. She'd come here to discuss his music. Besides, she didn't even like talking about herself; she much rather preferred drawing others out of their shells.

"Long enough to know a lot of people," she told him. "Living in town and teaching helps a lot."

She placed his second bag of groceries on the counter. "It looks like you're settling in well."

Matt glanced at her, but didn't say anything about her attempt to change the subject as he began to unload groceries. Haley noticed lots of red meat and fresh vegetables, including a couple of varieties she didn't immediately recognize.

"You cook?"

"I grill. It's a guy thing."

A smile tipped her mouth.

"You're very pretty when you smile. You should do it more often."

The smile quickly disappeared. "I didn't come here to fight," she said.

"Paying you an honest compliment means I'm picking a fight?"

Haley didn't know how to respond. Compliments from Matt made her feel vulnerable. And she definitely wasn't about to admit *that* to him. "I came to talk about this." She held up the now well and truly crumpled song sheet.

"What about it?"

"It moved me to tears."

That got his attention. Slowly he folded the paper bag. "And?"

Haley shrugged. "And I wanted you to know. I also wanted to hear the music."

It was his turn for quiet contemplation.

Haley bit her lip, wondering if she'd again said something improper or inadvertently impolite. She still felt bad about the dig she'd made at the church.

The silence grew uncomfortable, and she wished he'd say something—anything! But still he just looked at her. She tried not to squirm, but found herself unable to pull off the absolute stillness that he'd apparently perfected.

"What?" she finally asked when she couldn't stand the silence a moment longer and he didn't seem inclined to say anything at all.

"Have dinner with me."

Chapter Two

Haley's eyes widened, first in surprise and then in reluctant pleasure. She could think of worse ways to spend a Thursday evening. Settled in front of the television with a bowl of microwave popcorn came to mind.

She told herself curiosity about the song ''Acceptable'' made her want to take him up on the invitation. Her innate honesty, however, compelled her to acknowledge curiosity about the man himself. She'd never really been this close to anyone like him before. If Matt projected any image at all, it was that of rebel. Maybe it was the bike and the earring. And maybe it was the sense of controlled power she sensed whenever he was near. Whatever it was, she knew for certain that she'd never met anyone quite like him.

He shrugged out of the jacket and placed it over the back of a chair. She'd seen him in nothing but his casual clothes since the day of his final interview with the church council. Wondering if the suit he'd donned

for that meeting was the only one he owned, she studied him as his arms flexed when he tucked the paper
bag under the sink. Pulling out a colander, he ripped
lettuce and let cold water run over it.

When he turned to her again, her breath caught.

"So?"

More than slightly confused, and painfully aware
of her awkwardness, Haley just stared back. "So
what?"

He held up a plastic-wrapped butcher package that
contained two thick center-cut steaks. "Dinner?"

Before she could answer, the telephone rang. "Excuse me," he said as he walked across the kitchen to
an old-fashioned gossip bench. He picked up the
phone.

A moment later, a smile curved his mouth. He
glanced at her and shifted a bit so his back was to
her. He spoke in the quiet hushed tones she'd seen
her college roommate use when a boyfriend called
and said something naughty.

Haley blushed. She quickly glanced away.

Then she looked over her shoulder at him. His low
murmur and chuckle made her wish someone talked
like that with her on the telephone. But Timothy, her
first and only long-term boyfriend, had never been
one for flowery compliments or long conversation.
That was one of the reasons Haley eventually realized
it would never work between them. They had everything—and nothing—in common. A man of action,
Timothy wasted precious little time on social niceties
unless it was with a client. To Haley, that seemed so
cold. And so unfair. Over time, until he'd finally

called things off between them, she'd learned to live without.

Now, half-listening to Matt, she wondered what it might be like to have a man whisper sweet nothings to her.

Despite his dinner invitation, probably issued because he wasn't used to eating alone, Haley realized she intruded. She picked up the song sheet, smoothed out the wrinkles in the paper and tucked it in her pocket. Without disturbing his conversation, she slipped through the rooms headed toward the front door.

She'd just pushed the screen door open when he called out.

"I thought you were going to have dinner with me. You know, we have to at least put forth some sort of effort at compromise."

Haley paused.

While her mind had been running along another track entirely, Matt remained focused on their mission.

Inexplicably, Haley felt on the verge of tears, her emotions raw and on the surface. Something about Matt brought out a soul-deep longing in her while at the same time a fear of the very thing she longed for. He wasn't afraid to embrace life, while Haley preferred the comfort of things she knew best.

"I can't," she said. And then she fled.

From his door, Matt watched her leave. Something had frightened her. He glanced back in the house, not sure what it could have been. He finished the conversation with his grandmother, apologizing for keeping her waiting, then, unfortunately, turned his attention to an evening meal for one.

After grilling steak and vegetables for dinner, he spent the rest of the evening in the room he'd been using as a makeshift studio. Upstairs, it had the best light and a decent view of the town square. If he stood just so, he could see the gazebo where, he assumed, bands played during the summer. That's the sort of small-town activity he'd seen on television. And Wayside, at least its downtown area, looked and felt as if it had been towed straight out of a studio back lot.

Matt had been in Wayside for all of two weeks. He'd been in Oregon, though, for several months. He loved Portland and took every moment he could get to go into the city for books, good coffee and record stores with extensive gospel selections. He liked large cities because a person could be as anonymous as he wanted to be. And for a long time now, Matt had reveled in anonymity.

Lord, why did you lead me here? He'd been praying the same prayer, asking the same question...and inevitably getting the same response. Silence.

But Wayside had called to him. And long ago Matt had learned to listen to the still, small voice inside him. The one time he hadn't had cost him everything. That had been three years ago, time enough to do penance, time enough to reflect on how he should have handled the situation with Melanie.

Sitting at his favorite keyboard, his fingers moved over the keys and he sang of lost youth and innocence, of finding the way home, of being a prodigal son. As it had so many times before, time passed without his being aware of it. When he looked up, it was because shadows chased across the room as evening fell.

Matt prayed. There were a lot of things he could have asked for, including a return to the public glory and adoration he'd thrived on. Even after three years, a part of him still yearned for all he'd lost. But he had a different life now. He'd been given a clean slate and a new beginning.

Grateful for that gift, one he knew he didn't deserve, his prayer was one of thanksgiving and praise.

Friday dawned misty and cool in Wayside. The rain, as much a part of the environment as the community's hospitality to newcomers, always took Matt by surprise. His hometown was renowned the world over for embracing strangers, but it had been a long time since he'd actually lived in New Orleans, the place he called home.

"Have a good morning," the town baker called as Matt left with a dozen mixed doughnuts. He'd never tell his grandmother, but these doughnuts rivaled her beignets.

"You, too," he said with a wave.

He'd traded in his red BMW for a four-wheel drive SUV before starting his cross-country trek to Oregon. In the rain today, the truck made much more sense than the motorcycle he usually drove.

As he headed toward Community Christian, he took in the small shops and businesses along Main

Street. The town boasted sixteen churches, a synagogue and two temples.

A small, private college lent the town an additional appeal, but with students gone for the summer, Wayside apparently didn't offer much open beyond nine at night. In the daytime though, people were out and about, another fact that always seemed to take him by surprise.

He sure wouldn't have picked it himself, but Wayside was as good a place as any he might choose to completely start over. As he pulled into the parking lot at Community Christian, Matt's thoughts turned to the ever perplexing Haley Cartwright. Without a doubt he knew he was attracted to her. Was that why she was so skittish, sometimes hostile toward him? Did he emit "I'm trouble" vibes?

Since he didn't see her white Honda, Matt figured it a safe bet that he'd have a quiet morning. Today was the first rehearsal he'd have with the choir. Until that gathering at three, he planned to further familiarize himself with the church's big pipe organ.

"Good morning, Eunice," he said. Hoisting the doughnut bag high, he added, "I brought a treat."

"I just put a pot of coffee on," she said. "I'll get us some cups."

Before long, they sat in Eunice's office enjoying the late-morning repast. She'd taken a fresh cup of coffee and two jelly doughnuts in to Reverend Baines, who was working on his sermon.

"So, what do you think of Wayside so far?"

Matt smiled. "I was just comparing it to New Orleans on the drive over here."

"It must be exciting to be from somewhere as famous as New Orleans. Me, I've never been beyond Portland."

"There's a great big world out there," Matt said. "Have you ever dreamed of seeing it?"

Eunice waved a hand. "Heavens, no. All that I've ever wanted or needed is right here. All my family is here. And I have good friends and a wonderful church family. No, I leave the traveling to you young people."

He chuckled as he sipped his coffee. He very much wanted to ask Eunice about Haley, but thinking of an opening that wouldn't seem contrived escaped him. As it turned out, he need not have worried.

"So, have you and Haley come up with a plan yet?" He detected a definite twinkle in her eyes when she asked the question.

"Not exactly. Did you have a suggestion?"

"Haley's a good girl. And even though she's a stickler for rules, we love her dearly. She's been hurt. So kid gloves are a good idea. She needs someone who will cherish her."

Matt cleared his throat. "I was talking about a suggestion on the music."

She looked at him and winked. "I know. But I thought you might want to know the other, too."

Wisely, Matt held his tongue. He finished off a doughnut and excused himself. "I'm going to the sanctuary to practice on the organ."

"All right," Eunice said. "And Matt."

At the door, he turned to face her. "Yes?"

"She's allergic to roses, but she loves lilies."

"I'll keep that in mind."

* * *

Haley overslept. She'd planned to clean her closet and do some baking Friday morning. While she couldn't claim to be a gourmet chef like Amber, she was hardly a slouch in the kitchen. But a restless night filled with shadow dreams left her tired and a bit cranky. Bagging her plans for the early part of the day, she decided on a little gardening. A peek outside, though, squelched that plan. Right now, the rain, which would undoubtedly clear up later, fell as gray and blah as she felt.

The telephone rang before she made a decision to just fling the sheet over her head and go back to sleep.

"Good morning, dear," Eunice's cheery voice rang through the line.

Running a hand through her hair, Haley sat up in bed. "Hello."

"Oh, my. I hope I didn't wake you. It is after ten."

"That's all right." She'd truly planned to be up at eight-thirty. "What can I do for you?"

"The vacation Bible school supplies arrived. The UPS driver just delivered them. I thought you'd want to know."

That news cheered her up. "Thanks so much. I'll come down this afternoon."

"I'll be here. Ta-ta."

Chuckling at the breezy way Eunice always signed off, Haley got up. She made quick work of showering and making her bed.

As Sunday school director, she was also in charge of the church's education and outreach program. Anxious to go through the materials she'd ordered, Haley dressed in chinos and a cotton top. She pulled her hair back into a ponytail and donned a pair of sandals. An omelette, toast and tea would provide sustenance until dinner.

A few hours later after running a few errands in town, she pulled into the parking lot at Community Christian Church where she saw several cars, but no sign of Matt's motorcycle. Not willing to peer too closely to see if she cared one way or the other, Haley locked her car and went into the church.

Figuring that Eunice probably had the supply boxes put in her classroom, Haley headed there. And sure enough there they were.

The summer program would be a lot of fun for the children and the teenagers. With ready-made handouts and activities for the youth from the religious-supply company, Haley would spend more time developing the program for adults. But right now, she'd enjoy going through all of the colorful fliers and banners and books for the kids.

She was so caught up in her work, she didn't notice Matt at the door looking in. He took the opportunity to study her. In the casual clothes, she looked a lot like the teens she worked with. Matt had often wondered how she'd appear in a different environment. And now, while still at the church, she'd clearly abandoned her prim-and-proper pumps and pearls for more comfortable clothes.

She hummed as she worked, and Matt smiled at the off-key melody.

Had they met under different circumstances they

might have been friends, maybe even something more. But that didn't seem possible, let alone likely. She'd made it pretty clear what she thought about him and his work. Yet, much like a moth flirting with a flame that would eventually consume it, Matt found himself compelled to get to know her better, to break down the defenses she'd built around herself.

Since he didn't want to again be accused of sneaking up on her, he cleared his throat and rapped his knuckles on the open door.

"Excuse me. Haley?"

She glanced up, a smile on her face. When she saw it was him, though, the smile faded. "Hello, Mr. Brandon."

"Call me Matt. Please."

She took a breath and put down a packet of promotional fliers. "What can I do for you?"

"I told Eunice you were okay with the plan for Sunday," Matt said.

"But I'm not okay with it," she said, putting air quotes around *okay*.

"Haley, this is the day she does the bulletin for Sunday. I gave you my changes yesterday. When you didn't voice any objections, which, I might add, I appreciated, I told Eunice everything was fine for Sunday."

"But everything isn't fine. We haven't discussed anything."

Matt folded his arms. "She's at the printer's right now getting copies made."

Haley wanted to cry out in frustration. But Matt couldn't be faulted here. She'd gotten so caught up in feeling sorry for herself last night that she'd run off without resolving the issue between them. "Well, we still have to come up with long-term recommendations for next week's council meeting. I'm free now. I was just finishing up with some vacation Bible school inventory."

"Sorry. I have plans." He smiled and Haley remembered the quiet conversation he'd had the previous evening. A date? The man had just moved to town and he had a date already.

She really couldn't blame the women of Wayside. Men who looked like Matt didn't come along very often. Forbidden fruit, that's what he was.

"Hi, Matt. Hi, Haley."

They both looked up to see who stood at the open door.

"Hi there, Cindy." He sent a smile the young woman's way and the girl's face lit up. "I'll be right there."

The teen's shy smile had Haley glancing between the girl and the musician.

"Haley, we're looking forward to seeing you tomorrow," Cindy said. "You will be there, won't you?"

"Wouldn't miss it," Haley said. She'd actually been looking forward to the surprise farewell party for Eric Nguyen, an exchange student who was headed home after spending the fall term in the United States. He'd been sponsored by Community Christian Church.

Haley's gift to him was a photo album half-filled

with images of Eric and his American friends during church activities. All she had to do was wrap it.

But the party was the least of her worries right now. Matt Brandon was the problem.

He'd been here barely two weeks and if the adoring look in her eyes was any indication, Cindy Worthington was putty in his hands.

Haley's eyes narrowed. Cindy was Deacon Worthington's only grandchild. She was young, sheltered, very pretty in a china doll way and just barely eighteen.

Matt cutting a swathe through the single women in Wayside was one thing; hitting on girls at the church was another entirely. Extremely protective of her young people, Haley's hackles rose.

Could Cindy with the sweet soprano voice have been the woman he'd privately whispered to yesterday?

"I have to get going," he told Haley. "I'll see you Sunday."

Troubled, Haley watched them go. He didn't put his arm around Cindy, but he leaned down to see whatever the girl had in her hands.

Matt Brandon thought he was slick. But Haley, already on to his tricks, wouldn't let him take advantage of anyone, especially her young people who could so easily be influenced by flash, dash and a sexy smile. Haley knew from painful experience that that potentially lethal combination led to nothing but heartache.

She'd have a talk with Cindy after Sunday school and then, depending on the outcome of that conversation, she'd voice her concerns to Reverend Baines.

And in the meantime, she'd ignore the stab of jealousy that arced through her and focus on what was really important.

The party was in full swing when Matt arrived at the home of Cliff and Nancy Baines. He'd been invited earlier in the week by Cindy and some of the choir members and hadn't planned to attend...until he'd heard Haley say she'd be there.

"Matt, I'm so glad you could come," Nancy Baines said as she ushered him into the house. "Everyone's down in the family room."

Matt could hear the laughter and conversation floating up from a nearby room.

"Food's over there. Help yourself."

He held up a small, but gaily wrapped gift. "I wasn't sure if I should bring something."

"Oh, how sweet. You didn't have to, though. You've never even met Eric. Sign the guest book, would you? We want Eric to return home with good memories of his time in Wayside. And you can put that on the table over there."

Matt found a place for the CD on a table already overflowing with presents, then wandered down into the family room, where a rousing game of charades was being played.

He grinned. Haley was right in front kneeling on the floor and yelling out answers.

"Baby. Infant."

"Rockabye baby!" somebody hollered.

The player's shoulders slumped and he started pantomiming again.

Reverend Baines joined Matt at the arched entry to the sunken room. "Hi, there. Nancy told me you'd come in." The minister pressed a glass of red punch into Matt's hand.

"Thanks. Looks like a great party."

"One for my baby!" Haley said.

The player nodded. Applause and high fives went up all around. Haley scrambled up and gave the previous player, a boy of about sixteen, a hug. As he took a seat among the twenty-five or so people gathered, Haley plucked a card from the box and read it on her way to the open area in front of the fireplace. "Oh, goodness."

"No talking, Haley."

"I know. I know. But this is hard." She furrowed her brow and then her face lit up.

Smiling, Matt relaxed against the archway and watched as Haley held up three fingers to indicate the number of words. Tonight she wore a pair of capri pants, with a long floral see-through jacket over a scooped neck top. Everyone settled down as she started the first word. She held her arms out at her sides and shook her hips from left to right. Matt's eyebrows rose.

"Aerobics," someone guessed.

"Hula hoop."

Haley gave a quick shake of her head indicating those weren't correct. She shook her hips faster.

"Hawaiian hula. A luau."

Haley slapped a hand over her head, then indicated she was starting over. She held her hands stretched out in front of her, closed her fists and turned them in opposite directions.

"Twist," Matt said softly.

"Yell it out," Reverend Baines told him.

"Not yet," Matt said as he studied her.

Haley held up three fingers telling the group she would work on the third word. She cupped her hands over her mouth and opened her mouth wide.

"Twist and shout," Matt said, this time loud enough for his voice to carry across the room.

Cliff chuckled as all eyes turned to where they stood. "Well done, Matt."

Matt accepted the applause and greetings as he made his way to the front of the room. Haley's eyes never left his.

"So, was that right?"

She licked her lips and glanced away. "Yes."

"Way to go," someone said slapping his back.

"Everybody," Reverend Baines said, "this is Matt Brandon, the new choir director at the church. I know some of you haven't met him yet."

Calls of "Hi, Matt" and "Welcome, Brother Matt" went around.

"No hug for me for guessing the right answer?" he murmured as she went by.

Her eyes widened and she gave him wide berth. She didn't take a seat back in front, but made her way to the edge of the group. Matt watched her fold her arms and watch him. His game card read "blue moon." It took a while, but he was finally able to pantomime enough for someone to guess.

The rest of the evening went by with a couple of

other games and then a video that someone put together of Eric Nguyen's adventures while in Wayside. Matt watched Haley interact with the teenagers and was impressed at her ease and their camaraderie. She'd obviously been a good choice to lead the church's youth department. Throughout the night he'd seen her making the rounds, talking with everyone, drawing the shy ones into conversation. She'd made no such friendly overtures with him.

"You've been avoiding me," he told her.

He'd stalked her to the buffet table. She paused in midreach for celery sticks.

"I've done no such thing."

"You did a great job with your turn at charades."

Haley glanced at him, but didn't address the compliment. "I didn't know you knew Eric."

"I don't."

"So you crashed a party at the pastor's house?" The censure came through loud and clear.

"I was invited."

She looked skeptical.

Matt turned his attention to the hearty spread Nancy had set out. He helped himself to some salmon then offered some to Haley.

"Thank you."

"I'm not going to bite," he said.

"Excuse me?"

He put his plate down and faced her. "Haley, you look and act as if I'm a wolf preying on your flock of lambs."

She lifted an eyebrow.

He sighed. "I'm here to do a job, Haley. We have

to work together, so we may as well get along while we do it.''

Before she could answer, Reverend Baines called for everyone to gather for a special tribute to the guest of honor.

Later when Matt looked for Haley he couldn't find her.

"Have you seen Haley?" he asked Mrs. Baines.

"She left about twenty minutes ago, Matt. She said something about a headache.''

Matt had no doubt that he'd caused it. And he was sorry he'd chased her from the party where she'd clearly been having such a good time.

Haley didn't sleep well at all that night.

"And it's all his fault," she said, petulance lacing her voice. Since she was home alone, she could get away with the whining, something she rarely indulged in and never let her students do.

She'd truly had a headache when she'd left the party. After a long soothing bubble bath, she washed down three aspirin and climbed into bed. But sleep proved to be an elusive partner. For a long time she stared at the ceiling in the darkness of her bedroom.

Even though her clock flashed that it was after eleven, her thoughts tumbled over each other in disarray that left her too keyed up to settle down. Why had Matt come to the party? She'd been having a great time until she'd heard his voice call out the answer to her pantomime. Her heart beat double time from the moment she spotted him.

She punched her pillow and turned to her side,

clutching the pillow to her body in a comforting embrace. It was bad enough that Eric Nguyen reminded her of her long-forgotten dreams. Once upon a time, she'd wanted to be a foreign missionary, working in Central America or Asia. But those dreams hadn't come true, so she'd created another life for herself and pursued other dreams right here in Wayside. Now Matt threatened the peace of mind she'd so carefully cultivated.

When she finally drifted to sleep it was on the thought that Community Christian's new choir director had been taking up an awful lot of space in her thoughts lately.

Chapter Three

Sunday morning dawned as a perfect late-spring day. The sun shone bright in Wayside, and Haley felt much better than she had the night before.

Haley took another deep breath of the fresh air and deliberately shut down thoughts of Matt, focusing instead on her Sunday morning meditation and quiet time.

By grace she had a place to call home and every day she thanked God for that. But Sundays were special. While she walked in grace and thankfulness each and every day of the week, Sunday afforded the opportunity for communal worship and fellowship. Sanctuaries had always soothed her, and the one at Community Christian never failed to fill her with such reverent peace that she always found a moment during the week to sit quietly in the presence of God. And she usually found a few minutes between Sunday school and the start of the eleven o'clock service to

meditate before the church filled with morning wor-
shippers.

She'd do it again today, too…if only Matt didn't
spoil it.

She huffed in exasperation. He was invading her
world and now he'd invaded her quiet time.

"Focus, Haley," she coached herself. She closed
her eyes, again trying to turn her attention to the
things she had to be thankful for.

"School's out," she said. That was another thing.
She loved her job, but by the time the academic year
ended, she was ready for a break.

With the official start of summer just around the
corner, today seemed even more blessed. She'd completed her fourth year teaching at Wayside Prep and
was looking forward to the full-time volunteer work
she'd begin next week. Before she knew it, her days
would be filled with activity, the sorts of things that
left her little time or energy for the pangs of loneli-
ness and longing that sometimes crept up on her.

But right now, she wasn't lonely. She couldn't be
as she basked in the joy of nature. Taking another
deep breath she filled her lungs with the clean Oregon
air before slowly exhaling. After watering her flowers,
she picked up her purse and her Bible, and with a
bounce in her step as bright as the day, she headed
to church.

That's where the day took a definite downward
turn.

"Oh, thank goodness you're here," Eunice said the
moment Haley stepped in the door.

"What's wrong?"

"Three teachers have called in."

Haley winced. "Three?" The Sunday school staff consisted of just seven teachers, including Haley. "Who?"

"Linda, Bob Thompson and Alicia Gordon."

Haley did some quick thinking. She normally taught the middle grade level. For today, she could combine Linda's elementary kids with her class. But with both the high school and young adult teachers out, that gap posed a significant problem. The first week after school let out and before family vacations kicked in usually meant a small upsurge in the number of teens at Sunday school.

"I can fill in in a pinch," Eunice offered.

"I think I'm being pinched."

Mrs. Gallagher patted her arm as they made their way down the hall toward the classrooms. "Just point me in the right direction."

"If you can take my class and Linda's, I'll handle the teens and young adults."

"Deal."

Twenty minutes later, the church bustled with the sound of laughter and talking.

Cindy came in, the hemline flounces on a bright yellow and blue sundress billowing behind her. Dainty matching sandals and a handbag completed the ensemble. Cindy looked like summer on parade. Haley couldn't help smiling.

"Do you have a moment, Cindy?"

"Sure, Haley. What's up?"

"I'm going to be filling in with your class today.

But I need to get Eunice settled with the younger kids. I'll be with you guys shortly.''

''Sure thing.''

Haley got Eunice tucked in with a Bible storybook and a game. She wouldn't have guessed that getting out of that classroom would pose the biggest obstacle.

''But I want to be with you today, Miss Cartwright.''

Haley bent low to give Amy Perkins a hug. The girl's mother had died a year ago, and Haley had been trying to fill in some of the gap. She could never replace or be Amy's mom, but Haley had more than a little experience with being a motherless child. She knew some of the fears the little girl faced.

''It'll be okay, Amy.'' She knew just the way to help Amy's insecurity while boosting the girl's independence. ''Eunice is going to have her hands full with all of the little kids today. I think she could use some help from someone who knows the ropes and can assist with prayer and offering.''

Amy's face lit up. ''I can do that.''

''Are you sure?''

With the girl's enthusiastic nod Haley steered her toward the front of the classroom, where Eunice sat in an oak rocking chair.

Breathing a sigh of relief, Haley closed the door, checked her watch then quickly made her way to the young adult classroom where the teenagers gathered.

The door was pulled to but not closed. Laughter spilled out of the classroom one moment and in the next voices raised in spirited debate.

"But the Bible doesn't say anything at all about makeup. Makeup wasn't even used back then."

"Not true," someone countered. "There was henna. And Cleopatra sure had a ton of it on."

"That was in a movie, you nitwit."

"No name-calling," a deeper voice said.

A smile tugged at her mouth. At least someone maintained order.

Haley pushed the door open. "Good morning, everyone," she called out brightly.

Her gaze scanned the group. About fifteen teens sat around the room, some of the guys more sprawled than seated. In the back, but nevertheless commanding attention, was none other than Matt Brandon. The urban cowboy pose with a booted foot in the seat of a chair and his elbow resting on bended knee wasn't at all very churchlike.

The only relief from his black slacks and a black suit jacket came from a sparkling white shirt with a banded collar. At his neck, instead of a tie, was a treble clef pin. He looked for all the world like a renegade priest on holiday.

Haley did notice that the earring she'd seen him sport all week was gone. Why was he here? If he wanted to attend Sunday school, he should have gone to one of the two adult classes.

Several of the teens greeted her, but Haley barely noticed. "What's going on?"

"We were just talking about some issues while we were waiting for you," Miguel said.

"And Reverend Matt here was telling us about a

church he was in where no one wore any makeup at all.''

"The women that is," one of the guys clarified to laughter around the room.

With so many issues thrown at her at once, Haley didn't quite know where to begin. "He's Mr. Brandon," she said addressing the easiest thing to correct.

A couple of the teens glanced at each other and shrugged.

Matt didn't say a word. But he did shift position and sit in the chair.

"Well, let's get started," Haley said. "Did you pray?"

"We were waiting for you," Cindy said.

Haley cast a glance Matt's way, but didn't say anything as the teens all gathered in a standing circle, clasped hands and bowed their heads.

"Father God," Haley began. "Thank you for this day. Thank you for the fellowship of your saints and children who have come to this house again to praise your name. Lord, as we study your word this morning, remind us to maintain a quiet dignity in your presence and to, as the Scripture dictates, keep our lives, our words and our actions in decency and in order.''

Murmured "amens" echoed around the room. When Haley looked up, Matt was looking right at her, *through* her it almost seemed. She could read neither his eyes nor his expression. When he sat down again, it was without the arrogant cockiness she'd witnessed earlier. Or was that merely an illusion, a trick of the light?

"This morning, we'll pick up your study of Psalms," Haley said. She was glad the teachers all coordinated their lessons. While she could hardly present to this older group the arts and crafts and Bible lesson she'd planned for her own class, she could easily adapt the Scriptural material to suit a discussion with the teens.

"Does anyone have a favorite?"

Cindy Worthington's hand shot up. "The Twenty-third."

Haley nodded. "A lot of people cite that one. Why do you think that is?"

The young people went around the room, each who wanted to say something taking a turn, some citing other Psalms, but most concurring that it was the soothing peace of the Twenty-third Psalm that made it so popular. When they got to Matt, Haley's breath caught as she waited to hear what he had to say.

"I'm glad you're studying the Psalms," Matt said. "As a musician, I can tell you that a lot of Christian music you hear today is based on the sacred hymns and poems of the Psalms. I have many personal favorites. One in particular is Psalms 150."

For a moment, the flutter of Bible pages turning was the only sound in the room. Then Josh stood and read aloud the short chapter, ending with "Praise him with the sounding of the trumpet, praise him with the harp and lyre, praise him with tambourine and dancing, praise him with the strings and flute, praise him with the clash of cymbals, praise him with resounding cymbals. Let everything that has breath praise the Lord."

Everyone in the room read the last line of the verse "Praise the Lord."

Haley bit the inside of her mouth. So, he wanted to play games, take their personal differences to an open playing field. That he'd use a tactic so low infuriated her. He'd already managed to ingratiate himself with the group at Eric Nguyen's going-away party. Now he thought he'd try to influence them to his way of thinking by planting ideas that would encourage them to accept his music.

Hiring this man had been a mistake. A big one. There was little she could do about it right now. But the next church council meeting would come, and in just days. Until then...

"Miss Cartwright?"

With a blink, Haley realized that a room full of teens waited for her to say something, to lead the discussion. Collecting her thoughts, she looked out at the expectant faces. "Thank you for reading, Josh. And you for sharing, Mr. Brandon. Let's talk a little about the reverence of worship."

From the corner of her eye, she saw Matt smirk. But he kept quiet during the discussion. Freewheeling, it ran the gamut from those who thought like Haley did, that worship service should be a time for quiet reflection, to a couple of teens who'd expressed an interest in the non-denominational but Pentecostal-type service held on the college campus during the year. Haley hadn't heard anything about it, but that these teenagers would be interested in fellowshipping with other young people didn't surprise her.

"Church shouldn't be boring," one of the teens said. "Why should I waste my time coming to something that's going to put me to sleep?"

"Because your mother makes you."

That got a laugh all around the room. Even Haley had to smile.

Community Christian Church had 250 members,

most of them over the age of forty. The younger families brought their children though, so the congregation had a pretty good mix of both ages and races. Haley's job as Sunday school director was to keep everyone, young and old alike, interested in the Sunday morning study of the gospel. She had some ideas about outreach efforts to draw more members to the Sunday school. But in the year she'd been in charge, the results had been mixed. Listening to the teens told her she might need to loosen up a bit and offer more activities that would appeal to them.

With just a few minutes remaining before the class ended, Haley breathed a sigh of relief that Matt hadn't challenged her again. Her relief was short-lived, though, when one of the guys turned toward Matt.

"You're the new choir director. What do you think about all of this?"

Matt leaned forward. Haley held her breath.

"I think everyone praises God in his or her own way. For some, it's quiet reverence, as Miss Cartwright puts it," he said with a nod toward Haley, who sat erect in her chair. "For others though, praise may come with a waving hand, tears, a shout of hallelujah or dancing."

"Dancing?" Cindy said.

Matt chuckled. "Not that kind. There are many Christians who believe that holy dancing is a form of divine worship and praise."

"We're out of time," Haley quickly interjected before this got out of hand.

"Oh, man," someone complained. "It was just getting good."

They said a final prayer; Haley then passed out a sheet with home Bible study suggestions and activities for the coming week and they began to disperse for the unity gathering.

Haley had smiles and hugs for the teens as they filed out of the classroom. She complimented Shannon on her new braided hair, and again thanked Josh for volunteering to read the Scripture in class and during the closing. She offered Miguel a word of encouragement as he left and overhead Jacob still talking about the end of their discussion.

"Jacob," Haley called, with the intent of answering a question he had about a scene in a movie that showed women dancing around a golden idol. But Matt touched her elbow. She knew it was him because the hair at her neck prickled with an uneasy awareness.

She whirled around, soundly closing the classroom door behind her. "How dare you?"

In the face of her anger, Matt took a step back. "Whoa, Haley. What's wrong?"

"How dare you bring something like that up in here? We're a conservative congregation, Mr. Brandon. If you think you're going to come in here and just turn things around and have people shimmying and shaking in the aisles, you're gonna be out of a job faster than you can say 'What happened?'"

"You know," he said, his voice a slow drawl. For the first time, Haley heard a bit of his Louisiana heritage in his voice. "I've typically found that the people who are most resistant to change are the ones who have the most to lose. What do you have to lose, Haley? I'm not here to take your position if that's what you're worried about."

"What I'm worried about is you putting thoughts

and ideas in those kids' heads. Things that will confuse them. This isn't a seminary. It's Sunday school.''

''Oh, well perish the thought that they might think and evaluate anything for themselves. Who died and made you gospel queen?''

Before she realized it, Haley's hand connected with his face. The slap resounded in the classroom.

He caught her hand in his, his grip strong and sure.

Mortified, Haley stared at the red imprint on his jaw. She'd never in her life hit another human being. Her mouth trembled and tears filled her eyes. But she didn't apologize.

She tried to tug her hand from his, but Matt held on, his blue eyes locked with hers.

''You try me,'' he said. His voice, while not cold, didn't hold any warmth either. An indefinable something gleamed in his eyes, though. A shiver raced through Haley.

''Let me go.''

His grip loosened a bit, but he held fast. Slowly, he turned her hand until her open palm was exposed. He bent his head, his eyes never leaving hers. And then he pressed a kiss to her hand.

''Jesus taught that we should turn the other cheek,'' he said.

He released her so quickly after that that Haley stumbled. By the time she got her bearings, the door had clicked closed behind him.

Chapter Four

He hadn't lied when he'd told her she tried him. Around Haley it seemed Matt's patience and his new-found peace was tested at every turn.

Did she do it deliberately? Or in some way was she yet another test of his faith, of his commitment to this new life he'd forged from the ashes of his disastrous past?

Today, right now as a matter of fact, his mind should have been on his formal introduction to Community Christian's full congregation. He was instead focused on the passionate blonde who sat on the right side in the fifth pew. The daggers she sent his way probably would have discouraged a lesser man. But Matt, in his day, had faced worthier and more formidable opponents. And that, unfortunately, is what Haley seemed to be...an opponent.

He still didn't know what had possessed him to place that kiss in her palm. It was there, her hand soft in his, her righteous indignation fueling the room with heat. He'd stared into her eyes and saw reflected there things she probably didn't want him to see: fear, yes, and shock that she'd actually struck him, but also longing and more than a touch of confusion.

As he waited for the cue from Reverend Baines, he wondered what made Haley so hostile toward him. Why she, one of the people he'd initially thought would be open to new ideas, so fiercely clung to tradition. She didn't even see that her outmoded ideas were sending her precious young people in search of something more in places other than the welcoming arms of Community Christian.

"This morning, it gives me great pleasure to introduce to you our new choir and music director," Reverend Baines told the congregation. The smiling minister turned to face Matt. "I think Community Christian has been blessed. We've grown so much that we now need a music *director*."

People in the congregation chuckled. "He comes to us from Portland where he's been living for a while. I think you're going to enjoy what he brings to us," Reverend Baines said. "Please join me in welcoming Matt Brandon."

Polite applause rippled through the sanctuary. On the electric piano, Matt played a few opening bars of the traditional hymn, "Holy, Holy, Holy." Then he motioned for the choir to stand. He edged the microphone closer, and made a mental note to order a headset unit.

While the choir hummed the first verse, Matt talked over them in prayer. "This morning, Father, we come before you, lifting our voices in song, our hearts in praise. You, Lord, are the holy one.''

The choir then sang that most cherished hymn of praise.

In her seat, Haley caught her breath. She'd been expecting a lot of things, but not this reverence and Matt's earnest prayer. And then his voice, solo, lifted in the second verse. The choir joined him for the last two verses, and then everyone in the congregation stood for the responsive Scripture reading.

She didn't know if the moisture in her eyes was a result of the beautiful hymn or her reaction to hitting him. Haley paid scant attention to the words printed on her bulletin. She instead prayed for forgiveness for what she'd done.

When she opened her eyes, she looked to Matt who had slipped onto the bench at the organ.

Had she been mistaken? Had she harshly and unfairly passed quick judgment without giving him the benefit of a fair hearing?

Those questions remained with her throughout the order of service, the answers elusive, darting through her consciousness much like lightning bugs in the dark of a warm summer night.

Then Matt sang the song ''Acceptable'' and Haley forgot why she'd been so worried. Not only was the organ music beautiful, the lyrics again drew her to tears. When he finished, Reverend Baines beamed and applause swept through the sanctuary as if a concert performance had just ended.

''I told you he was great. Let's give another hand to our new choir director.'' After everyone settled again, Reverend Baines glanced at his notes. "I'd like to call your attention to three special announcements in your bulletin."

Haley managed to draw her attention to her pastor and away from Matt, but not before she noticed quite a few other gazes lingering on the young and handsome choir director.

"Vacation Bible school will be starting in a couple of weeks. Haley, why don't you come up here and tell everyone about the new program you've planned?"

Her eyes widened. She hadn't prepared a speech. Talking in front of large groups, even when they were people she knew and for the most part loved, didn't come easy. The fear made little sense, Haley knew, since she stood before groups of children all the time. Adults were another matter entirely. But Reverend Baines stood at the pulpit with his arm outstretched toward her. Taking a deep breath, Haley rose. She smoothed the fabric of her purple dress across her stomach, fingered the embroidery at the collar then took a deep breath, and made her way to a small lectern in front of the congregation.

She explained about the program and the new features for adults, invited everyone to come out, then quickly made her way back to her seat. She passed the choir and felt Matt's gaze on her. When she turned to face him, her breath caught again.

He smiled at her, smiled as though there had been no sharp words between them. Smiled as though she'd never struck him.

Haley stumbled. She quickly reached out a hand to

grab the top of the nearest pew. After sitting, she clasped her hands together to halt their trembling. That's when she realized her case of nerves had little to do with speaking in front of the congregation and everything to do with the man sitting at the organ bench.

When she finally dared take a peek, she breathed a sigh of relief. His attention was elsewhere. Closing her eyes, she took a couple of deep breaths.

"The second special announcement," the pastor said, "is a reminder to everyone about Wayside Market Days coming up. I know all the ladies are busy planning their special picnic baskets. Fellas, that means it's up to us to bid on all that delicious food. Fried chicken, potato salad..." Reverend Baines turned toward the choir. "What else are you putting in yours, honey?"

Nancy Baines, sitting with the sopranos, smiled prettily. "A three-layer chocolate cake. But I think you have some competition again, Reverend."

"That's right," one of the older deacons called out. "I want some of that cake this year."

Everyone in the congregation laughed at the exchange. Each year, one of the deacons gave Reverend Baines a run for his money during the picnic basket auction. This year the bidding promised to be just as lively.

Reverend Baines stroked his chin. "Well, we'll just have to see about that." Turning to face the congregation again, he added, "Don't forget, all of the proceeds from the auction go to the library for acquisitions and for a scholarship for one of the city's young people.''

Haley always enjoyed Market Days, the town's three-day festival held mid-June every year in the town square. She'd even planned to prepare a basket this year.

"The last announcement before I take my seat is something I think you'll enjoy," the minister said. "And it has to do with our new choir director. For years we've had just one choir. On Tuesday night, there'll be an interest meeting followed by a rehearsal for people who might like to be a part of a new inspirational choir. And this is especially for the young and the young at heart. It's not a replacement choir, but a second one for Community Christian.''

Murmuring filled the sanctuary. Reverend Baines held a hand up. "That's all I'll say now," he said with a smile and a nod toward Matt. "Right?"

Matt gave him the thumbs-up sign.

Haley watched the interplay between the two men. Reverend Baines sure seemed to support Matt and his ideas. She had her doubts about this new initiative. She loved the Community Christian choir just the way it was. For the first time, Haley wished she could sing well enough to be considered for the church choir. But her talents didn't extend to carrying a tune. Nevertheless, she planned to be at that rehearsal.

After the offering collection and then a selection from the choir, Haley sat in her seat steaming, her earlier and charitable thoughts about Matt gone, drowned out with the beat generated from his electric piano.

The music, raw and nerve-wracking, jangled the calm she'd always felt in church. The toe tapping and hand clapping didn't help at all. She had no idea what Reverend Baines's message had been about. Her head pounded too much to decipher, let alone absorb, any of his words.

By the time service ended and Haley made her way to the fellowship hall, she was even more sure that she'd be at that Tuesday rehearsal. She'd be the voice of reason at the gathering. And she'd be able to keep an eye on Matt.

"Why are you afraid of me?"

She jumped at the sound of the voice in her ear. "Why are you always creeping up on me?"

"Creeping?" Matt smiled. "I'd hardly say that."

He handed her a cup of punch before she could say or do anything else.

She stared at the paper cup as if it contained liquid poison. "What's this?"

"Just a little refreshment," he said with a nod toward the ladies who manned the after-service cookies and punch table.

Haley found herself hard-pressed to hold a grudge in front of so many people.

"We still need to talk," he said. "I have a pretty busy week. Do you mind if we get together today? Maybe for dinner later."

Despite the dinner invitation, his "I just want to get this over with" went unsaid. Haley did, however, get the message loud and clear. He saw her as some sort of obstacle to be hurdled on his way toward conquering whatever he planned to conquer. If he expected Haley to be a pushover for his open smile and ingratiating attitude, he'd be in for a surprise.

"How about four o'clock? My place," he added. "You know where it is."

He didn't give her a chance to object or offer an alternative. He'd already turned to church members who tugged at his sleeve to compliment him on the morning's music and to welcome him to Community Christian.

Haley watched his back disappear into the membership as they fellowshipped after service.

"You seem troubled, Haley."

She swallowed, then plastered a sunny smile on her face as she turned to Reverend Baines. The smile didn't at all match what she felt in her heart.

"Hello, Reverend. No, I'm not troubled," she said, telling herself it wasn't *really* a lie since *troubled* barely described the extent of her discontent.

"How are the negotiations going between you and Matt?"

She cleared her throat. "Well, we haven't exactly—"

"I know you want what's best for our church. That's why I think the two of you will come to a fair and equitable compromise that will make everyone happy. This morning went well, don't you think?"

Haley wondered about his definition of the word *well*, but feeling the burden of his expectations weighing heavy on her, she nodded. "I'm sure we'll work out our differences."

"Excellent," he said, patting her arm. "Well, I'll see you at the church council meeting Wednesday."

Haley nodded and watched as he, too, disappeared into the throng. It dawned on her as she drove home, that she never seemed to be a part of the throng. Sure, she had friends at church, as well as people she liked, respected and looked up to. But she didn't have any hang-out-with friends from Community Christian. Matt had been at the church all of two weeks, and he had people, well, he had women of all ages, hanging on his every word. Haley could pretty much bet that he'd pick up a series of dinner, lunch and brunch invitations before the day was out. For some reason, that thought didn't sit well with her.

He's asked you out to dinner twice now, her conscience nipped.

That didn't count. He was just being nice.

But at four o'clock on the nose, she rapped on his front door.

It swung open and he greeted her with a smile. Feeling all the world like Little Red Riding Hood entering the cottage where the wolf waited, Haley stepped into the gloom of his living room.

"Come on back," he said. "The steaks are almost done. I figured we'd meet on the deck. Catch some sun while we talk."

Haley, still dressed in her church clothes, didn't quite know what to make of that. She hadn't come over to catch sun with him.

"Come on. Take a load off," he said, striding toward the back of the house, and apparently expecting her to meekly follow. "If I weren't renting this place completely furnished, my first order of business would be to dump everything in it and to knock out a wall that would let more light in. All of the dark, heavy furniture and drapes in here is depressing so I usually hang out outside or upstairs.''

Haley glanced around, silently agreeing with his assessment of the living room. ''You're acting awfully friendly toward someone who hasn't been very friendly to you,'' she told him.

''I'm just that kind of guy.''

Haley didn't believe that for a minute. But she also had nothing on which to compare him or his claims.

''What's your agenda?'' she asked after following him to the deck.

He glanced up from poking at the grill with a long, two-pronged fork. ''Well, it's pretty simple,'' he said, surprising her with his honesty. She hadn't expected him to answer.

''First, we're going to eat,'' he said. ''Then, I suppose we'll argue for a while. After that, if you don't storm out, we'll come to an understanding that you don't like and I can't abide. But we'll declare it the best we can do under the circumstances. And then you'll go home and I'll either go upstairs and play some music or read the latest book I've been meaning to start.''

Haley smiled in spite of herself. ''So that's the way it's gonna be.''

He glanced at her. ''Uh-huh. Unless, of course, you flip the script.''

''And how would I do that?''

''Surprise me,'' he said, opening his arms wide. ''I'm expecting you to fight me at every turn. To oppose any suggestion I make. To disagree with everything I say or do. So, do something unexpected and surprise me.''

Haley took the steps that put her in front of him. She snatched the grilling fork from his hand and tossed it aside. Then with both hands on her hips, she stared him straight in the eye. This close, Haley could see that the shade of blue was more like a cloudless sky than the stormy sea.

''Matt Brandon, new music director at Community Christian Church of Wayside, Oregon, I was truly blessed by the hymn you sang this morning. Thank you for that.''

His eyes widened and darkened. And then, taking advantage of the opening she'd presented, he kissed her.

Before she could protest or react or do anything except stand there dumbfounded, he pulled away. But the warmth of him remained, as did a not unpleasant aftershock that rippled through Haley much like the lingering effects of an earthquake.

She realized that she wanted that kiss to go on…and on, even though it had been unexpected. He'd asked for a surprise, but she was the one who'd gotten one.

''Now we're even,'' he said as he stepped away from her.

Haley blinked, trying to get her bearings. ''Even?''

''You took me by surprise this morning when you slapped me. I thought I'd just turn the tables so you could see how it felt.''

She nodded her head slightly, finally understanding. He hadn't kissed her because he'd wanted to kiss her; it was merely a way to best her at her own game.

And Haley knew about games. Timothy had played them. She'd come today, in part, to apologize to Matt. Mild-mannered Haley rarely, if ever, lost her temper or raised her voice. Too complacent, that's what her former fiancé had called her. Yet with Matt, she was anything but. Why couldn't she apologize and get it over with?

The pleasure she'd taken in his kiss diminished a bit—but not completely.

Haley might not have had that much experience with the physical aspects of relationships, but if he deemed a slap on par with a kiss, well, there were some fundamental things wrong with him.

The old saw about there being a thin line between love and hate came to mind. Since it obviously didn't apply here and she didn't quite know what to say to him, she focused on the original intent of her visit.

The time for games between them needed to end. Maybe he felt the same way.

"Let's just have our meeting," she said. "And let's begin by starting over. We got off on a rocky note and things have progressively worsened since then."

He nodded, then held out a hand to shake on the deal, an armistice at best. With all the niceties stripped away, they had little, if anything, to talk about. The weather, Reverend Baines's sermon, even the upcoming Market Days picnic could fill just so much time.

"Why don't you have a seat?" he said. "I'll get some iced tea."

Haley turned and for the first time noticed a table set for two at the rear of the deck. A crisp white tablecloth covered the small table. Dinnerware in a daisy leaf pattern graced each place setting. But it was a bowl of lilies as the centerpiece that caught her attention.

Did he know those were her favorites? He couldn't possibly. Haley went to the table and reached out to touch one of the flowers. She then peered toward the kitchen where Matt had disappeared.

A coincidence?

"You shouldn't have gone to so much trouble," she called out as she leaned forward to catch the fragrant scent of the flowers.

"No trouble at all," Matt said returning with a pitcher filled with ice and tea.

He watched her. And he wondered what in the world had possessed him to kiss her like that. Granted, it was something he'd wanted to do since the first time he'd laid eyes on her. That didn't, however, give him the right to just grab her and take liberties.

But she'd felt so good in his arms.

"These are pretty," she said as he put the pitcher on the table.

Matt glanced at her and bit back a knowing smile, glad that Eunice had given him the info about Haley and lilies.

Maybe he'd been more right than he realized. They *were* even now.

Matt wanted to believe that after a short sweet taste of her, he'd be rid of the woman who haunted his hours, waking or sleeping. The fact, however, was that he still found himself drawn to her. He'd been drawn to the knowledge of his first mentor in the music industry, drawn to the wisdom of his pastor back in Louisiana. And, unfortunately, drawn to the power of Melanie, the woman who'd guaranteed that his life would never again be the same.

He'd never, though, been drawn to anyone the way Haley called to him, on multiple levels, engaging all of him. She was a woman of strong principle, and he found that that appealed to him. She was also beautiful, and passionate about the things that mattered to her. He'd known her just a few weeks but he already knew that church and children were high on her list of priorities. He'd had relationships with women before, but true romance had never entered the equation. With Haley everything was different. Everything. And romance was on his mind.

Chapter Five

Matt knew a couple of ways to deal with the situation. He could pretend it didn't exist and see how far that farce got him. Or, he could own up to the attraction, put it on the table and let the chips fall where they may. Hands down he preferred the totally honest route. But right now, he had too much to lose to be that honest. He could, however, be straight up with her about something else, something less likely to send him into a guilt trip.

He retrieved the grilling fork she'd tossed aside, wiped it off and poked at the steaks.

"Haley, I need to be honest with you," he said. He leaned against the deck rail.

"Yes?"

"I think you're a very attractive woman. But I'm a man of faith and I'm not going to move on that attraction. Do you understand what I'm telling you?"

She nodded. "You kissed me to get back at me

physically for the way I hit you this morning. I understand that."

He was afraid that she'd take it that way. Maybe it was better this way. If she really knew the extent of his attraction, she wouldn't be standing there pretty as a picture—she'd run screaming out the door.

She might not recognize or understand what was happening between them. But Matt knew all about the instant attraction that could flare up between a man and a woman. He knew just how potent and dangerous it could be.

He grasped her arms. Then, quickly realizing that physical contact was a mistake, a big mistake, he let her go. "Haley, I need to apologize. I'm sorry for what I did."

Reading the confusion in her eyes, he realized that maybe even Wayside wasn't as far away from his past as he'd hoped.

"Matt, I'm the one who should apologize. I shouldn't have lashed out at you this morning."

He simply smiled. Then suddenly he was all business and efficiency.

"Have a seat," he said. "I'll get a notebook so we can talk while we eat."

Over the meal, they hammered out a deal. The compromise plan included an equitable mix of hymns during the services with Matt reserving the right to have the choir members get a voice in the decision-making process. He shared with her his vision for the music department, a plan that included more choirs and an ensemble that would perform in the community.

"A children's choir and a traveling ensemble? How about we just see how this inspirational choir of yours goes over."

Matt sighed. "It's not *my* choir, it's the church's."

Haley opened her mouth to argue, but changed her mind a moment before the words tumbled out. They'd managed to have a pleasant meal together. There was no need to spoil it.

As Matt had predicted, neither of them was truly happy, but they'd settled their differences long enough to come up with something to present during the meeting. And that's what mattered.

By the next day Haley was still replaying that kiss they'd shared. Even though it had meant nothing to him, she'd relived every moment of it. She couldn't recall ever dwelling that much on one of Timothy's kisses. While pleasant enough, they'd never left her wanting more or wondering where a simple kiss might lead.

And if that weren't enough, Matt had set his dinner table with lilies. Had that be a coincidence or a sign that he'd done some homework?

"Had to have been a coincidence," she concluded. The only other explanation would mean that he'd actually made an effort to be nice, to get to know her; that he'd actually asked someone about her preferences. And why would he do that?

When the kettle on her stove whistled with boiling water, Haley prepared a cup of tea and reviewed all that had transpired the day before. Sunday's events seemed more of a dream than any reality she could face.

She'd actually hit him. And *he* was the one who'd apologized. He'd kissed her. And she was the one who'd been flustered.

Since the debacle following Timothy, Haley didn't trust her judgment around or about men. She preferred to keep herself cloistered, surrounded by the church and community work that filled any void she might, at one time, have felt existed in her life.

But the memory of Matt Brandon's kiss lingered on her mouth and in her heart. With shaky fingers she touched her lips, remembering the many sensations that washed through her when he'd kissed her. Surprise, of course, but also something else. Something indistinct, but different. Something she'd never experienced: longing.

She'd been kissed before, of course. Maybe not as much as other women her age, but she knew how things were supposed to be between a man and a woman. She found it disconcerting that Timothy never inspired in her half of what Matt brought out in that one brief embrace.

Strong enough to realize that they were treading in dangerous territory, he'd invoked his faith as a deterrent, a reminder to them both. Haley, however, had been caught up in the moment. Now she felt nothing but shame.

Haley liked the comfort of being in control of her life and of her emotions. After years of being bounced around from relative to relative, she needed the security of sameness in her life. Matt Brandon had stormed into her world leaving her defenseless and vulnerable. But even more disturbing, Matt left her feeling like a missing piece of her life had finally fallen into place.

She needed to talk to someone, to get off her chest the many conflicting and confusing emotions that raced through her. With Kara out of town, there was just one person she was close enough to, to share those kinds of things. She reached for the telephone and called Amber, the cousin who was as close as a sister.

"Have you eaten?" Amber said.

"No. And I haven't gotten a single thing done today, either."

"Say no more," Amber told Haley. "You're in luck. I was just taking a roast chicken out of the oven. Set the table for two and brew up some of that wonderful tea. I'll be over in a jiffy."

"So," Amber said a little while later. The two cousins had just done some serious damage to a herb-roasted chicken that Amber served with vegetable strip bundles and wild rice. "This same guy has you tied all in knots. I think you need to stop avoiding the obvious."

"What's the obvious?"

Amber sighed. "Did I not teach you anything?"

Haley grinned. When she'd moved in with Amber's family, the two girls shared a room along with lots of secrets.

"Obviously not," Haley said on a dry note as she reached for another of Amber's made-from-scratch crescent rolls.

''Don't sass your elders,'' Amber said.

''Well, you *are* twenty-eight. I'm just twenty-seven.''

Amber gave her the evil eye, but spoiled the look by poking out her tongue. ''November's coming, missy. But seriously. The obvious with this Matt person is that you need to ask him out.''

''Ask him out? I don't even like him.''

Not true, not true, her conscience butted in.

''Then why were you all freaked out when he kissed you?''

Haley studied her reflection in the butter knife. ''I wasn't freaked out. I was just...'' She shrugged. ''I was surprised.''

''But you liked it,'' Amber pressed.

''Well, yes. Sort of.''

''And he said he was attracted to you but wasn't going to act on it? Haley, honey, you can't let this one get away. He's cute, chivalrous and a great kisser. What more could you ask for except him being great you know where?''

Haley blushed. She'd heard it before, but she still wasn't comfortable with Amber's openness about certain things.

''There won't be any of that,'' she said. ''I'm not like you, Amber.''

A shadow crossed Amber's face, and Haley instantly regretted her choice of words. She reached for her cousin's hand. ''I didn't mean it like that.''

Amber tossed her head back, quickly shielding her own vulnerability. ''I know. But back to Matt.''

"Are you sure you don't want to talk about it?" Haley gently probed.

Amber had had an awful experience. Her physical wounds had long since healed, but Haley knew emotional ones still existed. Her cousin had turned her back on God, instead finding refuge and solace in her kitchen.

"I'm sure." To emphasize the point, Amber got up and removed their dinner dishes from the table. "I have a chocolate cake roll for dessert. I'm gonna make some coffee."

On a sigh, Haley cleared the rest of the table. After the coffee brewed, Amber poured herself a cup, refreshed Haley's tea and the two women went into the country-style living room to enjoy dessert and finish their conversation.

"We don't have anything in common. He has an earring in his ear. He drives a motorcycle and he plays loud music."

"Mmm-hmm," Amber said. "You both go to Community Christian. His ministry and outreach, like yours with the Sunday school, touches youth. And there's obviously some kind of spark between you two."

"There's more to life than sparks."

"Yep. There's misery and fear and poverty and homelessness and despair."

The words weren't meant to be cruel, but they cut Haley nonetheless. Amber never realized just how adrift Haley had felt during most of her childhood and teen years. Before coming to live with Amber's family, Haley had experienced all of those things. And she well remembered the sting of being an unwanted, homeless child.

"I get your point," Haley said.

"Look, all I'm saying is that you should give this guy a chance. To me, it sounds like you're throwing up a lot of unnecessary defenses."

Was she?

It wouldn't be the first time someone said she was too rigid in her outlook.

By Tuesday afternoon, Haley still found herself wondering about just that. She planned to be at that new choir meeting and rehearsal at the church. If nothing else, she'd keep an eye on Matt for the sake of her young people. But, at the last minute, she was asked to stay late at the local library where she volunteered on Tuesdays.

In the face of the library director's need, Haley found it difficult to say no. That, Amber always told her, was the crux of her problem. She didn't know how to say no. But tonight wasn't the evening to begin a new assertiveness campaign.

Haley couldn't help wondering if divine intervention had anything to do with her not getting to that new choir rehearsal.

At the church, Matt looked out at the thirty or so people, a good mix of teens, college students and a few older adults, who'd come out to get information about the inspirational choir. He realized, however, that he was really looking for Haley. He'd thought for sure she'd be present to harass and distract him.

He bit back a grin at the characterization, one she'd

undoubtedly find offensive but was true nevertheless. He hadn't seen her since their Sunday afternoon dinner. Kissing Haley had to rank up there with being one of his few but notorious not-so-bright ideas. The memory of that kiss stayed with him, had kept him awake at night.

Haley was innocence and sweetness combined. She'd tasted like springtime and sunshine. And he couldn't afford to let his thoughts drift like this.

Someone moved aside and Matt's smile faltered. Edward Worthington sat stoically near the door. The calm expression on the older man's face didn't for a moment fool Matt into believing that the deacon's presence meant he condoned the idea of a new choir, or even Matt.

Glancing around, this time taking a careful look, Matt spotted at least two others who'd openly challenged him. So, this was to be a test of wills.

Well, the only will that would be done tonight was the Lord's.

He clapped his hands to get everyone's attention. "Thanks for coming out this evening," he said. "I'm very pleased with the turnout. We'll open with prayer and a song and then I'll tell you a little about what we have in mind for this choir."

Reverend Baines led the group in prayer, then said a few words of encouragement before leaving for another commitment.

Matt went to a box he'd stashed under a table and pulled out several tambourines and maracas.

"We get to use those?"

"Sure thing," he said. "What's your name?"

"Adam," the teenager said. "Adam Richardson."

"Well, Adam, help me get these distributed." They began passing the instruments out among those assembled. Edward didn't take one. When the box was empty Matt went back to the electric keyboard he'd set up. "All right. Does everybody know the song 'This Little Light of Mine'?"

A broad consensus of enthusiastic nods let him know he'd picked a winner, a tune that already had a little pep to it. "Well, I'm going to play, and I'll point to you when I want you to join in. Everybody ready?"

The group nodded. Standing up, Matt tapped out a beat with a sneakered foot and then launched into a rousing introduction to the song. He used the percussion components on the keyboard to fill in as if a full band also played along.

By the time he gave the signal for everyone to sing, tambourines were already ringing and the maracas rattled along with the beat. Those without instruments clapped their hands along with the music.

Matt easily slid from that song into other quick-tempo tunes that everyone knew. When he finally closed with a flourish, the new choir members cheered.

A scowling Deacon Worthington stormed out of the choir room followed by his old guard minions. Matt saw them leave and didn't try to stop them.

During the next hour, he separated the voices into alto, soprano, tenor and bass parts, designated a couple of people to be dedicated percussionists and then taught the group a jazzy praise song.

By the time he called it a wrap, Matt felt good about the progress they'd made.

"Are we going to sing on Sunday?" Adam asked.

"Yep," Matt told them.

"Cool!"

A couple of kids high-fived each other. Matt grinned. Getting excited about spreading the gospel through song is what it was all about. Despite the rocky two weeks with the church council, this one night had restored him.

"We need to rehearse again, though. Can everybody make five o'clock on Friday?"

He didn't get any objections. "Excellent. Let's gather in a circle for closing prayer."

"Reverend Matt, we can't!"

All eyes turned toward Cindy Worthington.

"We can't pray?"

"We can't sing on Sunday. We don't have any choir robes."

Worried expressions marred the faces of a few of the teenagers. A couple of adults smiled.

"Hey, guys," Matt said. "The Lord doesn't care about robes. It's what's here," he said patting his heart.

Some of the kids still looked troubled. Apparently they'd never seen a church choir sing without having on those heavy choral robes. They'd be shocked to know he'd sung before thousands in everything from ripped blue jeans to black leather.

Realizing he had a long way to go in convincing some of them that there were lots of ways to worship, Matt offered them a solution. "Tell you what," he

said. "We don't have robes or uniforms, and we don't
have to, but we can all still be uniform. Guys, wear
white shirts on Sunday. No ties. Ladies, you should
all wear white blouses. How's that?"

Nods that grew into smiles greeted the idea.
Breathing a sigh of relief, Matt took the hands of the
people standing closest to him, Cindy on his right and
another girl on his left. He prayed for those who gathered, for those who wanted to come and couldn't and
for those who would be blessed by the ministry of
Community Christian's inspirational choir. Before the
group broke up, he also added a silent prayer for those
in opposition and asked the Lord to keep him in His
perfect will.

A moment later Matt was surrounded by a sea of
pretty teenagers all vying for his attention. Cindy
stood on tiptoe to press a kiss to his cheek. And that's
what Haley saw when she opened the door to the
choir room.

"Mr. Brandon." Her voice, sharp and high, carried
over the buzz in the room. Conversation died off as
people turned toward the door.

Matt's eyebrows rose when he saw her. The group
parted, opening a clear path between Haley and Matt.
Tension arced between them.

"Oh, Haley, you missed it," Cindy gushed. "We
had a wonderful rehearsal."

Haley didn't spare a glance at the girl. All of her
attention, and her barely controlled anger, was directed toward Matt. "I'd like to speak with you, privately. Now," she added.

A couple of people exchanged glances at her unusually sharp tone. Matt extricated himself from the group around him, but took his time making his way to Haley. He shook hands with a couple of the older folks, members of the church choir who were interested in the new inspirational group as well.

"Thanks for coming out tonight," he told them.

Haley watched Mr. Browning slap Matt on his back and his short wife clasp Matt's hands in hers. "It was wonderful," she said. "I'm so glad you're here at our church."

Matt smiled. "That means a lot to me. Thank you."

"Mr. Brandon." Haley's tone was the one she used with the most recalcitrant of her students.

Matt's gaze lifted to hers, and for a moment she faltered. Raw emotion blazed in his eyes. But then, from her peripheral vision she saw a small group of teenage girls huddled together. They looked at Matt as if he were a rock star or the leading man in a Hollywood movie. And they looked at her as if she were the Wicked Witch come to do harm to their hero.

"Excuse me," she heard Matt tell the Brownings. She waited for him and then, certain that he would follow, she headed down the hall to a classroom far removed from the choir rehearsal room. The click-clack of her heeled sandals sounded on the floor.

She pushed open the door, flicked on the light switch and rounded on Matt with the ferocity of a lioness protecting her young.

"I told you once that I would not have you turning the heads of my girls. You come in here flaunting your earring and acting as if the world should bow to you."

Matt leaned against the closed door and watched her rage. She was beautiful to begin with. Anger just highlighted the appeal. Her brown eyes flashed, color filled her cheeks, and tendrils of her hair, most of which was caught back with a clip, outlined her face.

He could admire her beauty, but he wasn't going to stand still while she berated him for something he hadn't done.

She unjustly accused him of being a Lothario and Matt had had enough unjust accusations hurled his way, more than enough, to last a lifetime.

"You have a lot of nerve confronting me like this."

"I know what I saw, and I won't stand for it."

Matt had been slowly working himself into a mighty fine anger when a thought hit him—a most intriguing thought that evaporated his anger and explained a lot of her behavior.

Overly righteous indignation flared from her whenever she was near him. And she assumed the mother hen role with the church's young people. But, what if her animosity stemmed from another source entirely? Could she be jealous of the attention her young charges gave him? Is that why she was so upset?

Or, was she experiencing the insecurity of someone not used to dealing with the myriad emotions that swirled with mutual attraction? In an odd way, the likelihood of that certainty endeared her to him.

"This isn't about 'your girls,'" he said, bracketing

her words with air quotes. "And it's not about the music either, is it? It's about you."

"What?"

"I'm not interested in girls, Haley. I thought I'd made myself clear on that." He pushed off the door and took the steps toward her that put them face-to-face. Haley took corresponding steps backward.

"You're how old?" he asked. "Twenty-six? Twenty-seven?"

"What are you talking about?"

"I find you very attractive. We've already established that. But at this point in my life, I won't let myself get caught up in a relationship with anyone." He stood right in front of her now. "Even someone like you who can't seem to stop throwing herself at me. What is it you're afraid of, Haley?" he asked, his voice gentle as if he spoke to an injured child. "I didn't come here to deflower any virgins."

Her mouth dropped open then snapped closed. "How dare you?"

"I'm not interested in any of the girls out there, and they aren't interested in me beyond the music that I teach them to sing. But you," he said shaking his head. "You always seem to be right in the forefront, a one-woman force leading the opposition."

He lifted a finger and traced the soft skin along her face from her brow to her chin. "So beautiful. So angry."

His mouth lowered to hers.

He gave her time to object, time to push him away. But she did neither. He felt the soft exhale of her breath, smelled the sweet fragrance of jasmine in her perfume. And saw her eyes close in anticipation.

He angled his head to claim the inevitable and sweet kiss—and let out an earsplitting yelp as the heel of her shoe ground into his instep.

"What are you doing?" he hopped away from her. "Have you lost your mind? What are you trying to do, break my foot?"

This time it was Haley who did the advancing. She poked a finger in his chest even as he continued to hop on one foot. "You are on notice, buster. I'm going to do everything in my power to see you out of here."

The door slammed behind her. Matt slumped into a chair and tugged off his left Nike to see if she'd broken the skin or any bones with those lethal shoes.

He grunted as he rubbed his sore foot, mumbling about high-strung, repressed church women.

Chapter Six

❧

Between the altercations with Haley and the daggers sent his way by Edward and his crew, Matt wasn't sure if he'd still have a job when he walked into the church council meeting Wednesday. Haley wasn't there, and neither was Worthington. They probably had the pastor cornered in his office bending his ear about what they viewed as Matt's shortcomings.

Part of Matt was ready to fight for his job and his honor. But the other part of him was weary, tired of everything in his life being a struggle. He'd thought the move to Oregon and then settling in Wayside had been the right direction. But maybe he'd just wanted peace so much that he'd fallen straight into the latest snare, a trap disguised as small-town Americana. Maybe he hadn't heard the still, small voice after all. Maybe he'd just made a big mistake, the latest in a history of them.

"Reverend Baines will be in in a moment," Eunice said with a sympathetic glance in Matt's direction.

That was all the confirmation he needed. This meeting was going to be a long, contentious battle, one he didn't relish.

A few minutes later, the somber trio of Haley, Deacon Worthington and Reverend Baines filed into the room. For the next forty-five minutes the church council dealt with its usual business, with not a word mentioned about Matt's so-called infractions and disruptions. When Reverend Baines concluded the meeting, Matt glanced at Eunice, who shrugged.

Haley hadn't said a word to him the entire meeting. As a matter of fact, she hadn't even made eye contact with him.

"Matt, can I have a word with you in my office?"

At Reverend Baines's quiet request, Haley finally looked at Matt. Triumph danced in her eyes.

"Sure," Matt told the minister, but his eye contact was strictly with Haley. He stared until she glanced away. Only then did Matt gather his papers and rise.

He closed the door after following Reverend Baines into the pastor's study. A deep piled, blue-and-burgundy rug silenced their footfalls. The shelved walls behind the minister's desk and the one to the immediate left were filled with books and framed photographs of relatives and church members. Two big overstuffed chairs sat directly in front of the cherry desk. A computer and a small television were on an easily accessible console.

"Have a seat," the minister offered. He went to a sideboard and poured juice into a tumbler. "Can I get you something?"

Matt, still standing, folded his arms. "No, since I think you're about to give me my walking papers."

Reverend Baines looked up, surprise clearly etched on his face. "Why would I do that?"

"I'm supposed to believe that Haley and Worthington weren't in here rattling off a litany of complaints about me?"

Reverend Baines shrugged as he took his seat. With the other man seated, Matt reluctantly settled into one of the chairs.

"They were. But that doesn't mean I'm about to give you the boot."

"Why not?"

"Because I believe you'll be good for Community Christian. You knew when you came in that there would be opposition to your ideas and to your music." He lifted his glass up, indicating Matt's ears. "As well as to your style."

Matt fingered the gold hoop. "A little too hip for Wayside?"

The preacher chuckled. "Not at all. You'll find everything here in Wayside that's in the big city, including crime and poverty and other social ailments. But pockets of this community, this church being one of them, have resisted change for a long time. As a matter of fact, in recent years, we seem to have drawn an even more conservative group of members here at Community Christian. Part of that is my fault."

"How so?"

Cliff shrugged. "When I arrived here five years ago, I took as a focus of my pastorate bringing back into the fold members and families who, through the years, had drifted away. As it turns out, many of them were, let's just say, set in their ways about what the worship experience was supposed to be.''

Matt could understand the problem, but he didn't see how he could be a part of the solution. Going from one extreme to the other was bound to tear the church apart. A more moderate approach seemed prudent, and Matt knew moderation had never been his strong suit.

"You know what I'm about," he said. "You even know what happened to me three years ago. Why bring me in here if it's just going to be a struggle?''

"Life's a struggle, Matt. You know that better than most. Yet, through our faith and by grace we continue to fight the good fight.''

Matt sighed as he closed his eyes for a moment. Cliff was right. He knew all of this. That didn't make it any easier to deal with. "So you're suggesting what?''

"Continue doing what you're doing. I've gotten several calls this week from excited teens and parents thanking me for starting up this new choir. Of course, I took all the credit for thinking of it,'' the pastor said with a grin.

Matt chuckled. "You are the shepherd of this flock.''

Reverend Baines's expression turned serious. "And I try to keep a so-called finger on the pulse of the congregation.''

"Meaning?''

"Meaning some days may be more arduous than others.'' Leaning forward, the pastor put down his juice glass and clasped his hands together. "There's something you need to know about Haley," he said.

That got Matt's attention and he leaned forward again. "What about her?"

Haley settled in front of the television and VCR with a bowl of popcorn and her favorite movie, which always lifted her spirits and they were nothing if not low today. It had been a horrible week marked by nothing but conflict and dissension—two things she tried to keep at an absolute minimum in her life.

All she'd ever wanted was a quiet, stable existence in a place she loved. In just a few days, Matt Brandon had turned her orderly world into chaos.

Scrunching down to get comfy on the soft pillows of the sofa, she propped the popcorn bowl on her tummy and adjusted the volume so she could hum along with the opening credits. In the privacy of her own home, it didn't matter if she couldn't carry a tune.

The carriages and cars were approaching and people scurried through rainfall when Haley's doorbell sounded. She glanced up, not at all certain of what she'd just heard. The door chimed again.

"Who in the world...?" Haley never had visitors. Amber always called before stopping over and school was out, so it couldn't be an anxious parent. She put the movie on pause, set the popcorn aside and went to the door.

"Oh, I'm so glad you are in," said a trim woman in a sporty pink suit. Three others stood behind her.

"Mrs. Attley, Mrs. Forest." She glanced at Deacon

Worthington and Gladys Paumroy. "What can I do for you?"

"We'd like to speak with you, dear," Donna Attley said.

"Sure, come on in," Haley said opening the door wider so the delegation from Community Christian could come in. "Right this way."

She led them into the living room. Wondering what would bring this imposing committee to her door, she quickly turned off the television and VCR and put the remote controls in a caddie next to the sofa.

"Have a seat," she invited her guests. "I was just getting ready to watch a movie."

Donna picked up the videocassette sleeve. "Ah, I do love this film. They don't make them like that anymore."

"They sure don't," Gladys said. "And that's why we've come, Haley."

"You want to talk about old films?"

Deacon Worthington harrumphed. "Hardly. We've come to discuss with you the problem we have at Community Christian."

"Problem?" Haley said, even though she had a pretty good inkling of the problem they all shared. Its name was Matt Brandon.

"That's right," Donna said. "We think that a group of like-minded people of the church should present to Reverend Baines and the church council a petition for the immediate removal of that so-called choir director."

Haley sure agreed with the "so-called" part, but a petition? "Isn't that a little drastic?"

"My point exactly," Deacon Worthington intoned. With his silver hair and steel-blue eyes he put Haley more in mind of an elder statesman than a retired hardware store owner. His strongly held convictions were as intractable as those of any senator defending a bill on faraway Capitol Hill.

The ever fashionable and always impeccable Mrs. Attley didn't roll her eyes, but the effect was the same. She clearly disagreed with Edward.

Haley glanced between the two, then looked at Roberta Forest who'd yet to say anything at all.

"Why don't I get some refreshments and then we can talk," Haley said. "Make yourselves comfortable. I'll be right back."

She returned with a plate of Amber's raspberry cream cookies and a carafe of raspberry iced tea. "I put coffee on. It'll be ready soon for anyone who'd like some."

After seeing her guests served, she took a seat and clasped her hands together. "So, you were saying?"

"I was saying that we need to just cut our losses and immediately begin a new search for a musician who respects the sanctity of our church."

"We've been unable to agree on the method, though," Gladys said. "That's why we've come to you."

"You have a good head on your shoulders," Deacon Worthington added. "Reminds me of my late wife, a woman of strong opinions and good sense. I told them how you questioned that Brandon's credentials and raked him over the coals during the interview process."

Haley cringed. "Well, I wouldn't characterize my questions as raking anyone over the coals."

"That's neither here nor there," Donna said. A raspberry cookie perched delicately on a small napkin in her palm. "The point is, you don't care for his music either. Am I correct?"

Haley slowly nodded. But she didn't at all feel comfortable with what seemed to be unfolding in her living room.

"Cindy told me how you practically yanked him out of that choir rehearsal last night," the deacon said. "I hope you gave him what for. I left after hearing the total desecration of a wonderful children's tune."

Again Haley wished she'd been able to tell the librarian that she couldn't stay late. She'd really wanted to be at church to keep an eye on Matt, to help avoid exactly this sort of outcome.

"They're supposed to debut that noise during Sunday's service," Gladys said. "It's an abomination."

"You heard it?"

"We were all there last night."

"Was anyone else from the church council present?" Haley asked.

"No, just me," Deacon Worthington said.

"Well, it seems like a majority of the council will need to be present and then make a decision," Haley suggested. "Everyone is likely to be at service Sunday. Why not hear what Mr. Brandon is going to present and then go forward?"

"Is he really a minister, an ordained minister?" Donna asked. "I heard Cindy, Adam and some others calling him reverend."

"Probably from some fly-by-night home correspondence place," Deacon Worthington said.

"Be that as it may, we're stuck with him for now," Haley said.

"But hopefully not for long," Mrs. Attley added.

Their plan agreed upon, the group decided to give Matt one more Sunday to prove his mettle. If his presentation proved as objectionable as what he'd done so far, the committee of five would launch Operation Restore Faith, the name a contribution from Mrs. Forest, who obviously watched too much cable news.

Haley wasn't at all comfortable with what seemed like a coup committee, but when she got in bed that night, she slept well for the first time in days. The security and comfort she'd come to rely on at Community Christian had been threatened, but everything would be in right order soon.

When Matt got in bed that night, his thoughts were on Haley and the things Cliff Baines told him. He felt a little sorry for her, but at least now he had a better idea of why she so stridently opposed him.

Orphaned at a young age, she'd been bounced around from relative to relative until finally landing with an aunt and uncle who raised her. That early instability had apparently had a deep impact on her. As an adult, the security of sameness, things she could always count on—a routine so to speak—grounded her. She'd sought the same in a relationship with a banker, Cliff had told him. But things hadn't worked out there. The happily-ever-after that Haley sought had been ripped out from under her.

Being dumped three weeks before your wedding could do that to a woman.

Matt felt sorry for the pain she'd suffered, but at least he better understood why she could be so prickly at times.

He smiled. All the more reason to turn on the charm.

"Stop it," he scolded himself a moment later. He was supposed to be in Wayside to minister, to heal the wounds of his own past, not start something new with a woman who intrigued him.

But, he knew, it was well too late to claim disinterest in Haley.

Sleep proved elusive so he got up and went to his music room. By the light of a gooseneck lamp, he composed at his piano, something he hadn't done in a long, long time. He hadn't been inspired to write new music in so long that he'd almost forgotten how much he enjoyed it. He'd been far too busy running—from God, from his past and from himself—to find pleasure in any part of his former life.

But now, in this unlikely town, he'd again found not just inspiration, but focus. Many songwriters put words down first and then found or created music to fit; but for Matt, the process of creating had always been integrated, lyrics and melody arriving almost simultaneously. And that's what was happening now. He jotted notes and words on a pad even while the melody burst through him. He kept one hand splayed on the keyboard and one wrapped around a mechanical pencil.

It seemed to be shaping into a song about a woman

who'd found her way home after searching for truth. He hadn't done any original composing in several years, so long that he'd almost thought he'd gotten it out of his system. Then along comes a small church, a fiery blonde and a new revelation. The song was about redemption and forgiveness, but the image in his mind was of a woman with sun-streaked hair, sparkling brown eyes and strong beliefs that she held dear and ferociously defended.

Matt didn't need a lightning bolt from heaven to alert him that their paths crossed for a reason. He just prayed that the reason was something other than a test of his faith and willpower.

At three in the morning Matt had finally made his way back to bed. While the eclectic early American furniture in the Amends House didn't exactly suit his personal tastes, he had not a single complaint with the superb bedding. Matt stretched on the big mattress then sat up to contemplate his options for the day. He'd slept late and now had less than an entire day before him.

"You need to get a job," he muttered to himself.

Wayside, Oregon, population 17,800, wasn't exactly a booming metropolis. Unlike in Portland, he couldn't just fade into the relative obscurity of the big city. Here, people, particularly at the church, might notice if an able-bodied man didn't work. Being choir director at Community Christian did not a full-time salary make.

Matt had no need to work; he had more than enough money salted away, the fruit of his former life. But there was the matter of his conviction that when he'd walked away from that life, he'd left all of its trappings behind as well, including the cash.

For the last three years he'd survived on odd jobs and grace. When he liked a place and decided to stay a while, he usually found a position in a national chain bookstore, the bigger the better. The owners and clerks at small and independent specialty shops had a tendency to closely follow their stock and the industry. They kept abreast of what was going on in the world. In the larger chains, clerks weren't expected to read; they just had to know how to work the cash registers and make espresso. He'd done some voice-over work in Denver, and had even done a stint as a radio newsman for an all-talk station. The one thing he religiously avoided at all costs was any and all entanglement with music.

Until Wayside.

He swung his legs over the edge of the bed. "Lord, I hope you know what you're doing."

Wayside had a couple of radio stations; maybe he'd stop by the offices to see if any positions were open.

"And if all else fails, you can commute to Portland."

That thought didn't sit with him very well, but Wayside didn't seem to have much to offer. Then again, other than the grocery store closest to the house, the bakery and his trips to the church, he hadn't spent a lot of time exploring the town. Cliff Baines had assured him that it wasn't as small as the downtown area made it appear.

Today he could rectify that oversight. Maybe he

could even find a place to buy some more lamps for the living room. And while he was out and about he'd scope out the employment prospects.

After getting dressed, he glanced at the music he'd written in the middle of the night. A fat lot of good it did to compose again when that chapter of his life had The End stamped across it in big bold letters.

He balled up the paper and tossed it in the trash.

"No turning back, Brandon. There's no turning back."

He parked his truck at the library then walked along Main Street. Despite the small-town look, Wayside was very much a part of the twenty-first century. A cyber café boasting twenty Internet workstations for rent by the half-hour did business next to Pop's Ice Cream and Malt Shoppe. Next door, an art co-operative shared space with the Chamber of Commerce.

By the time Matt made it to the library, he figured he may as well go in. He hadn't owned a library card since he was a kid. Maybe during his sojourn in Wayside he could catch up on some reading. A long time ago he liked to read mysteries and Westerns.

As he pushed the door open, he chuckled. Those two genres probably appealed because his life was a mystery and as long as he could remember he'd yearned to travel west. The two interest areas had finally managed to collide.

His first impression of the library was its smell and the light. Like everything else he'd encountered in Oregon, a clean, fresh scent permeated the air. Natural light poured in from skylights all around the perimeter. The last time he'd been in a library, the place had been hot and dimly lit. Maybe that's why he'd avoided them all these years. This building, though, obviously of new construction, welcomed him in a way he hadn't expected.

Children to the left. Reference to the right. Circulation straight ahead. Matt spotted the bent head of a librarian there so he approached the desk.

"Excuse me, I'd like to get a library card."

The librarian looked up and Matt caught his breath. If they'd looked like this when he was growing up, maybe he'd have spent more time checking out books.

"What are you doing here?" Haley said, surprise at seeing him clear in her voice.

"I could ask you the same question. I came to get a library card."

For a moment, he thought she might refuse to assist him. But then, after apparently considering her options, she put a sheet of paper and a pen in front of him.

"Fill out this form," she said. If he hadn't already known it, he'd have guessed in that moment that she was a schoolteacher. The voice brooked no nonsense. The extra note of hostility was, he suspected, undoubtedly reserved exclusively for him. If she'd hoped to send him packing, her plan backfired. The more he came in contact with her, the more intrigued he found himself.

What he'd heard of her background from Cliff Baines only reinforced what Matt already suspected. There was, however, a part that didn't fit. Reverend

Baines had described her as intensely devout, totally dependable, unfailingly unshakable and one of the few people he could count on to always have a kind word and a smile at the ready. But so far in Matt's experience she'd been intensely hostile, totally unpredictable and her feathers so ruffled that he could stuff a pillow or two with the fallout. As for kind words, the kind he'd heard from her would make a lesser man turn tail and run.

So what was it about him that so unhinged her?

Right then and there he realized that finding out just what it was meant a lot to him. Matt didn't understand the compelling need to know; he just trusted that his gut knew the answers. Something about this beautiful woman touched him on all sorts of levels.

The fact that he'd spent half the night writing music, music inspired by her, was enough to fuel his curiosity.

"Ms. Cartwright, we've obviously started off on the wrong foot. Our paths are going to continue to cross at church and, I'm sure, in town. Tell me what I've done to irritate you so much and I'll try to do better."

Haley stared at him as if he'd sprouted a snout and horns. Didn't he know that just his presence sent her into a state of abject discombobulation?

"You threaten everything I hold dear."

Chapter Seven

He blinked, looking as surprised as if she'd struck him. "Beg pardon?"

Haley took a deep breath, surprised herself at her honesty. She'd not intentionally planned to say that. It had just come out. Now, though, she couldn't say she was sorry. And since she'd started it, she may as well finish.

"You ride into town like a dark angel. You swoop into our church with your motorcycle and jeans and earring and turn everything upside down. There are ways to do things, Mr. Brandon. And your way is going to cause a lot of confusion and disruption in the congregation."

"Well, you don't hold back, do you?"

Haley folded her arms. "Actually, I do. You, for some reason, seem to bring out the worst in me."

Matt knew why. He represented change; and change threatened and frightened her because it meant an uncertain future.

He smiled then and Haley's heart did a little flip. She refused, however, to credit it to Matt's presence or his smile.

"Let me try to reverse that," he said. "May I buy you lunch? On my walk along Main Street I spied a little café that seems to have a great menu."

"Bouillabaisse," she said. "They make stews and soups."

He nodded. "That's the place. Then you'll have lunch with me?"

Haley bit her lip. Saying yes would be like consorting with the enemy. But hot on that thought came the realization that she could possibly affect more change by starting with a clean slate. She could show and tell him what Community Christian was all about. And maybe she could make up for some of her abominable behavior with him. It was true that he seemed to bring out the worst in her.

Besides, despite everything she told herself, a part of her, the part that had nothing to do with choirs or youth programs or anything else, wanted to spend some time with Matt. She'd do well to stop avoiding that fact.

"Yes," she said.

His smile grew broad. "Really? Great. One condition, though."

"I've agreed to go to lunch with you and now you're making demands?"

"Just this," he said. When he paused, she leaned forward.

"What?"

"Call me Matt."

Haley finished up her volunteer shift on the circulation desk while Matt roamed the mystery stacks looking for something to read. When he appeared before her again he had two mystery novels, one from the shelves of new books and one classic, as well as a copy of *How to Win Friends and Influence People*.

She raised her eyebrows as she took the books to scan.

"Is there someone you're trying to win over?" She slapped a hand over her mouth. The saucy question had popped out before she could stop it. "I'm sorry. That was out of line."

"No. It wasn't. And yes, there is someone I'm hoping to win over." His direct gaze and slight smile left no confusion about who it might be.

Warmth suffused Haley. When she reached for his next book, her hand was just a little unsteady. She didn't dare meet his gaze. She knew it was on her though, intense, questioning and all too male.

She stuck a Wayside Community Library bookmark into one of the novels and shoved his short stack toward him. "I need to tell them I'm leaving."

As she checked out with Mrs. Johnson, the head librarian, Haley chided herself for once again sinking to a newer, lower depth each time Matt got near. What was it about the man that made her lose her equilibrium? She knew she had to find out, though, and she planned to begin the search for answers at lunch.

Haley ordered a chef salad while Matt went for the heartier sandwich with fries and a bowl of soup. The animosity between them tempered for the moment, they shared a loaf of hard bread and settled into the easy, nonthreatening conversation of two people getting to know each other.

"Do you volunteer at the library during the school year as well?"

"Yes, but not as many hours. When summer break begins, I come in two or three days a week. I also do some work with the Girl Scouts and at the community center. And I'm on a couple of boards."

"That's a lot," Matt said, wondering why she felt compelled to keep so busy.

"I like staying on the move. You know what they say about idle hands." *Work also keeps my mind off things I don't have,* she added to herself.

"This is good," he said while enjoying the last piece of bread. "I'll have to admit this about Wayside, the food is great here."

"There's even an annual Make It or Fake It bakeoff during the Founder's Day celebration."

Matt grinned. "Make it or fake it?"

"Part of the town's lore. Women who can't cook learn how to fake it. During the bakeoff the town's cooks go for it. There are two categories for youth and adults."

"Making it from scratch or faking it, right?"

"You're quick."

He chuckled. "So, tell me. Which category do you enter?"

"Let's just put it this way. I leave that particular competition to the experts like my cousin Amber."

"Do you have a large family?"

She shook her head. "Just Amber, her older brother

and their parents. I have some way distant relatives but I don't keep in touch with them anymore." Not after the way they'd shunted and shuttled her to and fro all those years. As far as Haley was concerned, Amber was her sister and she had no living relatives save for Amber's family.

"What do you—"

She held up a hand cutting him off. "You've been asking all the questions, it's my turn."

With a tip of his hand, he invited her to ask away. But his smile engaged and distracted her, so much so that for a moment she forgot the question.

Buying herself time to remember, she added sweetener to her iced tea. Taking an unconscious deep breath, she asked the question that had been nagging at her since he'd first interviewed with the church council. "Why did a big-city guy like you settle in Wayside?"

Matt's gaze met hers head-on. He remained quiet for a while and inexplicably Haley held her breath.

"I was looking for a place to call home."

She exhaled on a slow, unsteady breath. Something clicked inside her, settled into place. It was something she hadn't even recognized as out of kilter until just now. For the first time in a long time, she relaxed, truly relaxed. Had she found in Matt a kindred spirit?

The well-traveled territory of searching for a place, for roots, was ground she'd covered many times over. She could handle this with ease, even aplomb.

"I feel the same way about Wayside. Do you know the town's history?"

When he shook his head, she smiled and leaned

forward, bracing her arms on the table to settle into the tale. "Wayside's roots date back to after the Lewis and Clark Expedition. It wasn't a town then, of course. Just a little way on the side of the road where travelers could rest."

"Don't tell me. You're also a member of the town's historical society."

"Don't scoff. You lucked out by having lunch with a Northwest history buff."

His smile encouraged her to proceed. "So when did it become a town?"

"The late part of the 1820s. One of the early settlers following the path set by the expedition decided not to go any farther. His wife was soon to deliver a child and after the long journey from Missouri, they just couldn't make the rest of the trip. Today, we get on the interstate and travel to Portland in about forty-five minutes. By wagon, the journey took many days."

A waitress cleared their table, sent a saucy smile Matt's way, then refreshed Matt's coffee and Haley's iced tea. Matt muttered a thank-you her way then again turned his undivided attention to Haley.

"When I was growing up," she said, "I wanted to be a pioneer, one of the people who settled the Northwest Territory."

"And then what happened?"

"I realized I probably wouldn't have made it one week on the open trail. Those people were made of sturdier stock. They knew hardships we can't even fathom."

"You seem pretty sturdy to me."

Haley would have taken the remark as a dig, since she carried an extra thirty or so pounds. But the look in his eyes reflected admiration, not censure or reproach.

She cleared her throat and glanced away.

"Well, the founders, Edwin Cherry and his wife, Sheridan, ended up staying right where they stopped. They worked with some of the fur traders and trappers and by the time the flood of settlers came in the 1840s, Wayside was a settled little place."

"With a name like Cherry, why didn't they name the town after themselves? Cherryville or something?"

Haley grinned. "They tried. But everyone just knew it as Wayside. Today, there is a street named after them to honor their attempt. A lot of the big, old houses are over on Cherryville Drive. It's a very pretty street."

Matt was about to ask a question when a shadow fell across the table.

They looked up to see Donna Attley. Today she wore a chic navy suit and carried a small square handbag, just the sort of bag Haley would carry if she, like Mrs. Attley, had bags to match every pair of shoes she owned.

"Well," Donna said. "Fancy seeing the two of you here. Together."

Even as he rose to greet her, Matt wondered what Mrs. Attley might be up to. She could hardly be called a fan.

Haley attempted to show a good front for Donna's benefit. She smiled and said politely social words.

Until this very moment, with the obvious censure oozing from Mrs. Attley, Haley had actually been enjoying the time with Matt. Now, though, she just felt conflicted, as if she'd been untrue to herself and the people depending on her.

"Would you care to join us?" Matt offered. "We were just about to order dessert."

Donna cast a critical glance first at Haley and then at Matt. "No, thank you," she said, her tone crisp. "I'm meeting Gladys, for lunch. We were going to discuss the work of a new committee we're both on." The last part was clearly directed toward Haley.

Right then and there Haley wanted the floor to open and swallow her. She was sure word of her defection would get back to the others. Not only had she been consorting with the enemy, she'd been enjoying it.

With what could only be described as a sniff, Mrs. Attley left them.

"You're very quiet all of a sudden," Matt said.

Haley blotted her mouth with the pale-cream napkin then set it aside. If she were to truly be effective, she needed to refocus the conversation, try to salvage what she could of this meeting. She wouldn't take into consideration that she'd simply been enjoying herself with an attractive man. Suddenly she was no longer simply Haley, but an emissary of the church, a role model for young people, a pillar in the community.

The weight of the burden bore heavy, but she'd been cast in the roles so long that the oppressiveness didn't bother her, nor did the fact that sometimes she very much resented not being free to choose the path she walked. At least that's what she told herself.

"I was just thinking about this coming Sunday."

"What about it?"

"Well, I know your new choir will be performing."

"Ministering. And it's not *my* choir. It's a part of the church."

She blinked, and then nodded. "Yes, of course."

Haley struggled to find the right approach for what she wanted to say. With the exception of the moment with Mrs. Attley, they'd managed to dance around the central conflict between them: a fundamental difference in philosophy. If they disagreed on this, she suspected that they'd have doctrinal differences as well. Earlier, she'd found herself reluctant to broach the topic, but since he'd opened the door...

"The music... The music you had the choir sing Sunday, that's what you call ministry?"

"Yes. What would you call it?"

"I..." Haley reached for and twisted the napkin. "I don't know."

Matt leaned forward, his elbows braced on the table. "As a schoolteacher, you know that children learn differently. Some are visual learners and need pictures and images to process information. Others are aural. They learn best when they hear lectures or explanations. They need the words. Still others prefer charts and handouts to best understand the concepts presented by the teacher. A good instructor knows to incorporate all of the methods so no student's need is overlooked."

"That's all true. But a classroom of 25 nine-year-olds is a lot different from a congregation of adults."

"True. And among those adults are people who find God and discover themselves in a variety of ways."

She shook her head. "I'm losing the thread here and the connection, if any, you were trying to make."

"All right. Consider this. Say you're thirsty."

At her nod, he reached for her almost empty goblet of water and pushed it to the middle of the table. "You could drink water to relieve your thirst. That's a universal thirst quencher. No one can deny that fact."

He then pushed a glass of iced tea damp with condensation to the center of the table. "But you could accomplish the same goal, soothing a parched throat with this." Next he reached for and placed his cup of coffee near the water and tea. "This would also work. It's very different, though. It has a different taste, a different consistency, a different temperature. But, the bottom line is, it works just as well."

Haley stared at the three, the goblet, the glass and the cup. Her gaze slowly lifted to his. "I see your point. But you're overlooking one fact."

"What's that?"

Without a word she poured some of the iced tea into the water goblet. Then she topped it off with some of his coffee. She quickly wiped up the liquid that dripped from the side of the cup.

"What you have when it's all mixed together is a mess. Not a concoction fit to quench thirst."

She would have liked that point to have been her

parting salvo, but she needed to know something else. "You'll be introducing other changes in the music department?"

"A few."

She waited, but he didn't elaborate. When the silence between them stretched to awkwardness, Haley cleared her throat. "You're going to run into some powerful opposition."

"I'm here to do a job, Haley."

"If you don't tread carefully, your tenure here will be very short."

"Is that a threat?"

Instead of answering him, Haley reached for her purse that dangled from the back of her chair. "This was…" She paused, searching again to find the right word. *Interesting* seemed too bland; *fun* would give the wrong impression. *Exhausting* was more like it, but she settled for another truth. "It's been enlightening."

"You didn't answer my question."

"I don't threaten people, Mr. Brandon. My role is to guide the church's Christian education program. That means a lot of people, young and old and in between, look to me for guidance and direction. My life, the reflection I send to the world, has to be spotless."

"No one is perfect. Not even you, Haley, no matter how hard you try to be."

"You don't know me, so don't judge me."

He was thoughtful for a moment. "I wonder if you

let anyone, let alone me, get close enough to know you.''

It was her turn to stare at him for a long time. Then she pulled a ten-dollar bill from her wallet and placed it on the table. "For my part of lunch and the tip."

"Keep your money, Haley. I asked you to lunch."

"I was planning to eat here anyway." She settled the strap of her handbag over her shoulder then stroked it as if she were drawing courage from the soothing repetitive motion.

He gestured for their server, but when Haley took a step away, he placed a ten on the table on top of hers. "Keep the change."

"Thanks. I didn't get your name," the waitress said. "I'm Sarah."

He glanced toward Haley, but she was already winding her way through the tables and to the door. "I'm Matt. Everything was great. Thanks."

The waitress scooped up the money and tucked it in the pocket of an apron folded over at the waist. "Waste of time pursuing her," she told him. "She's nothing but a holier than thou."

Matt was beginning to agree, though he didn't say anything to the waitress. His new personal challenge was to break down the emotional walls Haley had constructed.

Outside, he caught up with her. Without actually running, she'd put a lot of distance between them.

He grabbed her hand. "What are you running from?"

That stopped her. "I'm not running *from* anything.

I told you I have an appointment, to which, if you don't let me go, I'm going to be late.''

"I want to see you again," he said.

"You will. In church. I'll be the one leading the crusade to have you ousted."

Ouch. Well, at least he knew where he stood with her. Haley was a woman of strong convictions. Is that why she'd managed in such a short time to get under his skin? Another man would take her brush-offs, pick up his bruised pride or ego and find someone else to pursue. But Matt couldn't do that. Something about Haley compelled him to stay, to attempt to get behind and beyond the defensive wall she'd constructed.

"I enjoyed having lunch with you."

Her answering grunt sounded like "Go away."

Matt refused to give up. "Just tell me this one thing."

She sighed. "What?"

"Is it me, the music or a combination of both?"

Her glare, evidently meant to encourage him to back off, had the opposite effect. But she didn't need to know that.

Chapter Eight

Matt wasn't at all surprised to find Haley sitting in the back of the music room at the inspirational choir's next rehearsal. She smiled and chatted with the young people, but when they separated into their vocal parts and all faced him, Matt couldn't miss the intense scrutiny she sent his way.

If she wanted this to be a test of wills, Haley Cartwright didn't know it, but she played way out of her league. He'd done battle with the best. And no one was going to chase him away before he did what he'd been directed to do in this town.

Of course, Lord, the mission would be easier if you'd just clue me in as to what it's supposed to be.

Matt didn't question that he'd been led to Wayside and to this church in particular. If he'd been tapped to do something other than music, that something had not yet been revealed to him. Until it was, though, he'd stand still.

The rehearsal went exceptionally well. Haley slipped out after the second song.

She was reluctant to admit it, but Matt had a way with the teenagers. They seemed to open to him, responding to him as he encouraged and prompted them through the rehearsal. It couldn't be an age-relevant appeal. She guessed Matt to be in his early thirties, thirty-two at the most. But the teens responded to him in ways they'd never done with her. She'd always considered her relationship with them healthy and open. But watching their faces blossom, their easy laughter and the way they all seemed to anxiously await his next word or move made Haley realize that she received quiet respect from them while Matt seemed to be making personal connections.

''New-kid-on-the-block syndrome,'' she told herself. If not that, she'd have to face the unpleasant idea that she did harbor a streak of puritanism that was off-putting. She'd also be forced to admit that a touch of jealousy at his easy acceptance into her domain hovered around her as well.

The Committee of Displeased Christians, as Haley had taken to calling Edward and the ladies, didn't make another appearance at her front door. But Haley felt their collective disapproval Sunday morning when the twenty-voice inspirational choir made its debut.

Haley's stomach was in knots. She hadn't slept well the night before. And she didn't know if she was nervous for Matt or dreading the fact that the stability and tradition she loved so much was threatened.

The first thing she noticed when she took a seat in

her usual fifth-row pew was the number of faces she didn't recognize. Community Christian's congregation occasionally saw visitors; usually a family's out-of-town relatives or a college student home for the weekend with a roommate. But today, remarkably, there were lots of new faces, most of them young.

She opened her Bible and glanced at the book-marked page. She read the Scripture in Psalms, but two minutes later couldn't recall a thing about it. She closed her Bible and studied the bulletin. The inspirational choir would sing three times.

During his remarks and introduction of the choir, Reverend Baines asked everyone to keep an open mind.

Haley tried to do that. She tried to focus on the lyrics instead of the tambourines and shakers and the shouting out that was apparently intentional. She tried, but couldn't get past the fact that it all seemed so sacrilegious.

Intellectually, she knew there were people who worshipped this way. But she'd been drawn to Community Christian because it didn't swing with every new trend in the market.

She glanced around, saw on the animated faces of some of the visitors a true enjoyment, heard a few hands clapping from regular members and felt the foot tapping from the person next to her. But Haley could find no joy in it. She couldn't even understand what the choir members were saying half the time. The only song she recognized was what sounded like a disco version of ''This Little Light of Mine.''

Despite Reverend Baines's enthusiastic support of

the new choral group and a spirit-filled sermon about acceptance, Haley had a raging headache by the time the benediction was finally said at twelve-thirty.

Quickly gathering her purse and her Bible, she headed to a side door to slip out.

"Well, I liked the music," she overheard someone say.

A peek around a pillar showed Haley it was Janice McDonald with her sister. Haley paused to listen to the commentary.

"It was all right. A little on the loud side," Joyce Porter said. "But I'm more worried about my roast. We've been in there so long it's probably shoe leather by now."

"Oh, dear. I didn't even think about that. I had a chicken in the oven. I'll call you later, all right. I hope the house hasn't burned down."

Haley smiled as the two women hurried down the steps. With the extra music, the service had been extended about fifteen minutes to accommodate the second choir.

By the time she got home, changed clothes and got some water boiling for tea, Haley felt a little better. When the phone rang and Amber invited her over for dinner, Haley quickly accepted. A person would have to be crazy to turn down an invitation when Amber was in the kitchen.

A while later after finishing off a fruit salad for dessert and cleaning up the dishes, the cousins decided to take a walk to work off their rich meal.

"I figured you'd want to talk about the baskets," Amber said.

"The baskets?"

Amber waved a hand in front of Haley's face. "Hello? For Market Days. You're on the committee and I cook your food. That thing."

Haley smiled. "Ah, those baskets. Yours will probably go for top dollar again this year. You should reconsider your policy."

"Having a date, even spending one afternoon with some guy who has just one thing on his mind is not my idea of fun."

"Everybody's not like Raymond Alvarez."

Amber shuddered at the name, and Haley was instantly contrite. She reached for her cousin's hand. "I'm sorry. I shouldn't have mentioned his name."

Folding her arms tight around her chest, Amber looked straight ahead as they walked. "I should be over it all by now. Sometimes it just hits me hard and I jump at shadows."

"Have you given any more thought to getting some counseling? You could talk to Kara. She's terrific. Her office is..."

"No, Haley."

"What about Cliff Baines? As a minister, he's..."

"No," Amber said again. "The only counseling I need is putting distance, physical and emotional, between me and him."

Haley wanted to tell Amber that she couldn't run forever, but they'd had this conversation. And each time Amber rebuffed Haley's attempts to help, her offers to assist Amber in finding some closure.

"What'd your preacher man do today?"

Haley blinked, surprised at the swift change in the

conversation. Did Amber really want to know what Reverend Baines preached about?

"Well, his text was out of the Gospel of Mark, when Jesus had the disciples..."

"Not that preacher," Amber interrupted. "*Your* preacher, Matt Brandon."

Haley bristled at the connection. "He's not a preacher or my anything."

"Uh-huh," Amber said as she picked up the pace of their walk. "That's why any mention of him or what happened at church today was conspicuously absent from our dinner conversation."

"I don't know what you're talking about."

"Mmm-hmm. Denial is not a river in Egypt, you know."

Haley stopped walking. Amber looked back at her.

"I'm afraid," Haley said.

Amber was at her side in an instant. She tucked Haley's arm in hers and they walked the way they did when they were girls. "What are you afraid of?"

"Do you think I'm close-minded?"

Amber took her time formulating an answer. "I wouldn't say that necessarily. You're cautious. You're far more conservative than I am."

"That's a nice way of saying you think I'm close-minded."

"I think you don't necessarily give a fair hearing to ideas that conflict with your own."

Haley stiffened, but Amber pulled her along. "Close-minded, bigoted and overweight. Great. It's no wonder I'm still single."

"You're a terrific woman, Haley Cartwright.

You're beautiful, and you have a gentle spirit that a lot of us could use.''

The words were kind of Amber, but Haley knew what was valued in society. So instead of focusing on her shortcomings, she thought about the problem at hand. It bothered her that Matt's music concerned her.

''I think I need to talk to him.''

''Your Matt?''

''Please stop calling him *my* Matt. He's not my anything.''

''He's the guy who, unlike anyone else who's come through here, has gotten under your skin. If I were you, I'd spend a little time asking why. You're obviously turned on by him.''

''Amber.'' Haley's tone clearly indicated that she'd had just about enough.

''Don't 'Amber' me. You try to pretend that being religious means you're not human. Well, church people fall in love and have physical relationships too.''

''Amber, please.''

''I'm not saying you need to hop in bed with the man. I'd be disappointed if you did. That's not your style. Never has been. But,'' she said, emphasizing the word, ''it's no sin to be intrigued with a man.''

Well, this was a switch; Amber lecturing Haley on sin.

Haley stopped walking.

''What?''

''Nothing,'' Haley said. ''A thought just hit me.'' And it wasn't at all a pleasant one. Had she been an ineffective witness to Amber and to everyone else she encountered because she lectured?

"Amber, am I a stick-in-the-mud and by-the-rules type?"

"Yes. Why?"

Haley's shoulders slumped. She hadn't expected Amber to be so blunt. But it was true. She was. And her teens knew it, that's why they gravitated to Matt, someone who accepted them as they were and didn't pass judgment, unspoken or otherwise. Matt was fun and hip and cool.

"I want to be cool," she said.

"You spend too much time at church and running around with your do-gooder groups to be cool. But being cool isn't everything. So before you get all huffed up, there's nothing wrong with all that volunteer work. You just don't leave any time for you. If you're single, it's because you choose to be. You don't allow any time in your life for anyone to get close to you."

Haley flinched. Matt had said exactly the same thing...and he'd known her for just a few weeks.

"So I'm antisocial to boot."

"You're getting the wrong picture."

"No. It's all becoming pretty clear to me," Haley said.

"Wayside might be on the small side when compared to Portland or Salem. But there are things to do and see here. People do have social lives in Wayside. I should know, I cater a lot of their events."

"All right," Haley said, her mind made up. "You're right, at least on that point. I could get out more."

Amber grinned as they turned to head back down

her street. "So you're going to ask that Matt Brandon out?"

Haley looked horrified. "Don't be ridiculous!"

"Then what's your plan?"

Haley glanced at her cousin. "I don't know. But I'll think of something."

"I'm not taking no for an answer, Matt," Nancy Baines said. "You're having Sunday dinner with us."

Matt acquiesced under the dual salvos. "I thought members were supposed to invite the pastor and his wife to dinner."

Nancy looped an arm through Matt's. "You're new in town. Besides, I'm sure a bachelor such as yourself doesn't always get a four-square meal."

Reverend Baines zipped the garment bag around his robe and reached for his briefcase. "For all you know, Nancy, he could be a gourmet chef."

She glanced at Matt. "Are you?"

Matt chuckled. "No. But I do know my way around a grill."

Since he'd taken an immediate liking to Nancy Baines, Matt looked forward to spending time with the couple.

The Baineses' house, like the people it sheltered, was warm and inviting. By the time they settled in the living room for coffee and dessert, Matt knew he was well on the way to forging a solid friendship with Nancy and Cliff. Overstuffed chairs, much like the one's in Reverend Baines's office at the church, and a chintz sofa flanking two matching Queen Anne chairs invited visitors to sit and stay a while. Matt and Nancy chose the sofa while the reverend kicked back in one of the chairs, an embroidered footstool tucked under his feet. After talking about the church and Matt's role as music director, they'd discovered a mutual interest in rock climbing and the great outdoors.

"You'll have to do some hiking up Mount Hood. It's gorgeous," Nancy said. "We frequently do day hikes. Would you like to join us one Saturday?"

"I would," Matt said, looking forward to the outing. "Wayside is much smaller than Portland."

"Don't let the size fool you. Seventeen thousand people makes it interesting."

Nancy clapped her hands together. "Oh, Matt. You'll have to bid on a basket at the picnic Saturday."

Matt smiled. "What's this about auctioning picnic baskets? That's all I heard this morning. I never did have time to get the full explanation."

"I'll let the committee woman fill you in on all the details."

Nancy Baines waved a dismissing but playful hand in her husband's direction. "Don't mind him. He's still holding a grudge from last year. He got distracted and one of the deacons outbid him for my basket."

"I did not get distracted. It was a deliberate setup. He just wanted your Boston cream pie."

Watching the byplay between the two, Matt smiled. His widowed grandmother raised him, so as a child he never experienced the easy camaraderie between a loving couple. He liked seeing it between Cliff and Nancy Baines.

"Don't let his griping fool you, Matt. He got off like a bandit because he ended up sharing Haley's basket with Deacon Prentiss."

Despite his sudden and intense interest, Matt tried not to show it. "Haley can cook?"

"Oh, yes," Nancy said. "She has a few specialties that everyone loves. But it's really her cousin Amber who is the dynamo in the kitchen. It's a well-known secret that whatever's in Haley's picnic basket was probably prepared by Amber."

Matt wondered if this Amber looked anything like Haley. The thought that two tall, striking blondes might be walking around town seemed a bit of a cruel fate to put on a man.

"How are things going between you two?" Cliff asked.

He shrugged. "Oh, about as well as you'd expect between the Hatfields and the McCoys or the Union and the Confederacy."

The minister winced.

"What's this?" Nancy asked glancing between the two men. "You and Haley don't get along? Haley Cartwright?"

"We kind of got off on the wrong foot."

She patted his knee. "Well, I know just the thing to straighten out the situation."

"What's that?" he asked.

Reverend Baines sighed. "Now, Nancy. I think Matt can take care of his own social agenda."

"Nonsense. A gentle nudge in the right direction is all I'm providing. Matt's new in town. Besides, you're the one who thinks they should—"

Reverend Baines suddenly broke out in a fit of coughing. Nancy glanced at him.

"Are you all right?" Matt asked.

"He's fine," Nancy declared with a shake of her head.

"What, exactly, did you have in mind?" the subject of their discussion asked.

"Why, it's simple," she exclaimed. "You'll have to be the highest bidder for Haley's picnic basket Saturday. Then the two of you can go someplace quiet and talk out your troubles."

Matt knew it wasn't that simple. He had no intention of chasing Haley or making any kind of public declaration for her. The picnic auction sounded charming, like something straight out of the 1950s. Unfortunately, it was the twenty-first century and not everyone in Wayside seemed to know.

But by the time Saturday rolled around, he'd gotten a pretty decent picture of just how much this so-called innocent auction meant to the busybodies of the town. And apparently, that club had a full membership.

No less than five people from church, two of them choir members, suggested that he bid on Haley's basket at the Market Days festival.

The whole town seemed to be on a matchmaking mission. Or was it just his imagination? If Matt had been a conspiracy theorist he'd be on red alert about now. It was one thing to be interested in a woman and quite another to have what was starting to feel like an entire community in on the courtship.

Upon awakening Saturday morning, Matt had a good mind to go explore the Mount Hood area. He'd been thinking about getting some hiking in. But he knew he wouldn't. Not today. If nothing else, his curiosity had been piqued about this whole picnic culture.

Colorful blue, yellow and red banners proclaiming it the annual Market Days flapped on every signpost and telephone pole in the downtown area. From window displays to radio spots, merchants offered discounts and specials.

And from what he gathered, the entire event was an excuse for shopping and gossiping, a throwback to the town's trading post and way-station roots. Matt couldn't imagine any such event in the cities where he'd spent most of his adult life. Memphis, Nashville, New York and New Orleans had other things going for them.

Donned in jeans, a white T-shirt and a sport jacket, Matt made his way downtown, an easy walk from his house. The gazebo in the middle of the town square seemed the focal point. Clusters of people stood on the grass while others seemed to be headed in that direction.

"Here you go, young man," an elderly woman said. Dressed in bright-pink sweats and matching sneakers and with a white shock of hair poufed out all around her head, she looked a lot like a live Power Puff girl. She pressed a neon blue flier into his hands. "Don't lose that discount card. You'll need it to get the best deals."

"Deals?"

She grinned up at him. "A newbie are you?"

Pointing to the detachable discount card, she told

him, "You take that to any of the stores in town, just about everybody participates, and you'll get a discount or a buy-one-get-one. Some of 'em even give away free stuff if you show the card."

Matt turned the flier over. "Sounds like a good deal."

"And it's valid for both today and tomorrow." She leaned in close. "If you have a special lady, the jeweler has a blowout going on bracelets and rings. All the young bloods wait until Market Days to get their sweeties a little something."

"I'll keep that in mind."

"And if you don't," she said, batting a fake eyelash up at him, "I'll have a picnic basket up for bid. I make a mean turkey sandwich. My name's Pearl."

He smiled. "Nice meeting you, Miss Pearl. I'm Matt."

Pearl waved as she headed with her handful of fliers to a group of women who were setting up lawn chairs. "Hi there," she called out to them.

Shaking his head, Matt continued along the perimeter of the town square. Flowers bloomed in profusion in neat rows that created a border around the square. And a tree, Matt guessed cherry, marked each directional corner. Everything about Wayside was sheer Americana—Norman Rockwell meets Mayberry R.F.D. at the Petticoat Junction.

Within minutes, the town square was full. He'd looked, but so far hadn't seen Haley or anyone else he recognized from Community Christian Church. Not that he'd have been able to actually see anyone in the crush of people.

Matt found a good spot from which to watch the proceedings. The auctioneer greeted everyone. After reminding the bidders that the proceeds would be split between the library's acquisition fund and a college scholarship, he announced that the minimum opening bid for all picnic baskets was ten dollars.

"So, what do you think so far?"

Recognizing her voice, Matt smiled, but he didn't turn to face her. "Quaint. Cute."

"You're making fun."

"No," he said, this time facing Haley. "It's all of the things we need more of. Good, clean, wholesome activities."

Haley surveyed the crowd. "Nice turnout today."

"Do you have a basket up for bid?"

"And if I do?"

"I was just making conversation."

She cast her eyes toward the ground. "I'm sorry. Not that you'd ever know it from any time we've been together, but I'm really a quiet homebody type."

"So I bring out the…"

Her gaze connected with his, waiting for those last words.

"… protective instinct in you."

Yeah, self-preservation, Haley thought.

It had taken her an hour to dress because she'd been through most of her closet trying to find just the right outfit in case someone interesting actually bid on her basket. Last year, she'd had lunch with Deacon Prentiss. Reverend Baines joined them after being outbid for his wife's basket. The year before that, she'd also shared a meal with Deacon Prentiss who'd promised to make a hefty bid on her this year, too.

Haley wondered if Matt would participate. She'd drawn a high number this year and would be one of the last to go forward.

Most of the lunches went in the twenty-five to thirty-five dollar range. Haley explained to Matt that the baskets usually contained enough food to feed four to six people, sometimes more, sometimes less, particularly if sweethearts bid for an afternoon together.

"Folks, we're in for a treat now," the auctioneer said a while later. He picked up a large wicker basket with a cheerful yellow bow. "This is Amber Montgomery's basket. Now everybody knows that no matter what's in here, you're gonna be in for some good eating." He glanced down at a notecard in his hand. "Amber won't be able to join the winning bidder for lunch, but she does say that if the winner remembers to return her picnic basket and pie plate, she'll exchange it for four of her pecan honey rolls."

A cheer and applause welled up from the crowd gathered around. Matt turned to Haley for the translation.

"It's her specialty. You can buy one over at the Wayside Inn Bed-and-Breakfast, but it'll cost you."

The bidding on the absent Amber's basket opened at twenty-five dollars. When it ended, one of the town's firefighters claimed it for $82.50.

Matt looked stunned. "For lunch? That's insane."

"It is an all-time high," Haley said. "Even for Amber's basket." She watched the firefighter claim his basket and wondered if he was sweet on Amber, or if it was just his turn to cook at the station house.

"And remember," she added. "It's all for a good cause."

Next up was Pearl. She waved enthusiastically while the auctioneer introduced her and read off what she'd prepared. The bidding opened at ten dollars and slowly went to eighteen fifty.

"Twenty bucks," Matt hollered out.

Haley's mouth dropped open.

"Hi, Matt," Pearl waved enthusiastically. "Walter, if you plan on getting any of that apple cobbler, you gotta beat that young hottie's bid."

The crowd roared, and all eyes turned to check out the hottie.

Haley's face flamed. She tried to edge away from Matt but he reached for and held on to her hand.

With a scowl directed toward Matt, Pearl's beau Walter bid twenty-two, and the auctioneer, who knew how to avoid trouble, quickly closed the bidding.

Pearl grabbed the microphone from him. "Don't you worry none, Matt. You stop by my house any afternoon and I'll make you a nice turkey sandwich and some cobbler."

"I'll take you up on that," Matt hollered back, to the delight of the crowd.

"How do you know Pearl?"

Matt stuck his hands in his pockets. "Oh, we go way back."

Haley instantly missed the warmth of his hand in hers. Before she had time to analyze that to death, they were calling for the owners of lots twenty-five to thirty-five to make their way forward.

"That's me," Haley said, excusing herself.

As she went to stand in line, Haley wondered for the umpteenth time why she did this every year. On some level, she supposed she'd always wanted a handsome and interesting man in the crowd to bid on her basket. Sitting on a quilt they'd share a meal and talk about their hopes and dreams. One thing would lead to another, and before long, Haley would be standing in front of the altar, the man who'd bid on her basket at her side as they exchanged vows.

The flaws in the fantasy were, unfortunately, two-fold. First, Wayside didn't have any handsome, interesting men who appealed to her, and second, the only men who ever bid for her lunches were elderly gents from church just being kind.

"I am not doing this next year," she vowed as she stepped up to stand next to the auctioneer.

"Ladies and gentleman, next up is Miss Haley Cartwright. She's a teacher and one of the Market Days committee members. Let's give a hand to Miss Cartwright for helping organize this annual event."

Polite applause rippled through the square.

Deacon Prentiss opened the bidding at fifteen dollars. Someone she didn't recognize took it to twenty. Haley scanned the crowd looking for Matt, but he was no longer on the edge of the square where she'd left him. He'd obviously lost interest and headed home or elsewhere.

"We have a bid for twenty-five, do I hear thirty?"

Haley's attention went back to the auctioneer. Who'd bid twenty-five?

Then, about three people deep in the crowd, she spotted Reverend and Mrs. Baines. Nancy waved and gave her the thumbs-up sign. Haley bit back something of a sigh. One of them had probably made the bid. They were just trying to increase the amount of money for the library and scholarship.

"Thirty dollars," Deacon Prentiss called out.

The auctioneer pointed to him. "Thirty going once, going twice."

"One hundred dollars," a clear voice rang out from the right.

The crowd gasped. Heads swiveled as people tried to get a look at who'd made such an outrageous bid.

"Sold," the auctioneer boomed.

Haley's heart beat triple time. No one had ever bid that much money for a Market Days picnic basket. Who would be that crazy?

The crush of people parted and Matt walked up. "I believe this is mine," he said, hefting the basket with one hand and holding his other out for Haley.

Chapter Nine

"Have you lost your mind?"

He smiled up at her. "Maybe. Come on. I'm hungry."

Haley had two choices: she could go with Matt or she could stand on the gazebo steps looking shell-shocked while almost two-hundred people looked on. Seeing as how being in the spotlight always made her a little queasy, she really had just one option.

She put her hand in Matt's.

It was strong, warm and completely enveloped hers.

Catcalls and applause followed her progress down the steps of the gazebo. With a big grin, Matt bowed to the crowd, but he never let go of Haley's hand or of his picnic basket. Haley thought she might die of embarrassment.

"Do you have to show off?"

He glanced at her. "Yes. I just got the best basket and the prettiest girl in Wayside, Oregon."

Her blush of embarrassment became another kind.

"Where to?" he asked as the auctioneer began introducing the next lot.

"I have a quilt spread out over there," Haley said pointing toward the far edge of the square, away from the crush of people but close enough to enjoy the band that would strike up again as soon as the bidding ritual ended.

Matt led the way to a well-worn blue, pink and white quilt. "Hmm, churn dash, right?" he said eyeing the pattern.

"Don't tell me you quilt."

He laughed. "Hardly." While Haley smoothed out an edge, he settled the basket in the middle. A small two-quart cooler and a canvas tote bag were already there. "My grandma is the quilter. She has a couple of favorite patterns. That one," he said with a nod toward Haley's quilt. "And the double wedding ring."

Haley glanced over at him at that, but she didn't say anything.

"Everybody in the family who gets married gets a wedding ring quilt from her."

"Do you have yours with you?"

He grinned and pointed at her with a nod. "Smooth."

Haley shrugged. "You opened the door."

He held a hand out to assist her in settling on the quilt. When they were both seated, Haley reached for the basket. "Let's see what we have here."

"Is that your way of saying you don't know what's

in there? I just paid a hundred bucks for a mystery lunch?''

She smiled. ''You did that anyway.'' She reached for his hand. ''Thank you, Matt. You didn't have to be so generous with your donation. As a member of the committee, I thank you on behalf of all of us.''

He covered her hand with his other one and warmth spread through Haley.

''I didn't get this,'' he said with a nod toward the basket, ''to make a donation to your cause.''

''Then why?''

''Because I seriously doubted you'd agree to a date with me otherwise.''

Haley snatched her hand away and sat up on her knees. ''This isn't a date.''

''What do you call it?''

''Lunch. A Market Days event. A charity benefit.''

He shook his head. ''I could have bid on and won any one of those baskets. But there was just one that truly held my interest.''

''Pearl's.''

''No, Haley Cartwright's.''

''Matt, please.''

''I thought you'd never ask.''

He closed the distance between them and pulled her to him. When his lips covered hers, all Haley could do was sigh. She leaned into the embrace enjoying the sweetness of the moment and the man.

But before she lost herself in it and him, he pulled back. His smile was gentle, even tender.

''Matt, we shouldn't...''

He placed a finger on her lips. ''Truce?''

Haley wanted to enjoy this afternoon. This was probably the closest she'd ever come to seeing her fantasy fulfilled. Was it so wrong to just spend an afternoon pretending her life resembled the one that inhabited her dreams?

"We have some differences, Matt. Differences that can't be resolved over chicken and turnovers."

He reached for the flap on the basket. "Hmm, is that what's in there?"

"Matt."

"I know, Haley. And I've been giving this some thought."

"You have? Why?"

For a moment, he didn't say anything. Then he replied, "We talked about this a little before. I'm supposed to be here, Haley. In Wayside. At Community Christian Church. I'm a long way from the place I used to call home. The more time I spend here, the more I'm beginning to think that *this* is my home now."

"But being here in Wayside doesn't mean you have to turn our church into a nightclub."

The relaxed contentment evident on his face a moment ago vanished. "Is that what my music sounds like to you?"

She bit her lower lip, but nodded, cautiously. It was already too late to salvage the bucolic serenity of the afternoon.

"I have an idea," he said.

She eyed him. "What?"

"Let's go back to our original plan and mission."

"Which was?"

"Let's, together, come up with a compromise. I think once we really sit down we'll find there are some things we agree on."

Haley sat back on her heels, contemplating his offer. "The last time didn't work out so well."

"That was before we knew each other."

We still don't know each other, Haley thought. But she knew that to be a fib. She knew more about Matt Brandon than she'd known about the man she'd planned to marry. Of Timothy, she knew what he did for a living, the kind of car he drove, where he went to school and that his grandparents were descendants of pioneers who settled the Northwest Territory. It wasn't until he'd broken her heart that she'd realized that the outer trappings didn't at all matter, at least not in his case.

Haley looked at Matt, this time taking her time about the critical assessment. Some women, scratch that, most women would find him attractive in that bad boy sort of way. Haley wasn't attracted to bad boys. She liked calm, rational, logical men.

"Haley?"

"I'm thinking about it," she snapped.

Then there was that to consider. Matt seemed to bring out the worst in her. Did she truly want to forge a relationship with a man who made her shrewish?

Vetoing the effort it would take to figure out the why of *that*, she said, "Let's just have lunch. We'll let this park be neutral ground."

He chuckled. "In New Orleans, that's what we call a grassy area between two streets."

"I beg your pardon?"

"The French and the Americans didn't get along in early New Orleans, but they needed to do business together. So, the grassy medians were declared neutral ground, places where no fights or quarrels or duels would take place."

She looked around. "This town square is our neutral ground."

"All right," he said. "For now."

Haley didn't at all like the tone of that "for now." It was as though he planned that they'd have yet another showdown. Would they eventually have to tag every grassy spot in the town as neutral territory? Haley didn't want to live her life with that much conflict.

There was an easy solution: maybe it was time to look for another church.

But Haley banished that thought as quickly as it formed. She loved her church, and she loved the Baineses. She wasn't going to let a philosophical difference with the choir director run her out of the sanctuary or from the people she'd come to love so much.

"There's raspberry iced tea in there," she said, pointing to the cooler. She popped the latch on the basket and began pulling out the meal Amber had prepared.

She'd have lunch with the man. He could call it a date if he wanted. But Haley knew what it really was: a strategic retreat.

"Haley?"

She glanced at him.

"In answer to your earlier fishing expedition, my grandmother has yet to make a wedding ring quilt for me."

Haley ducked her head and reached for cutlery. She fervently hoped Matt didn't see the smile that blossomed on her face.

But, of course, he did.

Across the square, Cindy Worthington and Amanda Attley peered in the direction where Matt and Haley sat huddled together.

"I told you all that hostility was just a show," Cindy said. "Look at them. Don't they make a cute couple?"

"Cindy, I think we need to stop spying on them."

"We're not spying. We're at the gazebo listening to the band and voilà! There's our Sunday school director and choir master snuggled together under a cherry tree. I think it's sweet."

"We shouldn't be intruding on them."

Cindy gazed at the couple, but Matt Brandon had her attention. "He's so dreamy."

Amanda hit her arm. "Eeww. Come on. The guys are waiting for us at the ice cream shop. And they're paying, so let's hurry before they forget that part."

"I'll bet he's a terrific kisser."

"Yeah, he probably is. But that's for Haley to decide." Amanda frowned. "He's not interested in teenagers like us. And if he is, we've got bigger problems." She grabbed Cindy's arm. "Come on, Cindy. You've been dying for Adam to ask you out. Don't blow it now."

Amanda waved a hand in front of Cindy's face. "Hello. Earth to Worthington."

"I'm here," Cindy said. "I was just wishing I were

ten years older and had Haley's pretty blond streaks. You know, those highlights are natural. I'd kill for that effect.''

Shaking her head, Amanda dragged Cindy away from the square and toward Pop's Ice Cream and Malt Shoppe where their dates waited.

The two teenagers weren't the only ones witnessing Haley and Matt's shared lunch.

''I didn't have to do a thing,'' Nancy Baines told her husband. ''Look at them. Her light to his dark makes a striking pair, a nice balance don't you think, dear?''

''I think you dropped enough not-so-subtle hints the other day that the man felt obligated to bid on her picnic basket. You made her sound like a hunch-backed hag who could only get a pity date from her pastor and a hard-of-hearing eighty-year-old.''

Nancy scowled at him. ''Don't be ridiculous. Haley is a lovely girl. She's just too focused on, on actually, I don't know what,'' she said cocking her head to study Haley's profile. ''Maybe it's work. Or community things. You know she volunteers all over town. She always seems so busy.'' Worry etched her brow.

''They say idle hands—''

She cut him off. ''I know, I know. But Haley just seems to always be on the go. I'm glad she's found someone to relax with. You were right when you said they'd make a good pair.''

''Now, Nancy…''

Nancy's smile blossomed again when she saw Matt hold a piece of fruit out to Haley. ''Isn't that sweet?''

"That's the most disgusting display I've ever seen," Donna said from her vantage point on the south side of the square. "Just look at that. You'd think the girl would show a little restraint. Flaunting herself all over the place. And look at him. Why I never!" she exclaimed.

"They're just eating lunch," her companion said.

Donna sniffed. "And what would you know about decorum?"

"Apparently, not a lot since I'm here with you. What would people think if they saw us together?"

"I am not amused."

Edward chuckled. "Well, I'm going to be on my way. I'll see you later tonight?"

"I'll think about it," Donna said. She focused again on Haley and the new choir director. "Not at all suitable."

She turned to make another comment but found she was standing all alone on the grass.

Matt hadn't planned to kiss her. Not out here in the middle of Wayside's public square where attention had already been on them after his outrageous bid. He hadn't planned to spend one hundred dollars for lunch, either. But the money meant nothing. Spending time with Haley meant everything.

The more he watched and listened to her, the more he realized how very much she cared for the people of the town and the church. That sort of dedication appealed to him.

He'd told her he'd been searching for a place to call home. As he watched her, as he spent time with her, it dawned on him that maybe he'd been sent to Wayside for more than just ministry.

Maybe Haley was the key to this whole thing.

Matt had never really thought about settling down. He'd always figured a wife and a family would come at some point in the future. After the scandal with Melanie, the last thing on his mind was a relationship. It had, however, been three years. Wasn't that enough time for absolution?

On his cross-country trek and in a couple of the places where he'd stayed longer than a month, he'd met women. But he'd made it abundantly clear that he wasn't interested. The more aggressive ones always decided to take him on as a project. But when their attention got out of hand, Matt simply packed his bags and moved on, ever west. At some point, he realized that he'd soon run out of land. But before he had to decide about heading farther west to Hawaii or Guam or Tokyo he'd found little Wayside. And in small ways, he'd started putting down roots here. A music ministry at a church, even one the size of Community Christian was a big commitment on his part.

"Matt?"

He blinked.

"Are you all right? You had the oddest expression on your face."

He smiled. "I'm fine. Blessed."

From her questioning expression, one she tried to mask with a polite smile, Matt knew she didn't quite know what to make of him.

It wasn't every day that a man had an epiphany, though. In that moment he'd known—so many things became clear. It was as though a portal had opened for him or a path revealed in a densely populated forest. He'd been sent to Wayside, to this tiny little place thousands of miles from home, not to find himself. Not to learn to minister in small ways, and not to fine-tune lessons in humility and sacrifice—though the good Lord knew he needed a double dose of those. No, he'd been led here for none of those reasons.

He'd been led here to find Haley.

Despite all their conflicts, or maybe because of them, he was falling for the blond beauty who took the word *dedication* to new levels.

She completed him. And it had all happened in just the few weeks he'd known her. It had happened in spite of her opposition to him, and in spite of her obvious reluctance in developing any kind of relationship.

Matt wondered if it had been this clear and apparent for his parents. Somehow, he doubted it. They'd apparently had a lot more to overcome than a difference in musical philosophy. According to his grandmother, his mother had loved deeply, but always the wrong men at the wrong times. And then, in the end, she'd loved something more than she did her own son.

Since he remembered nothing of her, Matt couldn't judge his mother. His grandmother had showered him with all the love he ever needed or wanted. He just wasn't sure if he was capable, particularly at this point in his life, of being completely immersed in another person.

It wasn't that he was incapable. He knew he could feel deep affection and emotion. He just didn't think there could be room in his heart to fully accept another person. His walk with the Lord filled him up too much these days, so much that he wondered just how Haley Cartwright had managed to slip beyond his own well-fortified defenses.

She handed him a plate and then served him from the basket, strips of marinated chicken, a salsa to go with the poultry. She then opened the lid on a small container.

"Hmm," she said. "This looks like couscous."

"I paid one hundred bucks and you don't know what's in the basket you prepared."

Haley giggled. Her face lit up with childlike pleasure. And Matt was eternally grateful that at least here in this town square with its flowers and gazebo, they agreed to look beyond their differences.

She swiped a stray tendril from her eyes and sat back on her haunches. "It's no secret among the people who support this event that Amber does up my basket, too. This year, I did make the dessert. Lemon tarts. And I brewed the iced tea."

"Then I'll have a lemon tart and a glass of tea, please."

She smiled. Then she pinched off a bit of the chicken. "Open."

He complied. When she fed him the piece of chicken, he caught her hand at his mouth and held on a moment too long. Their eyes met. Haley's widened.

"Mmm," he said. "This is good."

Haley snatched her hand back and busied herself with serving the couscous.

"This is *really* good," Matt said again, reaching for another strip of the cold chicken.

"I told you. Amber's a good cook. Matt, you can't keep doing things like that."

"Like what?"

"Touching me. Making me feel..."

She was hesitant to say whatever it was. For a moment, Matt thought he detected fear in her eyes and he was sorry he'd teased her. "I didn't mean to make you uncomfortable. I have a tendency to act first and think later."

And that's what got him in trouble with Melanie.

Since he'd learned his lesson well following that fiasco, it didn't take Matt long to make up his mind about his next move. Every step with her needed to be by the book, straight from a Currier and Ives image. He had nothing to lose and everything to gain— most important, Haley's trust and love. To gain those things, he couldn't overwhelm her.

Over the next half hour they enjoyed the afternoon repast and the band that played at the gazebo.

Matt wanted to stretch out, lay his head in her lap and doze the rest of the afternoon away. But Haley would have a stroke if he did that, so he knew it was time to bring their date on neutral ground to a close. He stood and held a hand out to her.

She eyed him. "What's wrong?"

"Thank you for a lovely afternoon." He shook her hand as though they'd just completed a business transaction. "It's been nice. Very nice."

Haley nodded, since she didn't have anything to add to his assessment. Was he leaving? Why?

"I'll see you at church tomorrow."

"All right," she said, hesitation and confusion evident in her voice and her eyes.

"Thank you again. For everything." But he spoiled a perfectly gracious exit by reaching down and pilfering the last strip of Amber's marinated chicken.

Chapter Ten

Much later, after changing into a pair of white shorts, cropped ankle socks and a Willamette University T-shirt, Haley planned to settle down on the sofa to watch a movie. She'd spent most of the day in unproductive analysis of her entire encounter with Matt. She liked the notion of neutral ground and was glad they'd declared some of their own. The only problem with that was once all the defense mechanisms were removed, she'd discovered that she liked him. Really liked him.

She'd been so rattled by that fact that she didn't even get to any of the shops, and she'd really wanted to take a closer look at some of the new items in the World Emporium, her favorite little specialty shop on Main Street.

Obviously, there was more to Matt Brandon than just his physical appearance and the fact he could play a piano.

Right up until the point when he'd kind of zoned

out on her, she'd really been enjoying his company. But then, before she could get a handle on what had happened, he'd shot up, shaken her hand and scurried away as if an airborne contagion surrounded her.

"Instead of feeling sorry for yourself, you ought to be out finding a life," she muttered. "Everyone else seems to have one."

The microwave pinged and she put that depressing line of thought on hold where it belonged. After dumping the popcorn in a big ceramic bowl and padding to the living room, she settled in to watch the video. This time though, it wasn't a knock on the front door that interrupted her film. The telephone and Amber's insistent voice on the answering machine managed the assault.

"Pick up the phone, Haley. I know you're there. Haley!"

A moment of silence. Then, "If you don't pick up the phone I'm going to start singing." Amber sang off-key onto the tape. Singing was not one of the talents their family had been blessed with.

The answering machine squawked and squealed when Haley picked up the receiver. "All right, I surrender."

"That's more like it," Amber said. "Your movie can wait."

"What makes you think…"

"Haley, please. You're as predictable as the tides."

"I resent that."

"You should. Which brings me to why I called."

Haley clicked the Stop button on the video and leaned her head back on the deep sofa cushions. She'd seen the film a hundred times already and usually recited dialogue along with the actors. Sometimes she longed for a hero like the one on the screen, someone who might transform her from a dishwater-blond schoolmarm into a— Well, that's just where the fantasy always fell apart. She had no desire to become a society belle. She didn't exactly know what she wanted to be transformed into, and she'd grown weary of trying to do the makeover by herself.

"My dyed-in-the-wool practical and predictable little cousin has apparently been testing out some newfound wings."

Haley sighed. When Amber got into riddle mode, the best thing to do was just go with the flow until you could figure it out.

When Haley didn't say anything, Amber cleared her throat. "I'm impressed."

"With what?"

"How you got all the tongues wagging today."

Haley had a pretty good idea of what Amber referred to, but she didn't want to think about it, let alone talk about it. Matt had actually kissed her. In broad daylight. At Market Days. After bidding an unprecedented one hundred dollars for a lunch date with Haley. Her head was still spinning over the entire afternoon. And, if the truth would out, not in an unpleasant way.

"Haley, I know you're there. You can stop playing like you don't hear me. He shelled out a lot of money to spend an hour or so with you."

"I don't want to talk about it."

"Too bad. Everyone else is."

Haley groaned. She covered her face with a throw pillow. "What are they saying?" she asked, her voice muffled.

"What was that?"

Removing the pillow, she sank deeper into the cushions of the sofa. "What are they saying?"

"They who?"

"Amber!"

Amber chuckled.

Beeeepp!

"Ow."

"Sorry," Haley said. "The machine was still running."

"So, my dear. Tell Cousin Amber all the juicy details."

And so Haley did. Afterward, she realized that talking about it took some of the embarrassment away. Though why she was embarrassed she didn't quite know. She was, after all, a grown woman.

She was about to pose a question to Amber when the Call Waiting function chirped in her ear. "Can you hold on?"

"Nah," Amber said. "I have muffins in the oven. More juicy details later?"

"There aren't any more."

Call Waiting chirped again.

She said goodbye to Amber and clicked over. "Hello?"

"Hi, Haley. It's Matt."

Haley couldn't have been any more surprised if the person on the other end identified himself as the president of the United States. "Matt Brandon?"

He chuckled. "So, you know more than one Matt, huh?"

She quickly got a handle on her scattered senses. "No, I don't. You took me by surprise. Why are you calling? Is something wrong at the church?"

She knew she sounded just as perplexed as she felt.

"I was thinking about this afternoon," he said.

Her mind had been there and on little else all day.

"And I was thinking maybe we could extend it."

"Extend it?"

"To dinner and a movie. Tonight."

"Tonight?"

"I know it's short notice. But I thought I'd call anyway."

Haley glanced at the clock on the VCR. Six-thirty.

She'd never done anything impulsive before and definitely not gone out on a spur-of-the-moment date. Dates with Timothy had always been well planned and coordinated affairs on the calendar for two or more weeks.

After the conversation with Amber and her own curiosity, Haley found herself sorely tempted. And after she'd gotten over the embarrassment of how it began, she'd enjoyed the afternoon with Matt. She wondered what it might be like to go out on a real date with him—a date that didn't include the entire town looking on.

"Don't say no," he said. "I'd like to show you that I'm not really a bad guy."

"I never thought that."

"I'm glad. How about it? I understand there's a cinema at Cherry Center Mall."

"Yes," Haley said. "Yes, there's a movie theater at the mall, and yes I'd like to go with you."

"Great. I'll pick you up in say thirty minutes."

Thirty minutes! Then, she thought, *Why not?* Dinner and a movie, that was casual stuff.

"All right." She gave him her address then realized if he'd gotten her number from the telephone book he probably already knew her address.

After hanging up, Haley turned off the TV and VCR saying, "Maybe another night, guys." She abandoned the popcorn bowl in favor of her closet.

Exactly twenty-nine minutes later, her front doorbell rang.

"Wow. You look great," he said.

And she was very glad she'd spent most of the time on hair and makeup. A pair of textured capri pants and a matching turquoise tunic with open-toe sandals completed her look. Haley owned and wore a lot of capri pants, the length and cut accented her height and flattered her somewhat full figure.

Matt wore a modified version of his uniform, this time well-worn jeans, a blue T-shirt and a casual jacket.

She looked beyond him but didn't see the motorcycle. A gleaming SUV sat parked at her curb. Her next-door neighbor Mr. Radabaugh must have traded in his van.

"Did you want me to drive?"

"We'll take the truck."

Matt waited while she got a small wallet purse that she draped across her body. After locking her front door she followed him.

"This is yours?"

"It's not always practical to ride the bike. Especially in an area that gets so much rain." He smiled. "Besides, I need some grown-up transportation every now and then."

He held the door for her and assisted her up by positioning her hand on the grab bar. When warmth suffused her, Haley wondered if he, too, had felt the spark when their hands touched. She chalked it up to fanciful thinking and tried to concentrate on small talk about the weather and the Saturday afternoon turnout for Market Days.

Twenty minutes later they were seated in a booth and had ordered sandwiches and fries.

"You seem to like feeding me."

He smiled. "Mealtime is a good time to get to know each other."

Since she was already going for broke, Haley decided to throw caution to the wind. "And why are you trying to get to know me?"

He reached for her hands and held them in his. His intense gaze locked with hers. "Because I think there's something that should be explored between us. Don't you feel it every time we're near each other?"

Haley thought of the heated exchanges they'd had and tried to pull her hands away. But Matt must have been divining her thoughts.

"And it doesn't matter if we're arguing or just standing there."

"Matt, we still have some basic philosophical differences."

"If we get to know each other better," he said,

''we'll each have a better understanding of the other's point of view.''

She couldn't argue with that. As a matter of fact, that was just the approach she used in the classroom when she taught her pupils about different cultures.

''You know pretty much everything there is to know about me from the interview process,'' he said. ''So, you start. Tell me about the churches you've attended and the way the worship services were done.''

Haley wanted to protest that she *didn't* know that much about Matt's background. As a matter of fact, she knew precious little and had made a point of that fact to the other board members in a church council meeting.

Telling her story first, though, could very well loosen him up a bit so he'd share some things about himself.

''My parents died when I was nine,'' she started. ''They were killed in a car accident. I was shuttled around among the relatives. Mostly down near Springfield and Eugene.''

''How'd you get here?''

''I actually started here. I got back to Wayside when Amber's parents returned home. They were missionaries in Peru,'' she added. ''Her dad got sick and they were sent home. When they decided to stay in Wayside, they sent for me. From the time I was eleven, until…'' She paused. ''Well, until, I lived with Amber, her brother and parents.''

''What's this 'until'?''

Haley hadn't meant to mention that part of her life.

She wanted to forget the entire Timothy episode. But thoughts of what-ifs with Matt Brandon inevitably made her think of her ex-fiancé. That she even had what-if thoughts about Matt was distressing enough.

"Ancient history," she told him. "Buried over, never to be excavated history."

He looked interested, but didn't press her. "They were missionaries so you grew up in church?"

She nodded. "I thought about becoming a missionary. As a matter of fact, that's what I intended to do with my life."

"Why didn't you?"

Haley sighed and sat back. Timothy wouldn't even consider it. His path to a vice presidency at the bank didn't include side trips to places like Honduras, Guatemala and Peru. He'd needed and wanted a full-time country club wife. When her goals didn't meet his, he found someone more suitable, leaving Haley to pick up the pieces of her life. Again. "Other things got in the way," she finally told Matt.

She saw the question in his eyes, but Haley didn't want to travel down this particular regret-lined path. Answering his original question seemed much easier now. "It's a long story. Not pretty. So the short version is I had to make a decision between personal happiness and spiritual fulfillment. I made the wrong choice and had to live with the consequences." She shrugged. "It made me stronger."

Watching her, Matt realized two things: she'd been hurt deeply by a man she'd loved and there was more to Haley Cartwright than she let on. He wondered if she'd ever love him deeply. Getting burned had a tendency to make people gun-shy the next go round. According to Cliff though, that relationship had ended a while ago. And while Haley might not view it as a positive, her steadfastness was a desired trait. Not everybody was willing to stick things out.

She chose her words carefully, so as not to reveal too much. But in doing so she told him a lot. He saw in her the vulnerability she tried to shield and he intuitively knew that she kept herself busy with church and community and volunteer work in an effort to fill the void in her life. The one created by the choice she hadn't made.

Matt knew all about making bad choices, wrong choices. He had a trail of them behind him, and despite his best efforts, he still carted some of that baggage with him even though he traveled light.

"Haley, there's something you need to know about me."

She leaned forward, arms resting on the tabletop. "What is that?"

Could he trust her with the story of his past, the real reason he'd left Louisiana and Tennessee, traveling miles away from memories?

The waitress showed up before he could answer the question to his own satisfaction.

"Dessert? We have a mean peach cobbler tonight. There's also tiramisu, chocolate torte and the house specialty, triple chocolate fudge delight."

Matt looked at Haley but she shook her head. A look at his watch showed they should probably be heading to the movie theater anyway. "Nothing, thank you."

The server left the check and Matt put down enough cash to cover it and a better than average tip. When he held a hand out to Haley, she placed hers in his and slid from the booth.

The theater's three offerings included a romantic comedy that was the perfect date movie, an action film that featured lots of guns and explosions and the latest animated film that was a kid-and-adult cross-over hit.

"Pick your poison," Matt invited.

The two-hour cartoon was just right. At the end, they walked out arm in arm laughing about the antics of the frog that saved the day. Matt drove her home and on the way they still talked about the movie.

"I would have thought you'd pick the romantic comedy," Matt said.

"That's why I didn't. A girl shouldn't be too predictable."

"But you were dying to see it, weren't you?"

Haley grinned. "Yep."

His chuckle warmed her. "We'll see that one next time."

Next time.

Haley realized she liked the sound of that. She met his quick glance before he turned his full attention back to the road. A few minutes later, they arrived in front of her house.

"Would you like to come in for coffee?"

Matt's gaze dipped to her mouth. "I'd better not," he said. "I have an early start tomorrow morning. You do, too."

Haley, suddenly a little nervous in the intimate confines of the truck, licked dry lips. "You're right. I haven't even completed my Sunday school lesson."

"I'll see you to your door."

A moment later, they stood there, sharing the awkward silence of a first date farewell. Matt stuck his hands in the pockets of his jeans. "I'm glad you decided to go out with me tonight."

Haley's gaze met his. "I'm glad you called. You saved me from a night of classic videos and microwave popcorn."

He smiled. "That doesn't sound so bad."

"It's not. It's just…" She stopped a moment before she said "lonely."

But she got the impression that Matt knew just what she'd been about to say.

He leaned forward. But he didn't move to kiss her as she'd thought. Instead, his hand traced the outline of her hair, the caress as soft as a butterfly landing in an outstretched palm. He tucked the crimped tress behind her ear. "Good night, pretty Haley."

And then he was gone.

For a long time Haley stood just inside her front door. The reverence of his touch lingered much more powerfully than a kiss ever would have. When she finally closed the door, she was smiling.

When she arrived at Community Christian in the morning, Eunice met her at the door. Wringing her hands, the normally cheerful church secretary rushed over to Haley.

"Oh, thank goodness you're here."

Haley smiled, ruefully. "What's wrong now?"

With so many emergencies to deal with during the week, Eunice probably didn't even remember that she'd rushed to Haley's side in much the same manner last Sunday.

"Well, first..." Mrs. Gallagher paused. "How did you know something was wrong?"

"You're going to give me a complex about that 'Oh, thank goodness you're here' line. It's always a precursor to a problem."

"Oh." Eunice patted her arm. "Well, that's because you're so good about handling things like this."

"What's going on?"

"Follow me," Eunice said. "They're ganging up on him. He can hold his own, of course, but having someone else on his side would even things out a bit."

Haley almost stopped, turned around and walked right back out the door. What kind of trouble had Matt gotten into now? Just because they'd shared a few moments together didn't mean she was on his side when it came to church matters. Steeling herself, Haley marched down the corridor behind Mrs. Gallagher. But when Haley stopped at the music room door, the church secretary kept moving.

"But Matt's probably in—"

"Hurry," Eunice said. "He could use some help."

A moment later, the older woman stopped, gave a sharp rap on a door and pushed it open without waiting for a response from inside.

There stood Reverend Baines besieged by the Committee of Displeased Christians.

"I understand your concerns," the minister was saying. "And a solution is already in the works."

"Reverend," Eunice called. "Haley just arrived."

All heads turned toward the door where Haley and Eunice stood. Donna, today in a sheath of sunflower gold trimmed in blue, sniffed. "Our Haley has certainly gotten to know the new choir director. Maybe *she* can convince him that Community Christian is no place for all of that—"

Reverend Baines took her hand, interrupting Donna's flow. "No one needs to be convinced of anything," he assured her. "We've already put into place a compromise that will suit everyone."

"Compromise? What compromise?"

Haley wondered the same thing.

Cliff beamed. He clasped his hands together and rocked on the heels of his feet obviously waiting for the others to figure it out.

After a moment, Deacon Worthington harrumphed. "The early service we've been talking about."

"Well, I don't see how that is going to solve anything," Donna said.

Haley was reluctant to cast her lot with the displeased crew, but in this they were correct. Double the problem didn't make it any better. This so-called compromise would only compound the problem.

Reverend Baines glanced around looking at the people crammed into his office. "Christian friends," he began. "No one said the eight o'clock service had to be a replica of our eleven o'clock service."

Folding her arms, Donna narrowed her eyes. "What, exactly, do you mean, Pastor?"

But Haley had already seen where he was going with this. "We let Matt do what he wants at one of the services, and the other is reserved for traditional worship."

"Exactly!" Reverend Baines said.

All of a sudden everyone was talking at once, offering their ideas on just what should be allowed and who would monitor.

The preacher held up a hand. "Eunice and I have already run though all of those issues. The costs, if any, will be minimal. What we'll do is have the early-morning service billed as a contemporary one and the late-morning will remain the same as it's always been."

Eunice went to the pastor's desk and opened a file. "I took the liberty of making these up to show you at the Wednesday meeting," she said. "No harm in showing them now, I suppose."

She passed around a prototype of a new bulletin that included the order of service for both early and late morning worship as well as upcoming church activities, volunteer opportunities and community mission information.

"Hmm," Donna said.

"That's not bad," Deacon Worthington reluctantly admitted.

"This looks great," Haley said.

Eunice winked at Reverend Baines. He smiled. "Today during my remarks I'll encourage those who want to attend a contemporary service to worship with us early next Sunday. In the meantime, if anyone has any recommended changes to the bulletin in this format, bring your ideas to Wednesday's church council meeting. And you're welcome to attend,'' he told the ladies who weren't on the council.

Knowing that Matt would have an outlet for his ministry made Haley feel a little better about her role in thwarting him. Now all she had to do was come to grips with how she felt about him.

Chapter Eleven

Matt was nervous. He'd been playing the piano since he was six and performing before large groups since the age of fourteen, and not since his very first time directing a choir did he ever feel as nervous as he did today.

What if no one showed up? What if lots of people came?

He paused in midstroke, the razor in his hand hovering just above his upper lip. Staring at his reflection in the bathroom mirror, Matt faced the truth. He wanted people to come out to the early service. And they would. He knew God would move and that souls who needed to hear the gospel would hear it in the music he wrote for the choir.

With that variable taken care of, just one remained. And *she* was the real reason for this unprecedented case of nerves.

Haley.

Would she be there today, sitting in the fifth row

just to the left of him? Or would she abandon the contemporary service in favor of the later one?

He wanted her there, at the early service, to hear his music. To give him a chance. He couldn't remember feeling this awkward and unsure of himself, even when he was a teenager working up the nerve to ask a girl out.

Disgusted, Matt rinsed the razor and then finished off his face. Haley couldn't abandon him. They didn't even have a relationship.

Yet he knew that somehow, someway, the reticent blonde with the soul-deep convictions about right and wrong, appropriate and inappropriate, had somehow, someway, managed to squirrel up under his defenses. And since, in her book, everything about him was wrong and inappropriate, there was no way he should be feeling for her the feelings he felt. That's what made his situation all the more lamentable.

"Lord, if this is a test, I'm flunking big time."

He didn't expect, nor did he receive, an answer to that miserable little entreaty.

Matt finished dressing and then made his way to the church.

The service went off without a hitch. Not only were Community Christian's young people in full force, they'd invited some friends. The sanctuary, while hardly full, held a respectable number of people, including the curious.

The one face missing from the congregation, though, was a fresh-scrubbed wholesome one that Matt had come to rely on to brighten his day. So while the

Spirit had its way in the hour-long service, by the time it ended, Matt's own spirit was heavy.

He didn't stay for Sunday school. He took that time to head home and make a call back East.

"How are you, Nana?"

"Blessed, son, blessed. I'm just here kneading some bread. A few of the ladies from church'll be coming over for dinner today so I went to the early service. And how are things out in Oregon?"

Matt settled onto the sofa, the phone snuggled in the crook of his neck, while batonlike, he ran a pen through his fingers.

"Fine," he lied.

"Mmm-hmm. Then why are you calling me? Shouldn't you be in Sunday school?"

Matt smiled. Few things changed with his grandmother.

"I just wanted to hear your voice," he said.

And now that he had, he couldn't very well say he'd called because he wanted to feel connected to someone, to some thing, to some place.

In a lot of ways, his childhood and Haley's were similar. After his mother abandoned him, he'd been raised by her mother. And Matt thanked God for that Christian upbringing. He'd often wondered how he might have turned out had he been raised in the drug houses where his mother eventually found solace. To this day, he didn't know who his father was. When he was old enough to understand, Nana had told him that not even his mother was sure.

In the end, though, he'd disgraced his grandmother just as his mother before him had done.

"Matt, honey?"

He closed his eyes and swallowed hard. "I'm sorry I put you through all of that back then."

"Matt, you don't need to apologize to me. Ever. I love you. I've always loved you and will support the decisions you make. You know that, don't you?"

He nodded, even though he knew she couldn't see him.

"I looked up your little town on the Internet. The Chamber of Commerce has a nice Web site. Has it rained much? That seems to be the only drawback."

Matt chuckled. Nana had been surfing in cyberspace longer than a lot of computer geeks. She'd insisted on it as a way to track his career. Back when he had a career.

"The weather's been beautiful," he told her.

"So why are you in such a funk on the Lord's day?"

Matt sighed. That was a good question. He had no business getting this weirded out over a woman who didn't even like him.

"I'm not anymore," he said. And that was the truth. Hearing her voice helped a lot. Matt had traveled too much through the years to get homesick. But every now and then he needed a dose of unconditional love from someone he could touch and feel and talk to.

"I love you, Nana."

"I'm sending you some beignets and some chicory coffee," she told him. "That should make you feel better."

"Your beignets always do."

And then he told her about Haley.

* * *

"Hello, ladies," Matt said as he walked into the church office Monday afternoon. Cindy, Haley and Mrs. Gallagher were there stuffing envelopes at a table. A bowl of tortilla chips within easy reach had apparently provided them sustenance.

"Hi, Reverend Matt."

"Now you show up when all the work is done," Eunice said. But the twinkle in her eyes told Matt she only kidded.

Haley glanced at him but made a studious effort to appear nonplussed by his presence. It wasn't easy. Not when her heartbeat kicked up a few notches and her hands suddenly seemed sweaty. She wanted to look at him, but dared not. He might see in her eyes the interest she attempted to keep close to her heart.

Eunice glanced between Matt and Haley, then bit back a not-so-small smile. "Well, that's about it," she announced. "Cindy, why don't you help me take these to the post office for mailing?"

"All right." Cindy gathered up the flat boxes filled with envelopes. "Bye, Reverend Matt. See you later, Haley."

With a sly look at Matt and Haley, Eunice ushered Cindy out of the room.

Haley studied her hands for a moment. "I think she has a crush on you."

"Hmm" was all he said in return.

"I heard the early service went well."

Matt nodded. "I didn't see you there."

"I wasn't..." She thought about, then just as

quickly discarded the truth—she'd had a raging headache. "No, I didn't attend."

"I didn't see you at the eleven o'clock service, either."

"No."

When she didn't add any other explanation, Matt shrugged.

Haley gathered up the remaining envelopes and supplies on the table.

"What were you all doing?"

"Huh? Oh, sending out information about vacation Bible school along with the church newsletter. It goes out quarterly to all the members."

"And you're the editor?"

She smile. "How'd you guess?"

He pilfered a chip from the bowl.

She may have been reluctant to admit it, but Haley liked being around Matt. Even though he made her nervous. Even though she apparently lost the capacity for coherent conversation whenever he was near. She could chitchat with the best of them when the situation warranted. But with Matt, she found she had little to say—and nothing to do with her hands, hands that very much wanted to stroke the wayward hair curling at his ear.

Clearing her throat, she glanced at him.

And her breath caught.

The expression on his face was filled with such longing, such open…yearning that for a moment all they did was stare at each other. There didn't seem to be enough air in the room.

Haley licked her very dry lips and his gaze tracked

the motion. She watched his chest rise and fall, his gaze remained locked on her mouth.

He took a step forward.

Haley took a step back. "I...we..."

The sound of her stammering voice broke the moment. Matt stuffed his hands in his pockets and took a deep breath. Haley did the same, though part of her was absurdly disappointed that the moment hadn't ended with one of his sweet kisses. Like the brief one they'd shared at the town square.

She watched him wander around the office, pausing to read a plaque on a wall or one of the many inspirational quotations Eunice kept around.

Haley had a question she needed to get off her chest. It had been bothering her for a while now.

"Why do you let them call you Reverend Matt?"

He turned around, facing her. "Why not? Matt's my name."

"But the reverend part." That, in Haley's book, wasn't right. Only men of the cloth should be called reverend.

Matt filched another chip from the near-empty bowl. "What about it?"

Haley waved a hand. Wasn't it obvious? "But you're not."

"Yes, Haley. I am."

"What? A minister? You? Don't be ridiculous."

Expressions stole over Matt's face, a mix of surprise, irritation and hurt. And, she noticed, his smile dimmed a little.

"Do you want me to show you my ordination papers? I thought you'd seen them from my interview."

Haley looked horrified. "You're serious? From a real church and seminary?"

He just looked at her.

"But...but..."

"But what kind of preacher wears earrings and jeans and rides a motorcycle?" he prompted.

"Yes," she said, the word just barely a whisper.

"The kind who knows there's more to ministry than the outward appearance. Excuse me." He wiped his mouth and left.

Stunned, Haley sat there. She tried to reconcile her long-held image of what a minister was supposed to look like and act like with the man who was Matt Brandon. Every which way she turned the view, it remained out of focus, off-kilter. Maybe people on the East Coast and in the South had different views of how a minister comported himself.

Community Christian's vacation Bible school program was in its fourth and next to last evening when the trouble started.

Matt didn't see her walk into the sanctuary. His mind on Haley and how, or even if, he should ask her out again, he'd been sitting at the organist's bench with the intention of getting in some practice. The sniffles alerted him that someone else was there.

Quietly he approached so as not to frighten the young woman. He took a seat on one of the padded pews across from where she sat.

"Sometimes it helps if you talk about it."

The girl jumped and squealed.

Matt held up both hands to show he was no threat. "I didn't mean to frighten you."

With eyes wide and a hand clutched at her throat, she watched him. When the panic receded from her eyes, Matt smiled. Her answering smile, though tremulous, reassured him that she probably wouldn't bolt. At least not immediately.

"You're Reverend Matt. The choir guy."

He nodded. "And you're attending the classes this week?"

She nodded. "I was. I came to church here on Sunday. One of my friends at school told me about it. Now I wish I hadn't come."

"Why?"

She shrugged, then wiped at her eyes.

He guessed she'd left the vacation Bible school class she was in. "What happened back there?"

"Nothing. Nothing that I'm not already used to." Her mouth trembled. "I just didn't think it would happen in a church."

Matt figured that if he waited for her he'd get the story. So he gave her the silence she needed to process whatever was going on in her head. Sure enough, after a few more sniffles, she glanced at him.

"My mom has AIDS. Everybody knows and they think I have it, too."

Father, give me the words to help this young woman.

"How's your mom doing?" he asked.

"Huh?"

She'd obviously been expecting a recoil or some other negative reaction from him.

"Your mother, how is she doing?"

The girl shook her head. "She has some good days and some bad days. Mostly bad though. It's just a matter of time now."

"And how are you with that?"

For a long time she just looked at him, assessing, determining in her own way his sincerity level. "I hate it," she said. Then she burst into tears.

Matt was across the aisle in seconds. He enveloped her in his arms while she cried. He rocked her and told her it was okay to feel the way she did.

Eventually her tears subsided.

"I didn't mean to get your shirt all wet."

"Hey, you just saved me a trip to the Laundromat."

She smiled, but it faded quickly. "I can't go back in there."

Matt didn't argue with her. "What happened?"

The teen shrugged. "We were put into small groups, and one of the girls refused to be in the group with me."

"Did you tell the class leader?"

The girl shook her head. "I just left and came in here. I'm used to it." She shrugged again. "I guess I didn't think church people would be like that."

"Everyone isn't."

"Yeah. Right."

Matt let the silence speak for a few moments. Then he asked her, "Do you sing?"

She shrugged. "I don't know."

He stood and held out a hand. "Come on. I'll teach you a song."

He led her to the piano. He slid onto the bench and made room for her. In his rich tenor, he sang the first verse of ''Oh, How I Love Jesus'' then taught her the chorus of the hymn.

When they finished, she sat there quiet for a moment. ''We don't go to a church. My mom never got into the Jesus thing. But my friend, she gave me this Bible when she found out my mom was sick.''

The small Bible had a light-blue cover and looked like the inexpensive ones used as gift Bibles for youth.

''What's your name?''

''Angela,'' she told him. ''Angela McReady.''

''Well, Angela McReady, do you mind if I show you something?''

She shook her head and Matt took her Bible. From a piece of paper he'd been putting notes on, he ripped two small strips to use as bookmarks. ''There are a couple of things in here that I think might help you.''

''What?''

He turned to the third chapter in the Gospel of John and pointed to verse sixteen. ''That's what we were just singing about,'' he said after reading the verse to her. ''Jesus loves you and wants you to have the everlasting life that only his Father can provide.''

Angela frowned. ''There's no such thing as everlasting life. I know because my mom's life is almost over.''

''The promises in this book aren't about the life we live on earth. They're about what happens after we die. Accepting that Jesus shed his blood for our sins, believing in Him to save our souls and then confessing that belief is what provides eternal life.''

She looked up at him. ''Sounds pretty easy.''

He smiled. ''It is. But it's a lifelong commitment.''

''I'll think about it,'' she said.

''Deal. And here's another one to think about. This one might help you handle your mom's illness.'' He bookmarked the Twenty-third Psalm and handed the Bible back to the girl. She read the indicated verses then looked up at him.

''The valley of the shadow of death. That's pretty scary.''

He nodded. ''But God's peace and love is always there for you. Even when you have to go through the scary places and times.''

She took that in. Then, as if making up her mind about something, she nodded. Angela scooted from the bench. ''I need to go now.''

''All right,'' he said. ''I hope we'll see you in service again. Eight o'clock on Sunday.''

She gave him the thumbs-up sign and walked up the center aisle toward the back door.

''Hey, Reverend Matt?''

He glanced back at her. ''Yeah?''

''I liked that song.''

He smiled as the door swung shut behind her.

Matt didn't see the side door quietly fall in place. Haley stood just beyond the door, marveling at the scene she'd just witnessed between the two. Matt had ministered to Angela's needs in a way Haley had never seen before.

* * *

"I saw what you did for Angela tonight," she told him later that evening. They were in the parking lot, the last two to leave the church. Haley put a bag on her back seat and closed the door, facing Matt.

"Angela?"

"The girl that one of our regular visitors nearly ran off." She walked up to him, crowding his space, making him edgy.

"Oh, that Angela. She's going through a rough period right now."

"Cindy told me what happened between them. One of her friends said something unkind. I went looking for Angela and overheard the two of you at the piano."

When he opened the door of the SUV, Haley reached for his arm. "Where did you learn to do that?"

"Do what?"

"The way you witnessed to her on her level without preaching at her the way a lot of people have. That was really impressive."

"It's not about being impressive, Haley."

"I know that," she said as she snatched her hand away. "And I didn't mean it *that* way."

On the one hand, Matt was glad she was back to yelling at him. That meant the situation was normal, and it helped keep his mind away from places that spelled nothing but trouble, with a capital *T*. On the flip side, he really missed the warmth of her hand on his bare arm.

"I've had a lot of experience in that area," he said, answering her initial question. "Back East, and at home...I...well, let's just say that that was one of my specialty areas.''

Haley nodded, apparently accepting that vague explanation. ''I'm going to have a talk with Cindy's friend Erica.''

Matt was glad for that. But his mind had already turned to other things.

The night held the scent of rain, but the scent of her perfume is what riveted him to the spot. If he asked her out now, she'd definitely say no. That answer would rid him of the near obsessive way he felt about her. He still couldn't believe he'd bid one hundred dollars on lunch just so he could share her company. How pathetic was that?

He'd asked her out once since their movie date, but she'd turned him down saying she had a library board meeting to attend.

''Where are you headed now?''

She blinked at the abrupt change in conversation. ''Home. It's late and I need to get started on the certificates for all the kids.''

''Go out with me Friday night after the close of vacation Bible school.''

Haley looked at him as if he'd truly taken leave of his senses. ''Why should I? We don't even like each other.''

''That's not true. At least on my part. And I thought we were beyond all that. I'd like to get to know you better. And I really want to kiss you. For real this time. And I'm hoping that maybe if you get to know me better you'll want to kiss me, too.''

Haley blushed and took a step backward.

So much for laying his cards on the table.

"You're a very strange man, Matt Brandon. I don't even try to understand what goes through your head. We were standing here talking about a teenager in need." Her hand encompassed the church and the canvas banner spread between two posts proclaiming it Vacation Bible School and Youth Week. "That's what the priority is this week."

"My prayers for her have already gone up tonight, a couple of times as a matter of fact. But my hopes about forging a relationship with you keep getting dashed."

Haley shook her head. "All right," she said, folding her arms.

"All right what?"

"All right, I'll go out with you."

He couldn't halt the grin that encompassed his face. "You will?"

She held up a hand, and then a finger. "On one condition."

Matt groaned. Take it or leave it. He knew he'd take it. "Name the condition."

Haley grinned. "We declare the entire evening neutral ground."

Haley had no idea why she'd said she'd date him. She didn't even think in terms of dating anymore.

"And that's the problem," she said as she stood in front of her closet trying to decide what to wear. She needed something that worked for church, but was also suitable for a date to... "Where?"

Would they again go to the movies?

She'd enjoyed that. A lot. But watching a movie didn't exactly equate with getting to know a person.

What, exactly, had he meant by that? They knew each other. They saw each other at least twice a week, on Sunday and at the Wednesday church council meetings.

A thought suddenly occurred to Haley. Did he have another job? The Amends House rented for a pretty penny; she'd seen the listing in the newspaper. He'd need some sort of full-time position to supplement the meager salary the church offered. And in this case she knew just how meager it was because she'd been on the losing side of a council argument about the church musician's salary. If Community Christian paid more, she'd pointed out time and again, they wouldn't have such a difficult time finding someone with talent to take on the job.

Then, along came Matt.

"So, what *does* he do?" she asked a pair of black slacks that she pulled out and discarded. That question begged another. Why would someone of Matt's obvious talent accept a job at little Community Christian?

Maybe he was independently wealthy or lived off of investment income. For all she knew, he could be a dot-com millionaire just out having an adventure.

She'd find out tonight, while they were "getting to know" each other.

She held aloft a red jumper, cocked her head considering what she might wear with it, then, with a nod, tossed the hangered dress onto her bed. She'd wear flats to church since she did a lot of running around, but tossed a pair of high-heeled red pumps in a bag just in case she and Matt ended up someplace fancy. Dress-up jewelry completed the presto-chango she'd do if needed.

"You really are a minister, aren't you?"

Matt and Haley sat at a booth at Pop's Ice Cream and Malt Shoppe sharing a double banana split. He shook his head. "Why is that so difficult to believe?"

Haley gazed at him. Her brow was so furrowed, he could only wonder what questions raced through her mind. "Go ahead," he said. "Ask."

"Ask what?"

"All those questions you've had bottled up about me."

She bit her bottom lip and mashed at the edge of a banana with her sundae spoon. "That obvious, huh?"

He nodded. "Ask away."

She did, the questions racing out in a blur: Did you go to seminary? What denomination of church ordained you? Where? *You* preach sermons? The last question came out as something along the lines of a horrified squeak.

When she'd first asked if he were really a minister, Matt had been irritated. But now, after giving himself some room to breathe, he realized her curiosity to be genuine. She'd told him that she'd been raised by a missionary aunt and uncle. Was her world and view of religion so narrow—or limited—that she couldn't even conceive of ministers in roles other than pastors?

The answer—yes—hit him like a ton of bricks.

That was why she'd been so opposed to hand-clapping, foot-stomping church music. That's why any deviation from what she'd been taught as "acceptable church behavior" made her bristle.

That's why they hit it off like oil and water.

"Haley, where I come from, ministers, ordained ministers, serve in a variety of capacities in and outside the church. Just because a man or a woman is called to minister doesn't mean he or she pastors a church."

She looked decidedly uncomfortable. "I don't think I could belong to a church where a woman was the pastor."

"Why not? Some of the best preachers I've heard are female. A lot of women pastor churches today. Some lead very large congregations.

"I can get you some tapes," he offered. "Or both videotape and audiotapes, if you'd like to see or listen."

Haley nodded. "You mean evangelist types? Women who go around and speak for programs at churches and conferences. Pastors' wives."

"No, like Reverend Baines." Then he shook his head, stroked his eyebrow and chuckled.

"What?"

"I never thought I'd be a leading feminist."

Haley did laugh at that. "We're so different." But this time when she said it, it didn't come across as a negative, just a fact.

She leaned forward. "Matt, why'd you come here? This place is obviously very far removed from the things you know."

He paused before answering. It wasn't Wayside that was far removed from everything else. It was this Rebecca of Sunnybrook Farm that he'd managed to fall for. *She* was the one out of touch with much of the rest of the world—at least the world he knew. But how and why could she be so sheltered, so insulated?

He remembered something Eunice had said the day she told him Haley liked lilies: *She's been hurt.*

But getting hurt was a part of life. Haley had obviously buried her emotions in a vain attempt to never again be hurt.

"Haley, the world is a big place. So is this country." He knew he needed to take this slowly. He didn't want to insult her, especially now when she seemed somewhat open to, if not accepting of, his ideas. At least she was listening, asking questions.

"It's not about East Coast or West Coast. The North or the South," he continued. "It's about proclaiming the Gospel. You've insulated yourself here. But there's an entire movement out there, an awakening that has little to do with traditions or denominations. Christian values haven't changed. We're still beholden to Biblical law. The Ten Commandments haven't changed one bit."

"But...?"

"But the way we live our lives has." He saw her frown and scrambled for an analogy that she'd relate to. Inspiration came from the cherries on their fast-melting banana split. "Think about the Wayside founders. The way that pioneering couple lived their lives is crude by today's standards. The wife, Sheridan, probably gave birth in a cabin, they lived off the land, hunted and trapped to put food on their table. The day ended when the sun set. Right?''

Haley nodded. ''I see your point on that. But where are you going with it?''

''Today, women go to elaborate birthing centers to have their babies. State-of-the-art equipment is there in case anything goes wrong. And the food we eat— meat comes from grocery stores, cleaned and neatly packaged. Most people wouldn't know what to do if an animal carcass was plopped in front of them with the announcement—'That's dinner.'''

She wrinkled her nose. ''That's disgusting.''

He nodded. ''But it's how our ancestors survived. The point is people still have babies and they still eat. It's the same with the good news of the Gospel. Reaching out today means using the tools and the technology available to us, the things that appeal to the younger generation. The message from the Christian rock groups and hip-hop artists and Christian comedians and writers is no different than the one presented when the disciples walked with Jesus.''

''I don't think the disciples went into the temple with a rhyme and a beat.''

Matt grinned. ''No, I don't suppose they did. But if they'd had the Internet and DVDs and MP3 players, they would have used them. And if the apostle Paul had had a telephone or a Web site, he wouldn't have had to write so many letters back and forth to the church.''

''Hmm.'' She smiled. ''You have a point there.''

Then, Haley was quiet for a long, long time. She pushed aside the melted mess of whipped cream, fruit and ice cream. Matt held his breath, wondering if she'd been so insulted that she was ready to storm out of the malt shop.

But Haley was far from insulted. She churned his words over in her head. Amber had pretty much said the same thing, though not as eloquently as Matt. Listening to him now, Haley felt a pang of regret over the life she didn't choose. Had she wanted it, she could be living in Portland, the wife of a banker, shuttling her children from their large house in an exclusive neighborhood to soccer fields and cheerleader practice. Or she could be living in a shanty in some underdeveloped country, teaching English and the Bible to people in the compound. But she'd instead chosen the comfort and safety of home, a small town where her traditional values didn't get trampled in the fray.

The choices Matt had made intrigued her.

"So did you come to Wayside to drag us into the twenty-first century?"

He shook his head. "The new millennium is already here. I've seen evidence of it as I've driven around outside the downtown area. You have poverty and homelessness here."

"Then why did you come to Wayside?"

"I needed to start over."

"Why? Did you want a church to pastor?"

"No," he answered, with impunity. "I've never been the pastor of a church and have never had a desire to. I've always been a musician."

Her knitted brows told him she still had trouble

with that concept. "So why be an ordained minister who only directs a choir?"

He sat back.

"I'm sorry. That probably came out all wrong. I just don't understand."

His ministry had gone far beyond *only* directing church choirs, but that wasn't relevant at the moment. He tried to hold in his impatience and frustration.

"There are lots of ministries, Haley. In some large churches everyone on staff, from the person in charge of the Christian Education programs and the person who runs the day care center to the bookstore manager is a minister. At my church back home, there are about twenty-five ministers on staff. Of that number, only eight or so preach from the pulpit."

She shook her head. "It seems like such a waste."

"Doing the Lord's work is a waste?"

"You're putting words in my mouth. That's not at all what I meant and you know it."

"Haley, have you ever been to a city larger than Portland?"

"I've never been out of the state. And I don't get to Portland very often. I think the last time was about a year ago."

Matt's mouth dropped open. "A year? Why?"

She nodded. "It was to some cooking show Amber wanted to see. She'd won two tickets."

"No, I mean why don't you ever leave, go visit someplace else?"

She looked genuinely puzzled. "Why should I? Everything I need is right here."

Eunice had said much the same thing.

"Have you ever been on an airplane?"

She shook her head.

"Aren't you even curious?"

For a while Haley didn't say anything. She scooped up a bit of whipped cream on the tip of a long blunt-shaped nail and licked it from her finger.

"A long time ago I dreamed of going someplace wonderful, someplace exotic where I could do great things."

"Why didn't you?"

She looked at him. The answer seemed so obvious. "Matt, I grew up."

Chapter Twelve

That wasn't the whole truth and Haley felt guilty about evading the truth. The fact of the matter was that she'd longed to travel, to see other parts of the country, maybe even the world. The stories her aunt and uncle told of living and working in faraway places and in sometimes primitive environments had always intrigued her even while they frightened her a little bit. Much like the direction of this conversation.

This getting to know each other business was exhausting—and felt more like an invasion of privacy, or more accurately, an invasion of emotions. This was territory she didn't like traversing.

"The world is a very big place," he said. "This country, too. I'd like to show you the places where I grew up. I think you'd like them."

She smiled, but couldn't imagine visiting, let alone living in a place as wild as his hometown.

"I grew up in a parish not far from New Orleans.

My little town isn't even on the map. We didn't move to the city until much later.''

"Tell me about your early years. When did you start playing the piano?"

Matt laughed. "My grandmother says I came out of the womb playing the piano. But I guess my earliest memory was three, maybe four. I got serious at six, though. I played hot jazz, boogie-woogie and I played in church."

"Jazz?"

He spread his hands out as if to say what you see is what you get. "I'm a Louisiana boy."

Haley liked it when he smiled. He looked even more handsome than he did the rest of the time. When Matt smiled, his eyes did, too. Looking at him this way shed some light on why the females, young and old, hovered near him at church. He had the same disarming effect on her.

"You look more like a rock-solid man to me."

Something in his eyes changed, and Haley both saw and felt the shift in the atmosphere. Silence moved between them in a rolling wave. Time seemed to stand still. Then Haley cleared her throat. "Tell me more."

Matt blinked, as if he'd suddenly walked out into the sun after being in a dark movie theater. "I... What do you want to know?"

"When did you start writing music?"

"When I was twelve or thirteen."

The faraway smile on his face as he looked just over her shoulder told Haley that he'd left her for the moment and once again lived the life he'd known back then. She wondered if he'd met with any success with his writing. Probably not. If he had, he wouldn't be here—not that there was anything wrong with the town. It just wasn't a musician's mecca.

Matt's mind was indeed back in the early days.

He'd struggled and clawed his way out of obscurity, but was always careful to send back to Nana his ten percent plus a little something for her. She'd taught him from a boy that the Lord's work got the first dime of every dollar he made. All these years later, he maintained his tithe, making the offering to whatever church he happened to be affiliated with, and if he wasn't, he sent it home for Nana to put in the tithe box at First Goodwill Church.

When a soft, warm hand covered his own, Matt blinked.

Haley sat across from him at the outside café of the ice cream shop. The sultry heat of New Orleans and the summer symphony of night sounds in Nashville had been replaced by a cool evening in late spring in the Pacific Northwest. A beautiful woman, one he cherished sat beside him and all was right in Matt's world.

"You were thinking of home just now weren't you?"

He nodded.

"What made you decide to leave that place you loved so much?"

The contentment that had been rolling through him suddenly congealed into an unpleasant hard knot. "Time. Circumstances. People."

Once before he'd almost told her the story. But

then, like now, he decided not to burden her with his tale of woe. Besides, that entire episode was behind him. Buried where it belonged, even though he didn't know what had become of Melanie. He'd heard rumors. But rumors, in his business at least, were as easy to come by as soloists.

Haley already looked at him as if he were a sideshow act at the carnival of dubious Christianity. There'd be time enough for true confessions if they ever truly got serious. He didn't need to, or particularly want to, get into it now.

As it was, Haley's smile seemed a little sad.

He traced her mouth with a finger. ''What's wrong, pretty lady?''

''We both seem to have pasts we'd rather not deal with.''

''I'll tell you my sad story if you'll tell me yours.''

She quirked an eyebrow and the edge of her mouth turned up in a rueful smile. ''This is supposed to be a fun date. Not a trip to the morgue.''

''My sentiments exactly.''

''Well then, let's leave the past where it belongs and concentrate on the present.''

''Deal,'' he said. ''I saw a miniature golf course the other day. And the sign said they were open until midnight.''

''You're on,'' Haley said. ''But I'm warning you. I'm good.''

''Not as good as I am.''

She leaned forward, a teasing smile at her mouth. ''Care to make a little wager on that trash talk?''

Matt wanted one thing. "All right," he said. "A kiss."

For a moment, Haley looked unsure. But that expression quickly changed to one so filled with anticipation that Matt's breath caught.

"You're on, preacher man. But you lose and it's a handshake at the door."

Matt played the best round of miniature golf he'd ever played in his life.

At her front door, he stood back, willing himself to slow down, to forfeit, if he had to, the sweet prize he'd won. He wanted this to be the perfect ending to an almost perfect day, not a moment to stress Haley or make her regret going out with him. After all, Matt wanted this to be the first of many fun dates—and kisses—between them.

Haley slid the key in the lock and pushed the door open. "It seems I owe you something."

Matt stepped closer. "No, Haley. You don't. I'm not going to pressure or guilt you into doing anything you don't want to do."

She looked up at him with those big, brown eyes. Matt could easily lose himself in those depths.

"What makes you think I don't want to kiss you?"

His heart slammed into his chest. Matt willed himself to calm down, to keep it light. "There's been a lot of trash talking tonight. You at that windmill hole comes to mind."

She poked him in the chest. "You cheated."

"I did not. That spoke just happened to fall, the wind caught it and poof!" Unfortunately, he couldn't quite keep a straight face while making his claim on how he'd won that hole.

As they both chuckled, he took her hands in his. "Haley, I really enjoy the time we spend together. I had fun tonight. Thank you."

"So you're saying you don't want to collect on our wager."

He took a shaky breath. "That's not the case at all."

"Then why don't you stop talking and kiss me?"

"Haley, I don't want to do something that you'll regret."

In answer, she stepped closer to him. Carefully, as if she expected him to vanish, she placed her hands on his chest. The soft cotton of the T-shirt didn't dispel the warmth or obliterate the sudden pounding of his heart. One palm slid down and he inhaled sharply.

"Haley?"

"Kiss me, Matt."

And so he did.

The kiss was a meeting of hearts and minds and dreams. Haley's eyes fluttered closed and her hands moved from his chest to around his neck. When he clasped her about the waist, a little moan escaped her. And then she forgot everything except the dance of his mouth and the heat of his embrace.

He was gentle with her, so heartbreakingly tender that she wanted to cry out. She ran her fingers through the hair at his nape.

Matt groaned and deepened the embrace.

Haley thought she was prepared. She thought she knew what it meant to be swept off her feet. But she'd never gotten weak in the knees before. She'd never moaned simply from a kiss. But now she knew she'd never been kissed. Not like this.

Matt thought he was prepared. He'd been anticipating this moment since their chaste kiss in the park a few Saturdays ago. He'd known it would be good when he kissed her completely. He hadn't, however, known it would be this wonderful, as if he were, for the first time ever, kissing a woman. And then he realized it was.

Love made the difference.

And because he knew how quickly things could get out of hand, even between people who knew better, he reluctantly ended the embrace, putting air between them. He tugged at her arms until they no longer surrounded him. Holding her hands in his, he stared into those deep-brown eyes that had enchanted him from day one.

Her eyes looked dazed, her mouth was kiss-swollen. "What's wrong?"

"There are things I want that I can't have. So before either of us gets to a place where this gets out of control, I'll say good-night. I had a great time tonight."

He kissed her on the forehead and turned to head down the walkway.

"Matt?"

He paused, but didn't turn around. If he turned and saw her, her eyes shining, he knew his resolve would crumble. And that would serve neither of them. He jammed his hands in his pockets. "Yes?"

"Thank you. For that."

He nodded, understanding exactly what she meant, then walked to his truck before he faced her again and asked to stay.

Long after his taillights faded away, Haley stood on her porch. She told herself she was just enjoying the evening, but the truth of it was she didn't trust her legs to carry her over the threshold. Her bones had turned to jelly and she didn't mind a bit.

The memory of that kiss buoyed her all that night and into the next day. When Matt called and asked if she'd like to drive in to Portland with him one afternoon, Haley did something she'd never, ever done before: she missed an historical society meeting. She made up for it, though, by picking up a book in Powell's to add to the society's permanent collection.

Their conversation about her early desires to be a missionary spurred Haley to check into the current status of the program she'd once dreamed of joining. The old passion for that work resurfaced, and Haley spent some time searching the Internet for new opportunities. Not, she told herself, that she'd never, ever just pick up her life and head off to Peru or some such place. But she was curious.

Over the next several weeks, Matt and Haley saw a lot of each other, mostly at church, but also on movie and miniature golf dates. Without realizing it, they'd declared the entire town neutral territory. They kept their good-night kisses short and chaste—and therefore infinitely frustrating.

Matt, however, maintained a careful control and always walked away before things got out of hand. Ha-

ley admired him for that. In addition to making her
weak in the knees, his kisses also seemed to addle
her brain. So she was grateful that one of them managed to keep a clear head.

Today, after running into each other in the Christian bookstore at Cherry Center Mall, they wound up
having dinner at Matt's.

He showed her the rest of the house, including his
music room where he had two keyboards set up and
a conference room table with sheet music spread out
all over it.

Haley, seated on a piano bench that Matt brought
up from the living room, encouraged him to submit
his songs for publication.

"There are places," she said. "Maybe in Nashville. A lot of the Christian publishers are there, so
the gospel music publishers are probably there, too."

Now that she thought of it, it made sense for that
to be the case. "I'm sure there's a company that
might be interested in your music."

"Yeah, maybe." He didn't meet her eyes. Instead,
he straightened some papers on his makeshift desk.

Haley didn't understand his reticence. She'd finally
come around a bit in her thinking, enough to try out
on a semiregular basis the early service where Matt
seemed to be thriving in his element.

Word had gotten out about the dynamic new choir
director and attendance was way up at both services.
Haley prided herself on the fact that she'd come to
understand his perspective a little better. She'd even
managed to call off the CDC. Deacon Worthington,
Mrs. Attley, Mrs. Paumroy and Mrs. Forest stuck to

the eleven o'clock service where the tempo of the music—and Matt's attire—remained toned down a bit.

The music still grated on Haley's nerves a little, and in the midst of an early-morning congregation dressed in jeans, sneakers and tank tops, Haley felt decidedly old and out of touch. But she'd finally realized what appealed to the younger people: an outlet for religious expression that didn't demand rigid decorum or a litany of thou shalt nots.

Even Reverend Baines's sermons were different at the early service, livelier. At times he cracked a few jokes or made pop culture references that sometimes went over Haley's head, but had everyone else laughing.

She didn't necessarily understand it, but she could respect Matt's contribution to Kingdom building.

So now, she didn't at all understand why he wasn't thrilled with her idea that he try to do something with his music. The inspirational choir sang at least one of his original praise songs every Sunday. And he had a pile of stuff here, sheets of paper with handwritten musical notes and lyrics scribbled in. He had a terrific voice. He'd be a shoo-in as a gospel singer himself.

Haley could just imagine his picture on the cover of a CD case.

Running into him at the mall had been perfect. She'd thought of this music submission plan just last night and couldn't wait to see him again so she could make the suggestion.

She'd expected him to be thrilled. But instead of

being receptive and inspired by the notion of sending his stuff out, Matt looked downright miserable.

She didn't understand it one bit. Then realization hit her fast.

"Oh, Matt." She went to him, kneeling at the floor near his chair. "I'm sorry. I wasn't thinking. Here I thought I'd come up with something wonderful and supportive and instead I'm rubbing salt in a wound."

"Haley—"

She reached for his hand and clasped it in hers. "Your music has been rejected by all those companies, hasn't it?"

"Haley, that's not it. I—"

She put a finger across his mouth. "Shh. Don't say anything else. I should have been more sensitive. I'm sorry."

"But, Haley—"

Her mouth replaced her finger. The kiss was light and sweet, another form of apology.

"It's okay," she told him. "You should try again. Don't stop trying. I'm sure there's an audience and a record company for you."

Matt closed his eyes and shook his head. Sighing, he pulled away from her and stood up.

"It's getting late," Haley said. "I'm going to head home. Cindy is coming by the house early tomorrow to help me stuff goody bags for the skating party lock-in. By the way, that was a great idea. The kids are really excited about it. I wish I'd thought of it," she added.

"Haley, we need to talk. There's something—"

"Matt," she said, reaching for his arm in another

gesture of apology and understanding. "Don't dwell on what I said. When the time is right, I'm sure things will happen for you on that front."

He ran his hands through his hair and stood there looking as miserable as she felt about pressing him on something that was so obviously a sore point.

She kissed him again, then waved and left Matt to his own troubled thoughts.

His first instinct was to run, to run away from the past that yet again had managed to catch up with him. And just when things had been going so well between them—just when he'd been lulled into thinking his new beginning was a solid one.

"You should have told her."

He'd tried.

"Not hard enough." He ran his hands through his hair again, wondering, but knowing, how she'd react if she knew his secret.

He should have told her while he had the chance. Haley thought he was a struggling songwriter, someone with lofty dreams of breaking into the big time.

He laughed, the sound not one of mirth, but a bitter, hollow one. Making it as a gospel recording artist was the farthest thing from his mind...and his ambitions. He'd been there and had done that. In the closet of this very room in a rented house he'd come to call home, Matt had a big box full of the evidence of his success in that arena: lots of Dove and Spirit awards and even a Grammy Award. They'd arrived special delivery, courtesy of his grandmother, who thought he should have them with him since he'd finally settled down.

What Haley didn't know was that Matt Brandon-Dumaine wasn't trying to break into gospel music. He'd spent the last three years of his life running away from it.

Chapter Thirteen

"**Y**ou should level with your young lady. Dishonesty will only bring heartache."

Matt sighed into the telephone receiver tucked in the crook of his neck. His grandmother had a way of sizing up situations.

"I've tried, Nana," he said in his own defense.

"When you control the situation, *you* control the situation."

"Unlike last time."

"Exactly, *mon petit*. Tell her."

But it wasn't that simple. He and Haley had come a long way in terms of both trust and her willingness to accept his brand of ministry. In Haley's book, his sin of omission would be just as severe as any other. And the deal with Melanie went down in a most unpleasant and public way.

"I will," he promised his grandmother.

He just didn't know how he would keep that promise. Or when.

By the time he arrived at the church for choir rehearsal, his mind remained on how best to approach Haley. Her gentle encouragement only made him feel guiltier. She was convinced he was a failed songwriter.

Matt toyed with the idea of approaching Cliff Baines about the situation. But talking to his grandmother, who'd been by his side through the worst of the scandal, was one thing. Talking to his pastor and employer about his relationship with a longtime cherished member of the church was another thing completely. That would have really pushed the boundaries of friendship and propriety.

As they began rehearsal, Haley popped in and waved before disappearing again.

Tonight, he promised himself. He'd call her tonight and they'd talk.

Angela McReady couldn't have been more than sixteen or seventeen years old, yet her mouth and eyes carried the lines and weariness of a much older woman.

She'd shown up at choir rehearsal and sat on the outer edge of the assembly, as if she wanted to be a part of the group, but knew her place and how she'd be received. Matt waved for her to join them, but she shook her head. When they came to a break, Matt invited her to come closer.

"I can't," she told him. "But I'd like to speak with you when you have a moment."

"Take ten," he called to the choir members. He

stepped away from the electric piano and went to where she stood. "How are you?"

She shrugged, and then she shook her head and looked away. Matt could have sworn he saw tears in her eyes. "Angela?"

"Reverend Matt. My mom died yesterday and I wondered if you would, well, if you could sing that song at her funeral. It's nothing big. Just at the funeral home. We can't afford.... I mean, well. Would you?"

"Angela, I'm so sorry."

And because she needed it, Matt hugged her the way a father would a child. Angela did cry then. But not hard, and not for long. She pushed away from him, wiped at her eyes and stood straight and tall, stoic.

The stories Haley told him about the Lewis and Clark Expedition and the people who later settled the Northwest came to mind. He was struck by the image that Angela McReady could have been one of those pioneer women. She was strong, capable and determined, despite the odds. Life kept knocking her down, but she continued to get up. Losing her mother, however, would be a blow that took more than platitudes and a song to overcome.

"What's going to happen to you now?" he asked. "Is your father or a relative around?"

"I have two brothers. One's older, one's younger."

"And your older brother will take you in?"

She shook her head. "He's in jail. Prison, really. Possession and distribution, and possession of a firearm by a convicted felon." She rattled off the criminal drug and weapons charges as though reciting a menu. "And my little brother, he's out on the street somewhere. He ran away a year or so ago. I haven't seen him or heard from him. Mom wasn't bad off when he left, so he probably doesn't know. Or care," she added.

"Of course I'll sing at your mother's service. Have you been talking to Reverend Baines? And would you like the whole choir as well?"

She glanced back, looking at some of the people who were already looking at her and Matt. "I'd like… No, they don't like me."

Matt, who'd turned with her, saw the reason Angela had so quickly changed her mind. Erica stood off to the side, near Cindy and Amanda. The pampered teens huddled together pretending not to be staring at Angela and Matt.

Anger roiled inside him at the way they'd treated this girl. But he tamped it down and turned to her. "Tell you what," Matt said. "You tell me the time and the place and I'll be there with a couple of people who'll be able to help you say a nice farewell to your mom. Okay?"

She nodded. "Thanks, Reverend Matt."

"Is there anything else you need?"

"No, not really," she told him.

Adam Richardson walked up. "Is everything okay?"

Matt faced the young man, a junior in high school who'd displayed a maturity not evident in some of the others. "No," Matt told him. "Angela's mother just passed."

Adam opened his arms to her, and Matt could see

Angela fighting against a new wave of tears. He wrapped an arm around the two teens and prayed.

After rehearsal Matt caught up with Reverend Baines and told him about Angela's situation and need.

"I know some people who work in family and youth services. I'll make a couple of calls in the morning. Which one is she?"

Matt pointed her out.

"Thanks," Cliff said, turning to go. "Hey, Matt," the minister said. "You're doing a great job with the choir and with the teens. You're just what we needed here."

Matt nodded. "Thanks. That means a lot to me."

In the hallway, Haley stood just outside her Sunday school classroom door talking with Cindy and Erica.

"May I have a word with you?"

Haley looked up, a smile blossoming on her face. "Me?"

The two girls exchanged glances and then smiles. "The gang's going over to Pop's," Erica said. "Gonna come, Cindy?"

"I... Why don't you go without me," she said.

Erica shrugged and headed down the hallway.

Cindy remained, looking concerned. "Is it true, Reverend Matt? Did Angela's mother die?"

"What?" Haley interjected. "When?"

Matt addressed Cindy first. "You and your friend treated her pretty shabbily. Maybe you can do better by her now."

Cindy looked at the floor.

Haley's glance darted between Matt and the teen.

"He's right," Cindy said. "Erica did it, but I'm just as guilty because I didn't make an effort to stop her. Do you think she'll forgive me?"

Haley squeezed her hand. "I think so."

Matt leveled a look at her. "I think she needs a true friend right now."

Cindy nodded. "Adam's taking her home, right?"

"They needed to make a stop at the funeral home."

"All right, then," Cindy said as she mumbled a goodbye. "I'm gonna go over to her house right now."

"I think she'd like the company."

When Cindy headed down the hall, Haley rounded on Matt. "What was that all about?"

Instead of directly answering, he walked into her classroom, taking what would undoubtedly turn into an argument behind closed doors.

"Your little holier-than-thou Miss Priss trio is doing more to undermine the work we do here than any influence outside on the streets."

"What are you talking about?"

"Erica and Cindy and Amanda. I know they're your pets...."

Haley whipped a hand up in front of his face. "Whoa, buddy. You obviously have some sort of issue and I don't appreciate your talking about anyone in that manner."

"They probably got it from you."

Haley headed for the door. But Matt blocked her progress.

"We're going to talk about this right now."

"Let me out."

"You're going to hear me out, Haley."

Haley sighed. "Look. You obviously have something on your mind. Why don't you start at the beginning, and tell me what you're so angry about? Maybe if I have some sort of idea, I'll get a better grasp about your ranting."

In the time since they'd gotten to know each other, Haley had grown increasingly confident in her dealings with him.

So he told her about Angela McReady and the taunts that had come from Haley's teenage charges.

"That doesn't at all sound like Cindy or Amanda. As a matter of fact, Cindy has such a crush on you I doubt that she'd do or say anything that might upset you. I don't know Erica very well. She just started coming to Community Christian a few months ago."

"I'm not interested in girls, Haley. You should know that by now."

Haley turned away from his intense gaze. "I didn't say you were."

"Then what are you saying?"

"That you're mistaken about them."

"Cindy, maybe. But not that Erica. Angela is going through enough right now without adding unnecessary and unkind censure from girls who are supposed to be showing Christian love and sympathy to her."

"Well, it looks like Cindy is going to make amends now. I'll talk to her later, Erica too. But you should make some sort of effort as well."

"I'm the music coordinator. You're the teen leader."

This time when Haley went to the door, he didn't

stop her. "No," she said. "You've been filling that role since the moment you got here."

She hadn't meant to bring that up. As a matter of fact, she hadn't planned on running into Matt at all. She'd hoped to slip into her classroom and put some things together for Sunday school then review the program for the skating party. It was the first one she ever coordinated and she wanted things to be just perfect.

Before she turned the door handle, Matt had a hand blocking her exit.

"What did you mean by that?"

Haley closed her eyes for a moment. She'd hoped, obviously to no avail, that he'd overlook that less than circumspect comment from her. But he hadn't. And he was so close she could feel his breath on her neck and smell the subtle scent of a woodsy aftershave or cologne.

"Haley?"

"Just let it go, Matt."

A moment later his hand left the door and Haley breathed an audible sigh of relief. But she'd dropped her guard too soon. His hand left the door and came to rest on her shoulder.

"Haley, I'm not trying to usurp your authority here."

"It's too late, Matt. You already have."

For a long time Matt stood there after she'd slipped away. *Had* he encroached on territory that Haley rightfully claimed? With the exception of his feelings for Haley, his sole focus at Community Christian had been the music, whether playing it or fighting for it in church council meetings.

"Lord, I need some help here. Show me what to do."

Matt closed his eyes and waited for the still, small voice that had always guided him. Even in the midst of his worst trouble, he'd listened to the Lord speaking to him through his heart. And now, even though the stakes weren't as high as they'd been then, he turned to the One who would lead and guide him.

He knew better than to expect a direct response as though a voice boomed from the heavens. But he did receive a gentle nudge.

Go after her.

Part of Matt wanted to argue. He was the last person she wanted to be bothered with right now. And that was all the more reason to go.

He caught up with her in the parking lot, the place where a lot of their confrontations began. At her car, she was trying to poke her key in the door lock, but seemed to be having a problem.

"Haley."

"Go away, Matt."

He furrowed his brow at the sound of her voice. Had he detected a hitch in it?

"Haley?" He reached for her arm and turned her so she faced him. Tears streamed from her eyes.

Matt felt as if he'd been kicked in the gut. "Haley, please, don't cry."

She wiped at her eyes then found the door lock. "Just leave me alone."

"Haley, you're upset. I'm sorry. Let's talk about this."

"There's nothing to talk about. Let me go, please."

Matt released her arm and she opened the door. She wasted no time getting in her car, apparently trying to escape him. But Matt didn't scare so easily. When she started her car, Matt headed to his truck.

When she pulled in front of her house, he was right behind her.

"Go away!"

"After we talk. All I want to do is explain something to you."

Haley took a deep breath. More than anything she wanted to run to her room, fling herself across her bed and have a good pitiful cry. But that wasn't looking possible. Not until she got rid of Matt, who'd had the nerve to follow her home.

It was bad enough that she had to watch him slowly and effortlessly usurp her authority at church. Now he wanted to talk about it.

"And how long do you think your explaining will take?"

"Just a few minutes."

Reluctantly, she let him in. But she refused to be hospitable. She didn't offer him a cool drink or a snack, even though there was raspberry tea and a tin full of lemon tarts in the kitchen.

Haley put her purse on the bottom stair and then marched to the living room where she took a seat in the room's only chair. Matt stuck his hands in his pockets and rocked on his heels.

"I never meant to step on any toes, especially yours."

Haley sniffed.

"All my life I've worked with music. In a church setting, people generally gravitate to the choir because it's a place where they can express themselves creatively."

When Haley didn't say anything, Matt went on. "At Community Christian it's no different. And the fact that the music department is doing something new only adds to the appeal. That doesn't mean that they've abandoned you."

"I didn't say I'd been abandoned."

But it sure felt as though she had. There was a time when Cindy and Adam, Joshua and Amanda and all the others came to her first with their problems. Now, Matt was their sounding board. He seemed to have every situation under control, from counseling to chastisement.

"I know how important it is to feel wanted, to feel that your work has a purpose. Yours does, Haley."

"It doesn't feel like it these days."

He approached her, sitting on the edge of the love seat that faced her chair. "Haley, a lot has been going on lately. Things that, well, under other circumstances, I would have ignored."

She glanced up at him, the question in her eyes.

"I'm talking about us," Matt clarified.

Haley swallowed. "What us?"

He took her hand. "The us that neither of us seems willing to discuss."

Haley pulled her hand out of his then inched her

way out of the chair and away from him. "I—I don't know what you're talking about."

Matt sighed. "Look, Haley, we can dance around it if you want, but it'll be better in the long run if we just face this thing head-on."

She did know what he meant, but something about his direct approach put her off, frightened her if truth be told.

Timothy had never been direct, there were always layers and shades of meaning in everything he said, every gesture he made, every gift he presented.

With Matt Brandon, none of the rules that Haley thought she'd known about relationships seemed to apply. For one, he, much like her cousin Amber, openly talked about things like kissing and male-female attraction. Haley wasn't comfortable with that or with showing her emotions.

"Haley, I think part of the reason you're feeling uncomfortable, even threatened by my work at the church and with the young people is because we—you and I—have some unresolved issues."

She shook her head. "I don't know how you grew up, Matt. But the way I did, people didn't just..." She waved an ineffective hand.

"Just what?"

"Talk about things."

He looked rather bemused. "Then how did they communicate?"

Haley didn't have an answer to that. Her aunt and uncle were so well attuned to each other's feelings that they rarely talked, at least not in front of Haley or their children.

"You've dated before," he said. "Surely you talked to your dates."

"Not about things that mattered."

The telephone rang before Matt had a chance to ask her about that. Haley, grateful for the interruption, excused herself and reached for the cordless phone.

A moment later she told Matt it was a call she had to take. With a sigh, and a two-finger hand motion indicating that he'd call her, Matt left.

Haley didn't linger on her call with the library director. After ringing off, she wandered into the kitchen with the intention of getting a cup of chamomile tea.

Maybe that would calm her nerves.

But on the counter she spotted a flier for the upcoming Skate for Jesus party. Matt could claim that he hadn't taken over on purpose, but the net effect remained the same: Haley was left out in the cold in the one place she'd found shelter.

What she wasn't prepared for was just how popular the contemporary service would be. Word had evidently spread not just in Wayside but in surrounding communities that something different was happening over at Wayside Community Christian Church.

In the midst of the excitement about what Matt did, Haley's work at the church seemed irrelevant, no longer needed. She blinked away the moisture at her eyes, refusing to cry over something that was inevitable. Is that why she'd been so reluctant to have Matt join the Community Christian family? Had she innately recognized him as a threat to her own niche?

She wanted to believe that she was above that sort

of thing, petty jealousies and competition. But now, with the wisdom and benefit of hindsight, she realized that *was* the case.

Haley stood there, staring down at the flier that encouraged people to Skate for Jesus, and questioned her calling. She wouldn't go so far to say she questioned her faith. In that regard she had no doubt. Once before she'd put aside the desires of her heart. She'd settled in Wayside, ultimately without Timothy, and made a life for herself.

"Settled," she said.

She didn't at all like the connotation. But that's just what she'd done.

"Just like the Cherrys." The founders of the town had been too weary to go on to the area that would become Portland. So they'd settled by the side of the road. And in stopping before they reached their goal destination, had they missed their blessings?

Haley pondered that.

Had she, in taking the road toward what she'd thought meant security with Timothy, turned her back on what her true mission in life was supposed to be? And then, when that fell apart, had she truly settled for less?

Instead of following her heart, instead of taking a chance on the unknown and becoming a missionary, she'd decided to follow the safe and secure path. She agreed to marry Timothy. Then, after her future had been set and she'd come to terms with herself about her choice, he'd dumped her.

After the Timothy debacle, she could have started training to become a missionary. It wasn't too late then. As a matter of fact, it would have gotten her out into the world, focused on something other than feeling sorry for herself. But again, she'd chosen poorly. She'd settled in Wayside, a safe and sheltering harbor.

A part of her wanted to lay the blame for her restless spirit at Matt's feet. But she'd been having questioning thoughts long before Matt arrived. Questions like *is there something more for me out there?* and *why am I so unhappy?*

She knew that no one who encountered her would think she was unhappy. She always smiled and had a cheerful word for everyone she encountered. She had a job she enjoyed and at which she made a decent living. She had a nice house, small but hers. She had fulfilling work at the church and in the community.

But despite the calendar that always seemed full with meetings and appointments, she rarely had fun. Other than Amber and Kara, she had no close friends to speak of. And now, the very people she thought she was helping had found someone else, someone who spoke their language, who understood their needs far better than Haley did.

Obviously, it was time to step aside, time to give the church's Christian education department a chance to be directed by someone who knew how to run it properly.

With a heavy heart and much on her mind, Haley slipped the flier about the skating party onto the kitchen counter.

The decision didn't come easy. But by the next afternoon, she knew that's just what she needed to do. Haley booted up her computer and drafted a resignation letter to Reverend Baines. In it, she said she'd like to stay on as a Sunday school teacher if the new Christian education director had room for her.

After printing out the letter, she logged on to the Internet and looked up the site for the Interfaith Missions Project. Maybe it wasn't too late to become a missionary in Central America. There the focus was Christian education, and Haley's expertise could be put to use—and appreciated.

Chapter Fourteen

The funeral for Angela's mother took place two days later. About twenty people, mostly from Community Christian's inspirational choir, filled the chairs in the small chapel at the funeral home. Reverend Baines delivered the eulogy and Matt sang the hymn, "Oh, How I Love Jesus," that the teen requested of him. The church picked up the expenses that weren't covered and had taken a special collection to assist with Angela's future needs.

"Thank you, Reverend Matt. For everything," she said at the end of the service.

Matt gave her a hug, followed by one from Haley who stood next to him.

"I sent my brother a letter. I don't know if he got it yet. Dr. Spencer tried to call, but he's in solitary."

"I'm sure he'll get the word," Matt said.

Angela nodded, but she didn't look convinced. "Well, I need to go take care of some things."

Haley and Matt watched as some of the young people from Community Christian comforted Angela.

"This is the first funeral a lot of them have ever attended."

"Facing mortality can be scary," Matt said.

Haley nodded.

"Who is this Dr. Spencer she mentioned?"

"A therapist and friend. We're really close. Kara Spencer along with the people from youth services will be working with Angela."

"And this Dr. Spencer, is she any good?" Matt asked.

Haley nodded. "The best. She's an affiliate member of Community Christian, too. You haven't met her because she's been away on a fellowship."

With a final look at Angela and a handshake with Reverend Baines, Matt and Haley left together.

The next two weeks passed in something of a blur. Cindy, Adam and their friends drew closer, the funeral and Angela's situation apparently triggering in them a desire to help people in need. They spent time at a hospice center and visited seniors at a home for adults.

When Cindy and Adam announced that they were going to East Wayside to witness to the homeless, Haley got nervous. They'd never done this sort of thing before.

"You worry too much, Haley," Matt said. "They're just going to hand out some Bibles and meal vouchers. And I told them to make sure to take a cell phone. Don't worry. They know how to take care of themselves. And they should be back long before dark.''

Haley wasn't at all convinced that that was the case. The only thing that calmed her was knowing that the inner city mission teams traveled in groups of two or three.

When her phone rang at ten-thirty Thursday night, though, her fears came to fruition.

''Haley,'' Matt said. ''There's been some trouble. The kids are at the hospital. I'll pick you up in five minutes.''

Haley was at the curb when Matt rolled up in the truck. She was too scared and worried to be angry at him. That would come later.

The bright, sterile lights of the waiting room at the hospital's emergency entrance made Haley blink. She spotted Cindy's parents right away. Adam's father was talking to a man in green scrubs. Haley rushed forward.

''Are they okay? What happened?''

''Oh, Haley. You didn't have to come down here. But thank you. Cindy wanted to make sure you and Reverend Matt knew they were okay.''

Haley's eyes darted toward the swinging doors leading into the emergency room. ''What happened?''

''They were talking to a man and someone tried to rob them. Adam was cut.''

''Oh, my God.'' Color drained from Haley's face and she swayed. Matt was right there and steadied her with a hand splayed at the small of her back.

''And Cindy?'' Matt asked.

''She's all right. Just shaken up a bit.''

A few minutes later Cindy emerged from behind the swinging doors. She ran to her parents, who enveloped her in a hug.

"I was so afraid. I kept praying the whole time," she said. "Adam's okay, though. The doctor stitched him up and is giving him a tetanus shot just to be safe."

A little while later and just as they'd been told to expect, Adam was wheeled out. A white bandage covered part of his arm, but a big grin filled his face.

"Hey, Haley. Hi, Reverend Matt." He held up his arm. "I didn't have all my armor with me so a fiery dart got through."

Haley smiled despite the tears in her eyes. Just that Sunday the morning lesson had been from Ephesians about putting on the whole armor of God.

"Yeah," Matt said, ruffling the teen's hair. "But you're not standing."

Adam jerked his head back at the hospital attendant manning the wheelchair. "That's 'cause he won't let me."

"That's right," the orderly said.

When all the paperwork was done and their statements given to a police officer, Adam's father consulted with the doctor about a prescription for possible pain. Matt then called the group together for prayer and invited both the police officer and the orderly to join them. Haley refused to take Matt's hand and moved to stand between Adam's father and Cindy's mom.

Matt prayed a prayer of thanksgiving that the injuries sustained weren't more serious. He prayed for the people the teens had ministered to on the streets and for the one who'd attacked them. When he finished, the loudest "Amen" came from the orderly who still stood behind Adam's wheelchair.

Haley remained quiet on the walk across the hospital parking lot. She rubbed her arms as if she were chilly. Matt opened the door for her then settled in behind the wheel.

"This is all your fault."

Midway toward inserting the key in the ignition Matt paused. He sat back carefully. "My fault."

Then he looked at her, really looked. She was furious, so angry that she trembled with it. Her lips were a thin, disapproving line.

"You encouraged them to go running around town, poking their noses in situations that put them in harm's way. Now look what happened."

"Haley, you're making too much of this. Adam barely has—"

"He could have been killed! Both of them."

He closed his eyes. That *was* true. But it hadn't happened and she needed to realize that.

"I knew your influence was going to lead to trouble. I knew it. I hope you're happy now."

The was the last thing Matt could claim to be. "You're not being fair, Haley."

She grunted. With arms securely crossed about her, she stared out the passenger side window.

He'd barely pulled the truck alongside the curb in front of Haley's house when she opened her door and jumped down. She slammed the door shut.

"Good night to you, too," he muttered. But he stayed curbside until he'd seen her go safely into her home.

It came as no surprise to him when she refused to pick up the phone. After trying to reach her three times, Matt gave up. She could ignore him tonight, but it would be impossible tomorrow night—not when they'd be locked in a skating rink with fifty or sixty teens and adults from the church. The rink couldn't be big enough for her to hide all night long.

It wasn't.

But that didn't stop Haley from giving him the cold shoulder. No one seemed to notice except Matt. The hero and heroine of the hour were Cindy and Adam. The two teens found themselves in the spotlight, peppered with questions and concerns about the attack.

The party officially started at 11:00 p.m. Once the doors were locked, no one would leave until after breakfast at ten the next morning. Saying there was no need to fight gravity and that he was too uncoordinated to figure out how to use the crutches he'd need if he put on a pair of roller skates, the pastor planned to slip out after opening the lock-in and wishing them well.

"You can't ignore me all night," Matt said.

He'd caught her at the check-in table processing a few late arrivals. She handed each person a goody bag and pointed to a place where they could stash their sleeping bags.

"Yes, I can," Haley told him. "As a matter of fact, you don't even need to be here. You can leave with Reverend Baines."

Matt smirked. "You're not getting rid of me that easily. My gear is already laid out."

Set up out of the way and near the table where a deejay worked was Matt's electric piano, the box of music makers and a small gym bag.

In addition to roller skating, the night's activities would include Bible study, games, videos, lots of food and a mini-concert from the inspirational choir.

"I'm still very upset with you."

"I know. We'll work it out, though."

Haley's expression said she doubted it, but a question from one of the adult chaperons precluded her response. And someone called Matt away.

Haley was still angry with him. But she was more angry with herself. She'd let her feelings for Matt lull her into a complacency that resulted in a close call that even twenty-four hours later left her shaken and afraid.

Neither Adam nor Cindy seemed the worse for wear, though, and had, it appeared, earned bragging rights among their peers. The incident solidified the relationship between the two teenagers.

Matt's relationship with all of the young people had been cemented in rehearsals, during those early-morning church services and apparently at social events that Haley always seemed to find out about after the fact.

To add insult to her already wounded pride, *she* hadn't been the one who was called to the hospital. Cindy's parents had called Matt first.

Haley stared at the welcome table decorated with balloons and confetti. She felt disconnected from her teens. The skating party lock-in was exactly the sort of thing she should have thought up for the young people. But she hadn't thought of it. Matt had. And all the kids knew it. That Haley actually made it happen didn't seem to count for much. Not if the crowd around Matt was any indication.

With the weight of another failure weighing down her spirit, she realized she probably would have gently discouraged them from trying to organize such an event. Skating and the Lord's work just didn't seem to mesh.

But Matt had found a way to make it work. He knew how to take the Good News to the streets in a way that got people where they lived.

"And where they can be killed," she muttered.

"What was that, Haley?"

She glanced up at Cindy's mom. "Nothing, Elaine. I was just talking to myself."

Elaine Worthington reached for Haley's hand. "I know you're upset about what happened last night. So were we. But you know what?"

"What?"

"Adam and Cindy's faith in the middle of that led the homeless man to Christ."

"You're kidding."

Elaine shook her head. "He was waiting for us when we left the hospital. He was concerned about Adam. And said he wanted to talk about the God who gave them enough courage to come to a part of town that most people ignore and to seek out people who were invisible to most of the world. He even gave the police officer some additional description of the suspect.''

Haley found herself at a loss for words.

"We all went out for breakfast at the pancake house. He'll be at church Sunday."

"That's incredible."

Elaine squeezed her hand. "I just thought you should know that you and Matt have been a terrific influence on Cindy. Thank you."

Well into the evening Haley continued to mull over the conversation with Elaine. And she came to three distinct conclusions.

The first was that she wasn't cut out for foreign mission work. She couldn't even handle the domestic stuff. Just the thought of going not to another country, but to a neighborhood across the very town she lived in, filled her with trepidation. Yet, two teenagers, armed with nothing more than the Gospel in their hearts and a cell phone in a pocket, had walked straight into that unknown place.

Haley had unknown places right here at home, practically in her backyard that needed tending just as much as any foreign mission field. She could start missionary work right here if she really wanted to.

The second realization: She owed Matt an apology for the way she'd acted the night before. Her own fears shouldn't have been dumped on him. And she had been afraid. Afraid of what could have happened to Cindy and to Adam. But more afraid of her own growing feelings and dependency on Matt. They'd arrived at the hospital as if they were a team. Haley realized that she, and members of the church, had come to look at them as a team.

Her third realization and conclusion also involved Matt. She watched him lead a line of skaters. His head was thrown back as he laughed at something someone said. And there in the middle of a skating rink, with Christian rock blaring from the sound system, Haley realized she'd done the most improbable: she'd fallen in love with Matt Brandon.

The knowledge filled her with equal parts joy and despair. Until this moment, she thought she'd known what it was like to fall in love. She'd loved Timothy—or so she'd thought. Her deepest feelings for him didn't come close, didn't even rate, when compared to the depth of her love for Matt.

And therein lay the root of her despair. She and Matt were so different. They came from different backgrounds, had completely different takes on religion and worship. And though by mutual tacit agreement they'd come to terms on that part of their relationship, there were still things to overcome. Chief among those things was Haley's fierce streak of independence.

When people truly loved each other they married and made a home together. Throughout their long marriage, her aunt and uncle had called home everything from huts in East Africa to ramshackle shacks in Honduras. Haley, though, had built for herself the kind of home environment she'd always dreamed of.

But one look at Matt and she was willing to travel with him no matter where he roamed.

Her spirit soared at the heady euphoria rushing

through her. She hugged herself, sure that the joy
bubbling inside might spill out. At just that moment,
Matt made a turn on the floor and his gaze connected
with hers. He smiled and Haley's knees grew weak.
She waved at him.

On the floor of the skating rink, Matt nearly stumbled. He'd never seen Haley look as beautiful as she
did in that moment. She was the most enchanting
woman he'd ever met. Sure, some could claim that
Haley's face was too wide, her mouth not a perfect
bow. But she fit in his arms like a dream. She made
him smile and consider things from another view-
point. She was light and laughter in his life, and she
played a mean game of miniature golf. As far as Matt
was concerned, she was perfect just the way she was.
He just had to convince her of that.

On the next beat of the music, Matt disengaged
from the line. "I think you guys have the swing of
it," he said.

He skated to where Haley stood. She met him at
the counter ringing the rink. Something was different
about her. Her eyes shone with a light that brightened
her entire countenance.

"What are you smiling at?" He reached a hand out
and caressed the corner of her mouth.

"You."

"Me?"

Haley nodded. Matt leaned forward for a quick
kiss. But Haley halted his hand. She took his face in
her hands and kissed him thoroughly. Matt grabbed
the counter for balance.

"Wow," he said. "What was that for?"

"Just because." She couldn't tell him. Not yet, this was neither the time nor the place. But she could bask in her own secret knowledge of the love she harbored in her heart.

"I owe you an apology. I'm sorry about how I acted last night."

He cupped her chin in his hand. "You were scared."

She nodded.

"So was I."

She wrinkled her brow. "You were?"

Matt captured a stray curl and twisted it around his finger. "Very much so. I knew they could handle themselves witnessing. But I didn't think they would be in any physical danger."

"How did you know they were ready to do that? I thought it was some sort of residual effect of the funeral for Angela McReady's mother."

"That may have been part of it," he said, conceding the point with a slight nod. "But they were ready to spread the word because they've been trained by a woman who knows her business. They've had a solid biblical grounding by a prayer and Scripture warrior."

The word *Who?* almost tumbled out of her mouth when he gave her a look filled with tenderness…and respect. Haley knew she'd always remember that moment. Her heart filled with even more love for him.

When he leaned forward Haley met him halfway. The kiss they shared was filled with all of the things they each secretly felt.

Fireworks went off all through Haley. As Matt

handed it to her, almost graciously, instead. It's going to be all right, Angel thought, it's going to be all right, the two of us: for one whole minute believing it, maybe two. That night, she'd tried once or twice bringing the conversation round to Shane going to the police, giving himself up, but all he had done was scowl and tell her not to be so fucking daft.

'We've got to split up,' Angel said. The burger was finished and they were drinking Coke to swill away the taste. 'Just for a bit. A week or so.'

'No way.' Shane shook his head.

She came close and wound her fingers inside the cuff of his sleeve.

'We've got to. After what's happened. We're too obvious like this. Someone will spot us if we're together, you know they will.'

'They haven't before.'

'That was different. If Mum hadn't talked to the police earlier, she certainly will've by now.' She pulled lightly at his arm. 'Shane, it makes sense, you know it does.'

'How long?' he said after several moments. 'How long'd this be for?'

'Just a week or so, like I say. Then we'll meet up again.'

'You won't, though, will you? You'll bugger off. It's just an excuse to get away.'

'Don't say that.'

'It's fucking true.'

'No. No, it's not. I promise you. Promise. Look, we'll name a place, right? Motorway services, south of Birmingham. The M5. First services you come to, yeah? A week today. Early evening. Six or seven. We'll wait for

one another. Then we can go anywhere. Wales, like you wanted. Like you said. Okay? Shane, okay?'

'Okay.' When he looked at her there was sadness in his eyes.

'I'll be there, I promise.' She kissed him hard and stepped away, knowing she had to go now if at all.

The driver of the car transporter was on his way back from his break. 'Want a lift?' he said, seeing Angel now standing alone.

'Yes,' she said. 'Yes, thanks. Hang on, I'll just get my bag.'

Shane watched, then turned away.

◆

Happy to deflect the media from the true focus of their inquiry, the police did nothing to dissuade them from the view that Shane Donald was still the principal suspect in their investigation into Emma Harrison's murder. Public relations set up a press interview with Elder and agreed that he could be interviewed on local television on the clear grounds that nothing was asked which might be prejudicial to any future trial. So Elder graced *Midlands Today*, fielding his one minute and forty seconds of questioning about Donald brusquely if competently and then providing the young feature writer from the *Post* with sufficient material for a half-page, double-column side-bar in which the unsolved disappearance of Susan Blacklock loomed large.

Front-page photographs of Shane and Angel lined up along the newsagents' shelves. A couple of dangerous young villains on the run.

346

'*21st Century Bonnie and Clyde*' some sub-editor dubbed them, though as far as anyone knew they had yet to rob a bank or brandish a gun. Even the arts pages of the *Independent* got in on the act, publishing stills from movies featuring pairs of runaway fugitives: John Dall and Peggy Cummings in *Gun Crazy*; Farley Granger and Cathy O'Donnell in *They Live By Night*; Martin Sheen and Sissy Spacek as fictional versions of Charles Starkweather and Caril Fulgate in Terrence Malick's *Badlands*.

And all the while the search for Adam Keach was progressing; relatives, friends and associates were being traced and questioned as urgently as possible.

◆

Elder drove the relatively short distance to Crewe and talked to Eve Branscombe, whose injuries, fortunately, were less serious than they had at first appeared. She looked at him out of a round, doughy face and when she spoke of Angel her voice was filled with genuine sadness and concern: a good girl gone astray. When he asked her about Shane Donald, tears brimmed in her eyes but they were tears of anger and fear; describing how he turned on her, she flinched as if his hand were striking her cheek again, his foot driving into her side.

'He killed her, didn't he? That poor girl. Emma, isn't that her name?'

'We don't know, Mrs Branscombe,' Elder said.

'If she hadn't pulled him off me, Angel, he would have killed me too.'

◆

'Where have you been?' Maureen asked, when Elder walked back into the office. 'I've been trying to get you on your mobile.'

'Sorry. It was switched off.'

'Useful.'

'What was it anyway?'

'Angel Ryan.'

'What about her?'

'She's phoned in three times. She wants to meet you.'

'Why me?'

Maureen smiled caustically. 'Something to do with all this publicity you've been getting?'

43

Angel was sitting on a bench in the Broad Marsh bus station in Nottingham, head down, smoking a cigarette. Her blue jeans were stained on one leg with grease or oil and almost threadbare at the knees, grubby trainers on her feet; she wore a thin cotton T-shirt beneath a man's unbuttoned denim shirt, and over that a short rust-coloured corduroy jacket, new enough to have been liberated from somewhere like River Island earlier that day.

As Elder approached her, crossing from the underpass, she looked up.

'Angel Ryan?'

Taking one last drag at her cigarette, she dropped it to the ground. 'Recognised me, then?'

Elder glanced left towards a pair of men sitting hunched over their cans of Strongbow, right to where a harassed woman was doing her best to marshal four small children and stop them running out in front of oncoming buses.

'Not too difficult,' he said, and held out a hand. 'Frank Elder.'

'And you're not with the police?'

'Not exactly. Not any more.'

349

Despite the fact that it was far from cold, Angel began fastening the buttons on her jacket. Fastening and then unfastening nervously.

'Do you want to walk?' Elder asked.

Angel shrugged.

'Come on, no sense staying here.'

She followed him through the Broad Marsh centre and up the escalator on to Low Pavement, from there along narrow streets that ran between old Victorian factories which were gradually being renovated and remodelled into loft apartments, chichi little shops that seemed to Elder to sell things he neither wanted nor could easily afford.

As they walked Elder chatted about this and that, nothing substantial, seeking to put Angel at her ease. At the corner of Stoney Street and High Pavement, he pointed towards a bench inside St Mary's churchyard.

'Let's sit for a bit.'

Inside the church, someone was practising the organ, scales and then a tune, something Elder thought might well have been Bach.

'You wanted to talk to me?' he said.

'Yeah, I suppose.'

'About Shane?'

Angel glanced up at him and then back down at the ground. 'Yes.'

'Where is he?'

'I don't know.'

'Really?'

'Not where he is right now, no.'

'But you could get in touch with him. If you wanted to.'

350

'Maybe. Yeah, maybe.'

Angel looked at him again quickly. Old, about her father's age, she supposed. Nice hands. And not rushing her, she liked that. Pretending to be her friend. She'd had social workers who were like that, a few; psychologists too. She wondered if she could trust Elder more than she had them. If she could trust anyone, including herself.

'What if he wanted to give himself up?' Angel asked, her voice quiet, as if she herself didn't want to hear what she'd said.

'Is that what he wants to do?'

'If he did, though,' Angel said, 'what would happen?'

'That depends.'

'This girl, the one in the papers, Emma something, he didn't have nothin' to do with that. I swear.'

Elder nodded, thinking now that it was almost certainly true.

'He'd have to go back to prison, anyway, wouldn't he?' Angel said.

'No way round that, I'm afraid. He's what's called unlawfully at large. His licence would be rescinded and he'd have to serve the remainder of his sentence, that at least. And there'd be new charges, I imagine. The woman in Crewe, Eve was it? Quite possibly his probation officer, too. He'd likely be facing some serious time.'

Angel looked away.

'You've talked about this?' Elder said after several moments. 'You and Shane.'

Angel shook her head. 'Yes. No. No, not really. I mean, I've tried. Tried talking to him, but he won't. He . . . And I'm afraid . . .' She looked at Elder again, still trying to read something in his eyes. 'I'm afraid, if he just

carries on . . . if we . . .' She blinked. 'I'm afraid he might get too far out of control, kill someone. Not meaning to, not really, only . . .'

'I understand.'

'Do you?'

'Perhaps. I think so.'

'You were the one, arrested him before.'

Elder nodded.

'He was just a boy,' Angel said.

'A boy who'd helped kill somebody.'

'That was the other one, McKeirnan. Not Shane.'

'The jury didn't agree.'

'And you?'

Elder didn't answer right away. 'At the very least he stood by and let it happen.'

'And for that he has to spend almost half his life inside?'

'It's the law.'

'Fuck the law.'

A Japanese couple glanced round on their way towards the church door. The organist seemed to have finished his impromptu recital or possibly he was just resting.

'Has he ever been aggressive towards you?' Elder asked.

'No. Not really.'

'You're sure?'

'He wouldn't hurt me.'

How many times have I heard that, Elder thought?

'You're not afraid for yourself?' he asked.

Angel shook her head. An ailing lorry went past along the narrow road behind them, flowering black smoke from its exhaust.

'Does he know you're here, talking to me?'

'No.'

'And you really think he'd give himself up? Because if he would, all he has to do is walk into the nearest police station.'

'He wouldn't do that.'

'What then?'

'He'd talk to you.'

'Why me? Like you said, I'm the one who put him away.'

'He trusts you. Least, I think he does. One or two things he's said. That you were a decent bloke. For a copper. Straight. That's what he said.' Slowly, she turned again to face him. 'Is it true?'

'I try to be.'

Elder was already getting to his feet.

'Let's walk a bit more.'

They went down some worn steps at the far end of the churchyard and turned back on to Stoney Street. He was trying to reconcile Angel with the details, sparse as they were, that Maureen had received from social services. He had expected someone with even less confidence, someone who carried the scars of her early life more openly. But the places where Angel had cut herself with razor blades and fragments of shattered mirror glass were mostly healed over now, hidden from sight.

Who, Elder wondered, as he watched Angel cross the street a pace in front of him, was she trying to save most, Shane Donald or herself?

In a café off Stoney Street and High Pavement, Elder drank coffee and watched her while she ate soup and then a bacon-and-tomato roll.

'I'm gonna meet him,' Angel said. 'A few days' time. I could phone you, let you know when.'

'You could tell me now.'

'No, later.'

'You don't trust me.'

Angel blinked. 'You'll just talk to him, right? You're not going to grab him or nothing? Because if you do, he'll run. I know.'

'I understand,' Elder said.

'If he doesn't want to go with you, you won't try and stop him?'

'I'm no longer a constable,' Elder said. 'I've no powers of arrest.'

'And there'll be no police, you promise?'

'As long as he wants to talk to me, I'll talk to him alone.'

Elder wrote down his mobile number, went to the counter and paid the bill. On their way out towards the street, he pushed a twenty and two tens down into Angel's hand.

'You will be in touch?' Elder said.

'Yes. I said.'

'And afterwards? I mean, if he does decide to give himself up. What will you do then?'

'I dunno. Go back with the fair, maybe. Della'd always take me in, for sure.'

Elder nodded. 'Try and talk to him again,' he said. 'Work him round.'

They went a short way towards the Broad Marsh together and then he stopped and watched her walk away, hands stuffed into the pockets of her corduroy jacket, a survivor against the odds.

44

He woke with a head like so much wadded cotton wool. At first he thought it had been Katherine, treading round the edges of his dreams, but then he realised it had been Angel. Quickly dressed and feeling the need for space and fresher air, he drove the short distance from Willie Bell's to Wollaton Park and walked down past the house towards the lake. Deer grazed in the adjoining field or stood in twos and threes beneath the trees. If Angel did contact him with Shane Donald's whereabouts, there was no way he could keep them to himself, he understood that. He would have to tell Maureen, at the very least, and once he'd done that everything would be out of his hands.

Elder lengthened his stride; if he could convince them to let him talk to Shane first, there was a chance he might convince him to give himself up. A slim chance, but a chance all the same.

He was rounding the first curve of the lake, where the path opened out to afford an uninterrupted view back towards Wollaton Hall, when his phone began to ring.

'Frank Elder?' The voice was male and what would once have been called well-spoken. Maybe in some places it still was.

'Yes?'

'This is Stephen Bryan. You left your number, asked me to call.'

So much had happened it took Elder a while to connect the name. 'Yes,' he said eventually. 'That's right. A good few days ago.'

'I've been away.'

'It was about Susan Blacklock,' Elder said. 'You were at school with her, I believe. Chesterfield.'

'She hasn't turned up, has she?' With each sentence the regional accent lurking behind the received pronunciation reasserted itself more and more.

'Should she?'

'Depends whose story we're in.'

'Sorry?'

'Downbeat or sentimental. David Lynch or Steven Spielberg. George Eliot, if you like, or Charlotte Brontë.'

'This isn't fiction,' Elder said. 'We don't have a choice.'

There was a laugh at the other end. 'Do you still want to talk? Only if you do I'm afraid the window's fairly small. I'm off to Edinburgh the day after tomorrow.'

'Then how about this afternoon?'

Bryan gave him directions and Elder scribbled them down on the back of his hand.

◆

Clarendon Park was close enough to the centre of the city, the part of Leicester you lived in if you were a teacher near the top of salary scale; better still, a psychotherapist or university lecturer. Victorian villas with stained glass

still intact above the doors and Bosch ovens in brushed steel in their remodelled kitchens, Farrow & Ball paint on the interior walls.

Stephen Bryan's house was a part of a terrace of twelve with taller semi-detached villas at either end. From the upper storeys it would be possible to look back through the trees towards the railway station.

'*Stephen Makepiece Bryan*' read the card in black italic script alongside the front door. For someone who must still be only thirty or so, Elder thought, Bryan was doing pretty well for himself.

When he pressed the bell, Elder was treated to a burst of orchestral music, jarring and shrill.

'Apologies,' Bryan said, opening the door almost immediately. 'Bernard Herrmann, the music from *Psycho*. It's meant to scare away gas company cowboys and proselytising Baptists.'

Bryan was wearing blue-black jeans and a thrift-shop fifties print shirt. His feet were bare.

'I assume you're neither of those.'

'Frank Elder. We spoke on the phone.'

Bryan shook his hand and stepped back. 'Come on in.'

Elder followed him into a long and narrow hallway, one side of which was partly blocked by a confusion of cardboard boxes and bulging plastic bags.

'Lodgers,' Bryan explained. 'One lot moving out, another moving in. The bane of my life, in a way, but most months it's the only way to pay the bills. An aunt left me this place and I've been clinging on to it ever since – even if sometimes it does seem I've got half of De Montfort University living in it with me.'

There were posters from the Berlin and Telluride film

festivals and, midway along, a striking black-and-white photograph of someone handsome and young, lit by a spotlight on the opposite wall.

'Beautiful, isn't he?' Bryan said.

'James Dean?'

'Montgomery Clift. *A Place in the Sun.*'

Bryan ushered Elder through the doorway across from the foot of the stairs. The two main ground-floor rooms had been knocked through to make one large space with a square archway at the centre. Rugs on scuffed but polished wooden boards. Shelves, floor to ceiling, were crammed with books, videos and DVDs; the front half was dominated by a large, wide-screen television and separate floor-standing speakers; in the rear an old-fashioned wooden writing desk had been adapted to hold a computer and monitor, a printer on a table alongside. There was a framed painting, vivid with colour, above the tiled mantelpiece, a tall smoked-glass vase of flowers in the fireplace beneath; more flowers on a low table, hedged in by small piles of books.

'I can offer you Yorkshire tea, Nicaraguan coffee or plain water, take your pick.'

Elder shook his head. 'I'm fine, thanks.'

'You won't mind if I make myself some tea?'

'Go ahead.'

Elder sat on a sloping leather armchair and leaned back. Traffic noise was slight and there was very little sound from inside the house itself. Perhaps the last twenty-four hours had taken it out of him more than he'd thought, because he could feel his eyes beginning to close.

Shaking himself, he sat forward and looked at the books on the table: Charles Barr on *Vertigo*, *Wilder on*

Wilder, a couple by Bryan himself: a small, squarish paperback called *Forgotten Stars of the Fifties* and, more weightily, *Shakespeare on Film, Contemporary Interpretations*. The picture on the cover showed a young man in a garish jacket, holding on to a wounded comrade and brandishing a pistol.

'My thesis,' Bryan said, coming back into the room. 'With a few updates and excisions, but it still reads as if untouched by human hand.'

'Film,' Elder said, 'clearly your thing.'

Bryan flopped down on to the settee opposite, almost but not quite spilling his tea. 'Yes. I do a bit of teaching up the road, some criticism – radio mostly, there's a show called *Back Row* – introduce the odd movie at Phoenix Arts. Otherwise, I suppose I'm a bit of a *rentier*, raking in the shekels at the same time as unblocking the toilets and trying to make sure my guests don't annoy the neighbours with Coldplay at two in the morning or smoke anything more serious than cannabis in the common parts.'

'Some would say it sounds a pretty nice life.'

'Most days they'd be right.'

'I've talked to Siobhan Banham and Rob Shriver – it was Rob who gave me your number. Siobham said you and Susan Blacklock were close, that you spent a lot of time talking together.'

Bryan set down his tea. 'I suppose that's true.'

'Can I ask you what you talked about?'

Bryan smiled. 'Aside from contemporary interpretations of Shakespeare, you mean?'

'Aside from that.'

'Mostly, she wanted to talk about her father.'

'She was having problems with him?'

'No, that was Trevor. I don't mean Trevor, I mean her real father.'

Elder felt as if all the air had been suddenly sucked out of him.

'You didn't know?'

'No. I had no idea.'

'Ah.' Bryan drank a mouthful of tea. 'I suppose I knew she kept it pretty quiet, Trevor being her stepfather.'

'You sound as though you knew him?'

'Not really. But he used to pick her up sometimes, after drama club, things like that. Fussed over her, I suppose you'd say. Susan found it . . . well, claustrophobic.'

'But she never treated him as if he weren't her actual father?'

'No, not at all. And I don't think anybody else knew. In fact, I'm sure they didn't.'

'Can I ask how come you did?'

Bryan smiled, remembering. 'It was one of those conversations, in fact. About Shakespeare. We'd been reading *Lear*, doing bits and pieces of improvisation. We were due to see it, in Newcastle . . .'

'The production that was cancelled.'

'Precisely. Anyway, we'd been working in pairs on this scene where one of the daughters turns on her father and tells him if he thinks she's going to look after him in the style he's been accustomed to, he's got another think coming. I'm wildly paraphrasing, of course.'

'Of course.'

'Susan and I were talking about it afterwards and she looked at me, all serious, and said, "I'd never treat my father like that, no matter what he'd done." Well, I'd seen

360

her with Trevor, heard her moan about him often enough, so I must have looked at her a bit gone out and that was when she told me.'

'Go on.'

'Her mother got pregnant with her when she was just sixteen. She'd been seeing this man, older than her by quite a bit he must have been. Met him in the record shop where he worked. Chatted her up, asked her out. Nobody knew, big secret, then wham – secret no longer. At least, not the pregnancy part. According to Susan, her father didn't want to know. Did his best to persuade her mum to have an abortion and when she wouldn't, he washed his hands of her. Refused to speak to her, have anything to do with the baby after it was born.'

'And Susan knew all this?'

'Apparently.'

'And still she felt something for him? Even after he'd deserted her and her mother and everything.'

'Yes. I think so. She'd have forgiven him, no matter what. If she could. But I don't think she'd ever seen him, not knowingly. She certainly didn't know where he was, I'm sure of that, where he lived. I got the impression she'd tried asking her mother about it once and her mother had thrown a fit. So I think she probably spent quite a lot of time thinking about him instead, day-dreaming, I suppose. You know, what she'd say to him if he suddenly materialised one day out of the blue.'

'And, as far as you know, she never talked to any of the others, any of her other friends about this?'

'No, I'm sure she didn't. And she made me promise not to mention it to a soul.'

'And you've been true to your word.'

'Until now.'

Bryan picked up his tea but didn't drink it.

'Is it important?' he asked.

'Now I don't honestly know,' Elder said. 'But to Susan Blacklock it was.'

As Elder was leaving, a white van was drawing up outside to take away the departing lodger's things.

'If you do find out anything,' Bryan said, 'about Susan, I'd appreciate it if you'd let me know.'

'I will,' Elder said as the two men shook hands. 'And I'll listen out for you on – what was it? – *Back Row*?'

'*Back Row*, *Front Row*, all the same.'

Bryan raised a hand as Elder got into his car and then pitched in to help clear the mess from his hall.

45

'Why didn't you tell me?'

Helen Blacklock, eyes bleary from sleep, struggled to focus on Elder's face looming above her in the doorway. She was wearing the lime-green uniform she wore at the shop on the quay.

'I'm sorry, I must have dropped off after work. What did you say?'

'I said, why didn't you tell me?'

'What?'

'The truth.'

It was relatively early, eight thirty at best, a late summer evening with, as yet, no taint of autumn. Whitby Abbey, as Elder topped the gradient of Blue Bank, had stood out clear and precise against the sea.

Ice had all but melted in the glass Helen had filled with tonic and a splash of gin; the butts of two cigarettes were stubbed out in the ashtray; a magazine lay open and upside down on the floor where it had slid from her hands.

'I'm going to have another drink.'

'Go ahead.'

'D'you want one?'

363

'No,' Elder said a little too sharply, and then, 'Yes. Yes, all right then. I will.'

'Gin? I don't think I've got anything else.'

'Gin's fine.'

The room seemed smaller than in his memory, but then he realised he was comparing it to the spaciousness of Stephen Bryan's house in Leicester.

'Ice and lemon?' Helen called from the kitchen.

'Please.'

'Both?'

'Both.'

The hand with which she passed him the glass was less than steady and her eyes held his for no more than moments before angling away. She waited for him to sit down and then did the same, opposite and just beyond arm's reach should either of them have felt and acted out the need.

'When you say the truth,' Helen said, 'you mean about Dave?'

'I don't know his name.'

'Susan's father.'

'Yes.'

'David Ulney.'

'You never mentioned him.'

'No.'

'Let everyone believe Trevor was Susan's father.'

Helen nodded, still avoiding his eyes.

'The police, me, everyone.'

'Yes.'

'But not Susan herself?'

'I tried.'

'But she knew.'

Helen looked at him then. 'She found a photograph. She was nine, rising ten. Rooting through my things one day, you know the way kids do. Why I'd clung on to it, God alone knows. Dave Ulney in his brothel creepers and his Edwardian suit, velvet collar, drape jacket, the whole Teddy boy bit.' She paused to light a cigarette. 'Susan asked who it was and before you know it there I was telling her.'

'Everything?'

'That he'd gone off and left me, deserted her. Never given either of us a penny. Not that I'd asked. Yes, I told her that, why shouldn't I? And then I tore the damned thing up into little pieces in front of her eyes and threw them in the bin.'

Helen drew hard on her cigarette, holding down the smoke, then releasing it slowly. 'God, I fancied him. Fancied him rotten.' Her laughter was raw and self-deprecating. 'I was sixteen. What did I know about anything? I didn't even know enough to keep my legs together.'

'You knew enough to keep the baby; you made a choice.'

'I was afraid, terrified. Of having an abortion, I mean. And besides, my parents, it was what they wanted, when they knew. "We'll stick by you," they said. "Good riddance to the likes of him." My mum came with me up to school to see the head teacher, the doctor, everything. She was brilliant. She's in a home now, Scarborough, one of those big old hotels on the North Cliff. When my dad died, she fell apart.' For several moments she was silent, thinking her own thoughts. 'I'm sorry, where was I?'

'Having Susan.'

'Yes. I was lucky. It was a doddle, like shelling peas. And then, when she was no more than six months old, there was Trevor, so gobsmacked, bless him, that he practically worshipped the ground I walked on. For a time, anyway. Or was that Susan? Now I'm not so sure. Anyhow, he was prepared to take me on, complete with a little baby, ready-made family, I suppose, and I thought, if I'm to be honest, well, I'll not likely get a better offer. So we got married, just a small registry office job, his folk and mine, no fuss. If anyone asks, he said, tell them the baby's mine. And so I did. It didn't seem too much to ask, after all.'

Elder reached for his glass. Helen seemed to have used a more than liberal amount of gin and he was glad.

'How did Susan act when you told her?'

'How d'you think? Knocked her sideways, poor love. At first she went all quiet, you know, dead quiet. Thoughtful. And then she began to barrage me with questions, on and on, until eventually she twigged I was never going to answer them, and after that she stopped.'

'And do you know if she ever talked about it with Trevor? Asked him?'

'No, I don't think so. He'd have said. Had to.'

'Does that surprise you?'

Helen didn't answer right away. Somewhere a clock was striking nine. 'Now I think about it, yes, I suppose it does. They used to row enough once she was into her teens, heaven knows. Trevor was over-protective some-times, interfering. He didn't mean to be, meant it all for the best but . . . It was as if he had to try harder, prove to himself he was being a good father, doing what he thought was his duty. She could have blurted it out then,

366

in the middle of one of their set-tos, just to get back at him, you know, in anger, but no, I don't think she ever did.'

'And her father, Dave I mean, did she ever have any contact with him?'

'No, not ever.'

'You're sure?'

'I'd have known, wouldn't I?'

◆

They walked around the near side of the harbour, out to the West Pier. There was the usual smattering of fishermen, a few courting couples snuggling on the wooden benches, men in topcoats and flat caps walking small dogs. The lights from Sandsend just over a mile away were small and steady along the edges of the tide. Helen had changed into a pair of grey cord trousers and a bottle-green hooded sweatshirt; Elder had pulled an old anorak from the boot of the car. Anyone seeing them might have thought they were old friends, little more.

'If I'd told you right off, about Dave,' Helen said, 'it wouldn't have made any difference, would it? To finding Susan. I mean, How could it?'

'I don't know. You're probably right, but I don't know. I mean, we'd have been interested, certainly, followed it up along with everything else . . .'

'And when it didn't lead anywhere?'

Elder didn't answer. A little way along the pier they paused to watch a boat heading out of the harbour, night fishing, lights shining strongly.

When Helen turned to walk on, Elder stayed put

where he was. 'Dave Ulney,' he said, 'what happened to him?'

'How should I know?'

'He just disappeared?'

'As good as. Buggered off to the ends of the earth, first chance he got.'

Elder looked at her questioningly.

'New Zealand. He sent me a card – one – out of the blue after two years. Karori, wherever that is. '*Settled here now. Hope you're well. Dave.*' He didn't even mention Susan, the rotten bastard. He never as much as asked after his own child.' There were tears in her eyes. 'I set light to it there and then.'

'Susan didn't see it? She didn't know?'

'She was two years old.'

'But you didn't tell her about it later? After she'd found the photograph?'

'Why would I do that? It was hard enough for her as it was.'

There was anger still, resentment mixed up with the tears.

'You've never heard from him since? Heard anything about him?'

'Not a word.'

They walked on out to the end of the second, smaller pier and stood there gazing at the lights of a container ship creeping, snail-like, along the horizon. There was wind enough now for the waves to strike the underpinnings with force, water spraying up into their faces.

'I wondered if I'd see you again,' Helen said.

Elder kissed her and she took his hand and slid it up beneath her sweatshirt and held it against her breast. At

home, he undressed her slowly, kissing the roll and curve of her body, before turning on to his back so that she could undress him, looking down at him in the half-light, his shirt first and then his trousers. She made a slight gasp as she lowered herself on to him, and then it was slow and knowing, her nipple in his mouth and a tightening shudder of her body his final, all too sudden, undoing.

'I'm sorry,' he said, as she rolled off him.

'That's okay, pet,' she said, smiling. 'You rest, get your strength back.'

But both were sleeping when the sound of the phone awoke them, Elder uncertain for that moment where he was and not immediately recognising the sound of his mobile. Joanne's voice was distant and uneven. 'Frank, it's Kate. She's not come home. I'm worried sick.'

Elder lifted his watch from the bedside table, Helen's alarmed eyes following him. It was half past one.

'Have you called the police?'

'No. I wasn't sure what to do.'

'Phone them now. I'm a couple of hours' drive away. Maybe a little more. I'll be there as soon as I can.'

Helen was standing, naked, by the bedroom door. 'I'll make some coffee while you're getting dressed. A Thermos for the car.'

'Okay, thanks.' He was dialling Maureen Prior's number as he reached for his shirt.

46

Elder drove too fast, coming close to losing control at a curve on the narrow road between Pickering and Malton, then just catching himself drifting asleep, his eyes closing momentarily on the ouside lane of the M18 at between eighty and ninety, all that he could urge out of his ageing Ford. The touch of his outer wheels against the road's edge was enough to jar him awake before he drifted into the central reservation, and at the first service station he came to after switching motorways, he splashed cold water in his face and drank the remainder of the coffee Helen had made for him.

'She'll be all right, Frank. Don't worry.'

The irony of his own words, almost, coming back at him.

The fact that his mind was speeding, skidding from one scenario to another, proved a kind of blessing and prevented him from lingering over whatever images his imagination might have delivered. Imagination and experience.

There was a single police car outside Joanne's house, another, a blue Vauxhall that he recognised as Maureen's, parked close behind it. A uniformed officer opened the

front door and made Elder identify himself as he tried to push past. Joanne was standing in the centre of the vast living-room, adrift in space. When she saw Elder she ran towards him, stopped, and, as he reached out his arms, tumbled against him, the tears that she had choked back earlier falling without let or hindrance. Eyes closed, he pressed his face against her hair, her fingers gripping him tightly, her face pressed damp against his chest.

Embarrassed, the young WPC who had been talking to Joanne, going over the notes she had made earlier, looked away. Standing near the spiral staircase, Maureen Prior waited for Elder to raise his head and then exchanged a quick glance with him, a brief sideways shake of her head.

Elder held Joanne, allowing her to cry.

'I'll make coffee, Frank,' Maureen said.

The constable followed her in search of the kitchen, leaving Elder and Joanne alone and faintly reflected in a wall of glass, the garden dark behind.

'Oh, Frank . . .'

Elder led her carefully towards the long settee and, prising free her hands, gently lowered her down.

'Tell me,' he said. 'When you're ready, tell me what happened.'

Joanne felt for a tissue and wiped her eyes, blew her nose.

'Kate was . . . she was out at training, the usual, you know . . . Harvey Hadden Stadium . . . she'd finish somewhere around . . . oh, anywhere between eight and nine . . .'

'Surely by then it's dark?' Elder interrupted.

'Well, maybe it was half past eight, I don't know. Besides, it doesn't matter.'

'It might.'

'Frank, please.'

'I'm sorry, carry on.' He gave her hand a squeeze.

'Sometimes she'd come straight home, but not always. Quite often, I think she'd go for a drink or something, just, you know, hanging out.'

'You didn't know where she was, where she was going?'

'For God's sake, Frank, she's sixteen.'

'Exactly.'

'What's that supposed to mean?'

'It means that if she's only sixteen I'd have thought you wanted to know where she was of an evening.'

'Really? Then maybe if you were that concerned you should have stayed around.'

Elder bit his tongue.

'I'm sorry,' Joanne said.

'No, it's okay. Go on.'

'If she did stay out,' Joanne said, 'she was usually in by half past ten, eleven at the latest. Mid-week especially. When she wasn't here by twelve I started ringing round her friends, those I knew. Several of them from the athletics club had seen her at training earlier on, but not since.'

'Since when? Exactly, I mean?'

'Frank, I didn't get a precise time, I was too worried, I . . .'

'It's all right, it's okay. We can check . . .'

'We already have.' Elder turned sharply at the sound of Maureen's voice; he hadn't been aware she'd come back into the room.

'As far as we can tell,' Maureen said, 'Katherine left the changing rooms at the track between eight thirty and

a quarter to nine. One of the others offered her a lift, but she turned it down. Said something about catching a bus.' Maureen paused. 'That's the last sighting of her we've traced so far.'

A quarter to nine to half past four: Elder was doing the arithmetic in his head. Not so far short of eight hours since his daughter had gone missing.

'That boy she was seeing . . .' he said to Joanne.

'Gavin?'

'I don't think so.'

Joanne looked back at him, puzzled, as Elder searched for the name.

'Stuart, I think it might have been.'

'I don't know any Stuart.'

'He was in her athletics club; drove an old 2 CV.'

Joanne shook her head.

'It wasn't one of the names we had,' Maureen said. 'No one we've spoken to so far. I'll have it checked.'

As she left the room, the WPC came in with mugs of coffee on a tray.

'You mentioned Gavin,' Elder said, turning back to Joanne. 'Gavin who?'

'Salter. He's a student, at the university.'

'Which one?'

'Not Trent, at least I don't think so. No, the old one, I'm sure.'

'And Katherine's going out with him?'

'She was. I think they had some sort of a bust-up. Just before the end of the summer term.'

'Have you any idea where he lives?'

'Lenton, somewhere. I don't know exactly.'

'Christ!' Elder exclaimed, just under his breath.

Joanne pressed her forehead against the heel of her hand. 'Frank, please don't make it any more difficult than it already is.'

'There's coffee,' the WPC said.

Nobody moved.

'His name's Stuart Reece,' Maureen said, reappearing from the hallway a few minutes later. 'High jumper, apparently. Lives out at Lady Bay. Someone's on their way to talk to him now.'

Elder nodded and gave her the name of Gavin Salter. It was possible but unlikely, Maureen knew, that the phone book might supply a listing. He could be on the electoral roll, although with the migratory habits of most students that was far from a certainty. Most probably they'd have to wait till morning and check Salter's address with the university.

'Jo,' Elder said quietly, 'why don't you go up and lie down? Get some rest.'

'I couldn't sleep,' Joanne said, but she stood up nevertheless, though less than steadily, and walked towards the staircase, Elder beside her.

'Where's Martyn tonight?' he asked.

She looked at him without her expression changing and then turned away and walked slowly out of sight.

◆

Elder and Maureen Prior sat on the curve of concrete steps that went up to the front door. The door itself was on the latch, Joanne restlessly asleep above. The sky was already lightening noticeably towards the east. Both of the uniformed officers had reported back to the central

police station, where a separate inquiry team had been set up with Colin Sherbourne, a youngish DI who had recently transferred from Humberside, in charge. Sherbourne had driven out earlier to talk with Elder and assure him that they were doing everything they could.

'It's not that long since he started shaving,' Elder commented when Sherbourne had gone.

'He's a good officer, Frank. Organised. Not the kind to get into a flap easily.'

'He hasn't the experience . . .'

Maureen laid a hand on his arm. 'Frank, we've got a good start. You know that as well as I do.'

'Eight hours, more now . . .'

'Most cases like this, we likely wouldn't have been alerted till morning.'

Elder let out a deep breath, almost a sigh. 'This isn't a separate investigation.'

'Frank . . .'

'Come on, Maureen,' Elder on his feet now. 'Isn't that what you've been thinking ever since I first called you?'

'No.'

'No? You're a bad liar, Maureen. It doesn't come naturally.'

'What I think, Frank, is that, come morning, Katherine'll come walking back home. A little sheepishly, perhaps, but she'll be back. And not so many hours from now.'

'I'd like to think you were right.'

'You know what I think happened? I think she met up with her student – Gavin, is it? – they met up and made up and she spent the night at his place. Sixteen, Frank, likely not the first time, though you'll not thank me for saying so.'

But Elder was shaking his head. 'He's got her, Maureen. Keach. He's taken her, I know it.'

'Frank, you're not being logical. There's a hundred and one explanations more feasible.'

'Are there?'

'You know there are. And besides, why would Keach do such a thing? Just suppose for a moment it had crossed his mind and somehow he got close enough to have the opportunity, why take the risk?'

'Why kidnap Emma Harrison in broad daylight? Carry her body across open country? Why send a postcard advertising what he'd done? To impress McKeirnan, that's why. And what better way to impress him than to take the daughter of the man who was largely responsible for putting him inside?'

Maureen sat staring off into the gathering dawn; there was an electric glow pale behind a scattering of blinds and curtains now, the early barking of one dog answered by another, far off. What Elder was saying was conjecture and little more, but conjecture was pretty much all they still had. Conjecture plus a feeling in Elder's gut, a feeling that in the past Maureen had learned to trust.

Rising, she stood alongside him.

'There's a massive search on for Adam Keach. And it'll intensify now, I promise you that. If he's moving around he can't stay hidden for long. Meantime, let Colin Sherbourne get on with his job. I'll keep a watching brief on both inquiries, Colin'll not mind that. He'll expect it.'

'And I stand around torturing myself? Kicking my heels?'

'Get some rest, Frank. That's the best thing you can do.'

'You're joking, of course.'

'Stay here at the house, Frank. There must be a spare bed, all these rooms. Joanne'll need you when she wakes up.'

'What are you going to do?'

'Me? Catch a couple of hours. I'll call you round seven thirty if you haven't called me first.'

47

Katherine Elder didn't come walking back home, tail between her legs or otherwise.

A search of the area between the athletics stadium and the bus stop yielded nothing: no discarded articles of clothing, no torn-off buttons nor signs of a struggle. It would all be checked again, centimetre by centimetre, inch by inch.

By a little after two that afternoon, officers had traced all of the athletes who had been at training the previous evening and taken statements. Everything confirmed the story they had first been given: once the session was over, Katherine, sports bag on her shoulder, had gone off alone. Those who had thought about it at all had assumed she was setting out to catch the bus home. Of course, it was possible that she'd arranged to meet somebody, but she hadn't mentioned any such arrangement and no one could recall seeing any cars they couldn't identify parked nearby.

'This youth,' Elder had said to Colin Sherbourne earlier. 'Reece. When you talk to him, I want to come along.'

'I don't know, Frank . . .'

'I've met him, spoken with him.'

'Even so.'

Elder had rested a hand, not heavily, on Sherbourne's arm. 'I won't interfere. Embarrass you, lose control. I promise.'

With some reluctance, the DI had agreed.

Stuart Reece was clearly shocked to hear that Katherine was missing and anxious to help. He had been at the track for a good couple of hours that evening, practising his jumping along with some general fitness and speed training; yes, he'd chatted to Katherine, the last time just before she'd gone off to shower and change.

'How did she seem?' Sherbourne asked.

'Normal. The same as usual.'

'She wasn't worried?'

'No.'

'Preoccupied?'

'No.'

'And what did she say she was going to do later on?'

Reece made a loose, shrugging motion. 'She didn't.'

'You're sure?'

'Yes.'

'You have a car, don't you?'

'Yes, an old 2 CV. Why?'

'Did you use it yesterday evening?'

'Yes, I nearly always do. From where I live it takes an age otherwise, one bus into town and then another out, the same performance coming back.'

'You offered Katherine a lift?'

Before answering, Reece glanced towards where Elder was standing, just a few paces back from Colin Sherbourne's shoulder. 'Yes. Yes, I did. I said did she

want a lift home and she said no thanks.' Reece shrugged. 'That was it.'

'And did that surprise you?' Sherbourne asked. 'Her saying no.'

Reece reached up a hand to push the hair away from his eyes. 'Not really. I mean, there wasn't any sort of arrangement, you know. Sometimes she came with me and sometimes she didn't.'

'And you've no idea why, on this particular occasion, she said no?'

Reece shook his head. 'No.'

Elder took a pace forward. 'You like her, Stuart, don't you?' he said.

'Yes, of course. Katherine's great, always good fun. Everyone . . .'

'No, I mean, you like her. Really like her.'

Reece's feet performed an odd little dance. 'Well, yes, you know, like I say, she's . . . Yes, yes, I do.'

'The first time I saw you, the two of you together, you were kissing her.'

Reece flushed. 'That didn't mean anything, it was just . . .'

'Just a bit of fun?'

The redness around Reece's neck and along his cheeks deepened and spread.

'Because it looked more than that to me.'

Reece had to will his gangly body to be still.

'You know what Katherine said to me, Stuart? What she implied? After you'd driven away. That you wanted the relationship to be serious. Is that right?'

Reece was staring at the ground. 'Yes, I suppose so.'

'And how did my daughter feel about that?'

'She didn't want to know.'

'I'm sorry, speak up.'

'She didn't want to know,' Reece almost shouted.

'And how did that make you feel?'

'How d'you think?'

'Pretty lousy. Small. Rejected.'

Reece twisted his head from side to side and breathed deeply through his mouth. 'I'm not stupid. I can see what you're trying to suggest. That I got all screwed up because Katherine turned me down, didn't fancy me, wasn't interested. So screwed up about it that I . . . I don't know, did something, lost my temper, hurt her.' He stopped and steadied himself, looking at Elder directly. 'Look, I like her, you're right. More than she likes me. But that kind of thing happens all the time. There's scores of girls around. At school, athletics, everywhere. And when I get to university there'll be more. I'd've liked to have had a relationship with your daughter, I still would. But the fact that I haven't hasn't made me go crazy. What I told you about last night's the truth. I drove home alone and I was in the house by nine or nine fifteen and if you ask my parents they'll back me up. Okay?'

Elder held the youth's gaze for several seconds and then nodded.

'Thanks for your time,' Colin Sherbourne said. 'We'll speak with your parents in due course. All right, Frank?'

Elder nodded again.

'Katherine, Mr Elder,' Stuart Reece said, 'I hope you find her. I hope she's okay.'

◆

Tracking down Gavin Salter proved less straightforward. The university confirmed that he was a second-year student reading law and provided two addresses, one for term-time, one his parents' home.

The house he shared with six other students in Lenton was just off the main road, a three-storey building with paint flaking away from around the windows and dustbins out front which were overflowing. Four of the students were still around, but Salter wasn't one of them.

Later that morning, two officers from the Hampshire force drew up outside Salter's parents' house in Stockbridge. His mother was just returning from church and met them in the drive; Gavin's younger brother was washing down the Land Rover and Gavin himself was still in bed. 'Sorry,' he said blearily, fastening the belt of his dressing-gown. 'Bit of a night last night, I'm afraid.'

They sat at a round table in the drawing-room; having politely refused the offer of coffee, the officers watched Salter dissolve two Alka-Seltzers in a glass of water, then drink it down.

'Katherine Elder,' the senior of the two men began. 'When did you last see her?'

Salter's answers were cautious, careful: his training in law, perhaps, coming to the fore. He and Katherine had had a bust-up in early June, before the end of term. He'd wanted her to go away with him to France – take Eurostar and then the TGV to somewhere like Avignon – and first off Katherine had said her mother would never let her, but then confessed she didn't really want to go away with him anyway. Salter admitted to saying something rather unpleasant, accusing her of being a silly little schoolgirl

who didn't have a mind of her own and it had all got rather heated and nasty.

'How nasty?'

'Well, you know, a certain amount of shouting and bad language.'

'You hit her?'

'Good God, no.'

'The heat of the moment, you're sure?'

'Listen, it's not the way I was brought up. To strike women.'

'So how did you leave it? After this row?'

'We didn't. Kate went storming off, slamming doors – we were at the house in Lenton – and that was that, pretty much.'

'She was angry, upset?'

'I suppose so.'

'And you?'

'I think I was annoyed with myself for losing my temper as much as anything. I mean, Kate and I, we'd had a good time for a couple of terms and France would have been fun, but you know, it had just about run its course. So all for the best, in a way.'

'And did you see her again after that?'

'Not really. Once or twice, perhaps, in passing. Nottingham's not really such a big place, after all.'

'When was this? These one or two occasions?'

'It must have been the same month, June. I've been down here since the end of term.'

'And how much contact have you had with Katherine since you came down?'

'None. None at all.'

'Phone calls, letters? Text messages, emails?'

'As I said, none at all.'

A few minutes later, the two officers were back in their car and heading towards Winchester.

'What d'you think?' the first one said.

'Of him? He's an arrogant little prick who'll be a barrister before you or I get to inspector and he'll earn more in a month than we'll take home after tax in a year, but I believe him, if that's what you mean. I don't think he's involved at all.'

'Shame.'

'Yeah.'

◆

An hour, more or less, after Hampshire police had reported back on their interview with Gavin Salter, Elder took two calls on his mobile. The first was from Helen Blacklock, who had tried several times earlier, enquiring in a concerned voice if there were any news, asking Elder how he was holding up; the second was from Maureen Prior, there'd been what seemed a reliable sighting of Adam Keach in Cleethorpes, some twenty or so miles up the coast from where Emma Harrison's body had been found.

Elder's blood seemed to clot in his veins; the upper part of his left leg felt suddenly numb and he rubbed at it hard to get the circulation moving again. If Keach had taken Katherine within an hour of her leaving training, he could have easily have reached the coast with her by nightfall.

Colin Sherbourne had officers talking to the bus company, checking the times they would have passed

along that route, talking to drivers and showing them photographs: do you remember seeing this girl?

What else was there to do? What could he do himself?

◆

As Elder pulled up outside the house, he checked his watch. While the day seemed to be lasting interminably, time was racing away. Alerted by the sound of his car, Joanne met him, anxious, at the door; from the expression on Elder's face she knew there was neither good news nor yet the worst.

She held him quickly and then stepped back.

'Martyn's inside. He just got back twenty minutes ago.'

Martyn Miles was out on the patio, vodka tonic in hand; he was wearing a pale lavender shirt and olive-green moleskin trousers and he removed his dark glasses when Joanne led Elder through from the living-room towards him.

'Frank, I'm sorry,' Martyn said. 'You must be worried sick. Is there any news?'

'No, not really.'

'She's not a stupid girl, she wouldn't have just gone off without telling someone.'

'No.'

'She had her mobile, she'd have phoned.'

'Her phone's switched off,' Joanne said. 'It has been since I first tried last night.'

'Isn't there some way you can trace it anyway?' Martyn asked.

'Not without a signal, no.'

'There must be something can be done.'

'The police are checking with all of Katherine's friends, anyone who might have seen her or spoken to her in the last few days, anyone who knew her well.'

'That student she was seeing . . .' Martyn began.

'Gavin Salter. Down in Hampshire with his parents. Last night he was out getting drunk at someone's twenty-first, witnesses galore.'

'What about a search?'

'The area around Harvey Hadden's was checked over once first thing; there's a fingertip search going on now to see if there's any clue as to what might have happened. There'll be posters up all over the city by the end of the day, the railway station, everywhere. Bulletins on the local news, TV and radio.'

'And that's it? We sit and wait?'

'Until there's a break, it's difficult to know what else to do.'

'There must be something?' Flinging his arm wide, Martyn caught Joanne's arm with his hand and the glass went flying from his hand.

'Fuck it!'

'Are you okay?' Elder asked Joanne.

'I'm fine. But you could ask Martyn what all the sudden histrionics are about.'

Crouching down to pick up the pieces of glass, Martyn looked up at her. 'Meaning what, exactly?'

'Meaning the first thing you did when you walked in and I started telling you Katherine was missing was to ask me to calm down and get you a drink.'

'It was what I needed. And you were so agitated you weren't making any sense.'

'Now Frank's here you're making out you're really worried. As if you really cared.'

'Of course I care.'

'Do you?'

He stood abruptly, his face close to hers. 'Fuck you, Joanne.'

'Nice, Martyn,' she said, and turned aside.

Martyn let the glass he'd been collecting fall from his hands.

'Where were you last night, Martyn?' Elder asked.

'What possible business is it of yours?'

'Just asking, that's all.'

'Am I a suspect or something?'

'Everyone close to Katherine will be being asked the same questions.'

'But not by you.'

'Martyn was down in London on business, weren't you, Martyn? Staying at the Waldorf Meridien. Except that you weren't at the Waldorf because when I phoned there after twelve when Kate hadn't come home, they said they'd no record of you.'

'The night clerk on the desk made a mistake.'

'They'd had a reservation, but it had been cancelled.'

'All right, sweetheart,' Martyn said, 'I was with a woman in her flat in Notting Hill and we were up all night, the best part of it, fucking one another silly. There, now are you satisfied?'

His voice was exultant and loud and directed straight at Joanne's face.

She swung her open hand to slap him and he caught her wrist.

'Let her go,' Elder said.

Martyn relinquished his grip and stepped towards the door. 'Look at you,' he said with a sneer. 'You sorry pair. You deserve each other.'

Fist clenched, Elder started towards him but Joanne stepped in the way. 'Don't, Frank.'

Martyn laughed and took his time sauntering across the living-room floor; moments later they heard the front door slam.

'How long has it been like this?' Elder asked.

Joanne looked at him. 'How long hasn't it?'

48

Elder woke just short of five and was keying in Maureen's number on his mobile before his feet touched the floor. If Keach had Katherine and he were following the same pattern as before, he would have had somewhere secluded picked out in advance, no more than an hour's drive away.

Maureen answered on the fourth ring.

'The girl McKeirnan released,' Elder said. 'Michelle Guest. She was held north of Retford. And the car that was used in Emma Harrison's abduction was stolen from Retford station car park.'

'Frank, stop,' Maureen said. 'We've already made the connection. There'll be a search team on the ground at first light. A police helicopter. Dogs, everything.'

'Why the hell didn't you tell me?'

'I'm telling you now.'

Elder held his breath.

'Come in to the station,' Maureen said. 'We can go over things together on the map.'

There was a pause and then Maureen said, 'Frank – are you holding up all right?'

'I'll see you in an hour,' Elder said and broke the connection.

The Ordnance Survey map was detailed and clear on screen: farms, roads, electricity transmission lines, field boundaries, streams, public rights of way. Sunrise was at twelve minutes past five and on the ground the search was due to commence at six thirty; the police helicopter, equipped with thermal imaging equipment, would make its first pass some twenty minutes later. Elder and Maureen would be on site by a little after seven.

'Michelle Guest was held here,' Maureen said, 'is that right?' She was pointing to a spot on the old Roman road that linked North Wheatley and Clayworth.

'Yes,' Elder said. 'McKeirnan parked the caravan at this point where the road meets up with the Chesterfield Canal. Held her the best part of two days, then pushed her out here, just short of Bole Fields.'

Maureen nodded. 'The plan is to use North Wheatley as a centre point and spread out in an arc from there.'

'And if we find nothing?'

'Unless there's something else concrete to go on, we enlarge the area of the search.' She leaned back in her chair. 'Meantime Colin Sherbourne's running a check on all vehicles stolen in the Retford area.'

'The sighting of Keach in Cleethorpes?'

'We're still checking it, of course. But it looks less likely all the time.'

◆

As they headed north-east out of the city, the roads were mostly clear; Elder's driver mumbled a few quiet words

of sympathy and thereafter the journey passed in silence. The search was well under way by the time Elder arrived and he waited, watched and walked the edges of fields, all the while shutting certain images out from his mind. Almost succeeding.

By early afternoon, dispirited and close to exhaustion, Elder signalled that he was ready to call it a day. Just short of the Ollerton roundabout, a call to the car turned them back again. The thermal imaging scan in the helicopter had pinpointed something in a field near Oswald Beck, close to the power lines. Headlights and siren full on, they travelled back at speeds close to a hundred and ten. Alongside the driver, Elder breathed loudly, open-mouthed, sweat gathering in the palms of his hands.

A track just wide enough for farm vehicles to drive along led south and then west. Officers in coveralls were converging on a corner of the field. Blood racing, Elder ran between them, feet sliding on dry earth. Close by the hedgerow, near the broken chassis of an abandoned farm trailer, lay several sheets of heavy black plastic, humped at the point where they came closest to the hedge itself. Elder watched as gloved hands eased back a sheet at a time. Beneath and rotting into the ground lay the decomposing body of a dead sheep.

Elder held his face in his hands and wept.

◆

Back in the city, Elder checked in with Colin Sherbourne. Of fourteen vehicles reported as stolen in the Retford area, all but three – an almost new Ford Fiesta, a Mini Cooper and a Fiat van – had been traced.

The media, having feasted already on Shane and Angel, thought Christmas had come round again early. *DAUGHTER OF SPECIAL POLICE INVESTIGATOR MISSING. EX-SUPER COP'S KATE KIDNAPPED. COPYCAT KILLER ON THE LOOSE.* Files were ransacked for stories about Elder's more sensational cases. A photograph of Katherine crossing the finishing line at Harvey Hadden Stadium was sold and syndicated widely. Reporters laid siege to Joanne's house, begging her fruitlessly for an interview, sneaking shots through the upstairs windows of Martyn and herself in the bedroom, clearly arguing; Joanne alone in the garden, distraught. When Martyn Miles left the house that morning he had to push his way between half a dozen reporters and almost got into an altercation with a freelance photographer, threatening to take his camera and smash it on the ground. Returning, forty minutes later, with three large bunches of flowers, he was captured on video mouthing 'Fuck off the lot of you' before turning the key in the front door.

Reporters or not, Elder needed to talk to Joanne.

He hurried through the small posse of cameramen head down.

Joanne was sitting at a stained-wood table in the dining-room, albums open, photographs of Katherine scattered everywhere: Katherine on her own, squinting against the sun as she stared up into the camera on the beach at St Ives; Katherine nestled back against her father's upper arm, red faced and three days old; the three of them, mother, father, daughter, seated on a bench in a West London park, the camera set to remote.

'Is that what you should be doing?' Elder asked.

'Look at her here,' Joanne said as if she hadn't heard him. 'That bike – her fourth birthday, remember?'

He remembered everything and nothing; as if she were already slipping from his grasp.

'I'm sorry, Frank,' Martyn said, coming hushed into the room. 'Yesterday. I was being an arsehole.'

'What's changed?' Joanne said, without looking round.

Martyn went away and left them alone.

Joanne's skin was bleached of colour, close to translucent, her eyes unnaturally large. Her fingers were never still. Despite his better judgement, Elder sat with her and looked at the photographs. When his head had slumped forward and Joanne realised his eyes had closed, she nudged him awake and led him upstairs to the guest room, pulled off his shoes and closed the blinds. He fell asleep before she had left the room and slept for six hours straight.

When Joanne shook him gently she had his mobile phone in her hand.

'This was in your coat downstairs. There's a call. Someone named Helen?'

She withdrew and left him to it, and Elder talked with Helen Blacklock for some minutes, a halting awkward conversation, both aware of the minefields through which they were treading.

At a decent interval Joanne returned with soup and toast.

'I'm not an invalid, you know,' Elder said. 'You don't have to wait on me.'

'It's something to do.'

He thanked her and she sat with him, talking sporadically, while he ate.

'You don't think there's any news?' she asked.

Elder shook his head. 'Maureen would have phoned.'

Later he surprised himself by sleeping again, finally waking a little after three and going barefooted downstairs. The house was silent save for those small unattributable noises all houses, even new ones, make in the stillness of night. He made tea in the kitchen and sat leafing through back issues of Joanne's magazines, *Vogue* and *Vanity Fair*. Picking up a paperback by Anita Shreve Joanne had been reading, he carried it into the living-room and read several chapters before casting it aside. On his feet, he switched out the light and stood close against the glassed wall, staring out. He was still standing there when Joanne came down the spiral stairs in a long pink robe that swished silkily as she crossed the floor.

When she stood by him, Elder could feel the warmth of her arm against his side.

'Helen,' Joanne said after a while, 'who is she?'

'A friend.'

'And that's all?'

When Elder didn't answer, she threaded her fingers through his.

Their breathing was loud in the room.

He kissed her and she kissed him back and at first he thought it was going to be all right, but when, after a few moments, they broke apart and she said something about kissing a ghost, Elder thought it sounded like a line from the book he'd just been reading and stepped away. He kissed her on the top of her head and went back upstairs to get his coat and shoes. At the door he held her hand and tried not to look into her eyes.

At seven that morning, when the mail van arrived at Gartree prison, the officer on duty, who had been alerted, picked out the card addressed to Alan McKeirnan. The view across Whitby harbour was due north-west, showing the whalebone and the statue of Captain Cook clear near the cliff edge, the sands winding into the distance along the Upgang shore.

49

A police motor cyclist sped the postcard from Gartree to Bernard Young's office in the Nottinghamshire Major Crime Unit. The handwriting was recognisably the same as before. *'Alan – Come on in. The water's fine!'* Safe inside its plastic envelope, the card was passed from hand to hand: Young to Gerry Clarke to Maureen Prior to Colin Sherbourne to Elder himself and then back to the detective superintendent.

'I'm sorry, Frank,' Young said.

Elder looked at him but made no reply.

'I've been in touch with the Yorkshire force, we'll have full co-operation. By this afternoon there'll be fifty or more officers on the ground and twice as many volunteers. There are dogs, search trained, a lifeboat crew and a team of divers standing by.'

'Divers?' echoed Clarke.

'The water's fine,' Young quoted back at him.

'You think he means it literally, then?'

'I think it's a chance we can't ignore.'

It was Maureen who said what they were all thinking. 'As far as we know, when he sent the card from Mablethorpe Emma Harrison was already dead.'

She was careful not to catch Elder's eye.

'We don't know this is the same,' Young said. 'We must assume it's not. Pray to God we're right.'

The words as much for his sake, Elder knew, as because the superintendent thought they were true. Like the others, he knew Katherine could be already dead. Chances were she was. He forced himself to continue listening nevertheless. His daughter was in the hands of a murderer and they were still sitting there, more than a hundred miles away, the morning sun slanting across the room strongly enough for the motes of dust to shine brightly in its light.

'Frank,' Bernard Young said eventually. 'Your thoughts?'

Elder leaned forward. 'McKeirnan and Donald always denied any involvement in Susan Blacklock's disappearance. Keach might have chosen the location because he wants to show he can go one better. So the spot where Susan Blacklock was last seen – out by Saltwick Nab – that's where I think we should concentrate the search.'

The superintendent nodded. Clarke and Sherbourne were already on their feet.

'We'll find her, Frank,' Young said. He was about to add, don't worry, but stopped himself in time.

Elder was midway across the car park when his mobile rang.

Dread and anticipation all but trembled it from his hands.

'Hello.' The voice was a young woman's, faint and distant.

'Hello, who is this? Kate. Kate, is that you?'

'It's Angel.'

397

'Who?'

'Angel.'

The skin along the backs of his arms was taut and cold.

'Yes, of course.'

'The meeting place, with Shane . . .'

'Yes?'

'It's the M5. The first services south of Birmingham. We'll be in the cafeteria.'

'What time?'

'Half six, seven. This evening.'

Elder said nothing, shook his head. All around him car doors were opening, being closed, engines switched into life.

'Is that okay?' Angel said, her voice uncertain, anxious.

'Six-thirty today. Yes, that's fine.'

'You'll be there?'

'Yes.'

The line went dead. Maureen was standing alongside a dark blue saloon, waiting. There was no way he could handle this himself now, not any part of it. 'Maureen,' he said, approaching. 'Shane Donald, I've got a location.'

'Good,' she said. 'We'll sort it on the way.'

◆

A centre of operations had been set up in one of the Whitby secondary schools, with Rob Loake the senior officer in charge. Immediately he sought Elder out and, gripping him by the arm, conveyed both anger and concern, brusque but genuine. At a quickly convened meeting, he introduced Elder and Maureen Prior to the local team and priorities were agreed. The majority of the

other officers clearly found Elder's presence unsettling and, quick words of sympathy aside, avoided talking to him as much as they could.

From the police helicopter, Elder gazed down at the slabs and pinnacles of black rock edging into the tide round Saltwick Bay; and as they circled again, he could see below them the lines of slow-moving figures inching across the fields behind the holiday park, just as they had fourteen years before.

By dusk, each and every caravan in the park would have been inspected, the farm buildings between the coast and the road checked over two square miles.

Nothing would be found.

'Tomorrow, Frank,' Maureen said. 'We'll find her tomorrow.'

Elder nodded and turned away, his hurt mirrored in her eyes.

◆

Meanwhile, across the county, the West Midland force were responding to the request to pick up Shane Donald. Two teams of four officers were deployed, after descriptions of Donald and Angel Ryan had been relayed over the internet.

The plan was simple. Matt Jolley and Andy Firebrace would approach the pair of them in the cafeteria, with Rose Pearson hanging back by the entrance, Malcolm Meade at the foot of the stairs. The second, back-up team were in their vehicle outside.

Shane and Angel were sitting towards the far side of the smoking area, with a view down over the motorway.

Angel was flicking her disposable lighter at a roll-up, Shane half-turned away from her, glaring into space.

Andy Firebrace got to within twenty metres before he was noticed.

Suddenly Shane was looking directly forward, staring at him, and Firebrace, instead of continuing, stopped and raised a hand, fingers spread.

Scraping back his chair, Shane picked out Matt Jolley to Fairbrace's right.

'You bitch!' he yelled at Angel. 'You fuckin' bitch!'

'No, Shane!'

With a crash of crockery, Shane upended the table and began to run, dummying in one direction and then another. Firebrace, trying to turn, became entangled with a woman carrying a small child. Jolley collided with a table and lost his footing.

Ashen-faced, Angel stood with one arm outstretched, as if to claw him back.

Rose Pearson moved to intercept him and Shane kicked her hard below the knee and caught her with his elbow high on the cheek.

'Police! Clear the way, police!'

Andy Firebrace's voice pursued Shane downstairs, where Malcolm Meade had already lost him amidst a coachload of senior citizens on their way back from the Trossachs and desperate in their search for the toilets and a decent cup of tea.

Two sets of glass doors led out into the car park and when Firebrace pushed his way through there were perhaps two dozen people within sight, none of them Shane Donald.

'Where the fuck's back-up?' he called to no one in particular.

Rose Pearson was close to his shoulder now, holding her cheek and talking into her mobile phone.

Matt Jolley was running off right between the lines of parked cars and, yes, there was Donald, some thirty or forty metres ahead of him and almost level with the petrol pumps.

Firebrace set off in pursuit, shouting Shane's name as loud as he could.

The police vehicle, unmarked, came fast now but late along the slip-road behind the garage, braked hard to avoid swiping a Ford Mondeo side on, and skidded to a halt, officers jumping clear.

Shane, running along the perimeter, swerved and sprinted back the other way. Matt Jolley was slowing now as Firebrace called Shane's name and Shane, in response, vaulted onto the hard shoulder at the second attempt.

The driver of an eight-wheeler carrying metal casings south to Bristol saw Shane in the corner of his eye and, guessing his intention, struggled to pull across into the middle lane.

Firebrace's tackle caught Shane below the waist and sent him spinning but safe across rough tarmac. Before he could struggle or kick out, Fairbrace had his arms pushed up tight behind his back and was just reaching for his cuffs when Matt Jolley seized Shane by the hair and yanked his head right back.

'You're one lucky bastard, you know that? If it'd been me, I'd've let you take your chances with the traffic.'

Firebrace slipped the handcuffs into place and locked them tight.

◆

401

At about the same time that Shane Donald was being arrested, Don Guiseley met Elder outside the temporary heaquarters at the school. 'I couldn't be more sorry, Frank.' He took Elder's hand in both of his. 'Esme sends her love. She's thinking of you, your daughter too. Praying is what she said.'

They walked along the harbour and across the bridge to the Board Inn where Guiseley bought them both pints and they sat at the same table where they'd sat before.

'It's a bastard, Frank.'

'Yes.'

'This Keach, what d'you know about him?'

'Not a great deal. Oh, background and such, we know that. Pretty much as you'd expect. Shitty childhood and the rest.'

'Bit like the other lad, then. Donald.'

'Keach is more naturally violent, I'd say. All but killed someone in prison for no more than a chance remark. Brighter, too. High IQ. Took courses when he was inside, GCSEs and the like. But, yes, both loners by all accounts.'

'And both,' Guiseley said, 'thinking the sun shines out of McKeirnan's arse.'

'Yes.' Elder took a swallow of his beer.

'Some well-meaning bunch of paper shufflers,' Guiseley said, 'reckoned it was safe to let him back out.'

'Can't keep them locked up for ever, Don. Not everyone.'

'No?' Guiseley worked tobacco down into the bowl of his pipe. 'Keach and his like, my way of thinking, any doubt, you should make an exception.'

They sat there a while longer, lingering over their pints, but, despite Guiseley's efforts, conversation was

sporadic at best. When he left, an hour later, Elder walked around both sides of the harbour, then back inland to Helen's house, a light still showing through the curtains, Helen inside ironing, the radio playing. Elder had phoned earlier, said he would come and see her if he could, depending, and she'd told him she understood.

Now she held him and for only the second time since Katherine had gone missing he cried and she cried with him, the pair of them standing, arms wound about each other, sniffing back tears.

'Oh, Frank . . .'

'I know.'

Both knew too much: there was nothing they could say.

After a while, Helen offered Elder a drink and he shook his head.

'Will you stay?'

'I'd best not. You'd not thank me, like this. I've a room in town.'

'If you change your mind . . .'

'Yes. Thanks.'

When he walked back along the harbour, hands in pockets, there was a chill in the air that had not been there before and more stars than usual showed in the sky. Katherine, he kept repeating to himself, over and over. Katherine.

50

Elder woke at five, hair matted, his pillow beyond damp. The last vestiges of the dream clung to him, a blurry, rancid after-image that cleared only when he lowered his face towards the tap and splashed water, cold, up into his face.

When he sat back on the edge of the bed, his body was still faintly shaking, his feet and legs close to numb.

Some little while later, when he stepped outside, the gloom of early morning had been compounded by a sea fret, waves of mist rolling in off the sea and reducing everything to an amorphous grey. From the head of the road overlooking the east cliff, the light at the pier end was only dimly visible, the horizon unseen.

◆

Not far short of six, a runner, far enough inland for the air to be relatively clear, recognised the van from the pictures that had been shown on the previous night's news: a small Fiat, white with grey trim and a broken wing mirror on the near side. It was standing on the verge of the broad track that twisted down from the village of

Aislaby towards the junction of two roads, one of which bridged the River Esk.

He peered through the windows and, seeing nothing, continued on his way downhill, telephoning the police from a call-box a few hundred metres along the main road.

The duty officer had not long settled down to his desk, mug of tea close by his right hand, when the call came through.

Elder had walked into the communications room moments before, Rob Loake and Maureen there already, standing before the large area map on the wall. Loake chewing his way through the last of a bacon roll.

'Sir,' the officer said, stepping towards them. 'Ma'am. Seems like we've found the van.'

'Where?'

The officer pointed to the spot, just a few miles inland. 'There, sir. Just short of Sleights.'

'What the fuck's it doing there?'

They arrived within minutes, Loake smoking as he drove, headlights on, window down.

The van was parked at an angle, facing uphill; as they approached, birds rose clamorously from the tall trees above them and flew, black, into the still grey sky.

Elder, throat dry, stopped short of the van as Loake tried the handle with the forefinger and thumb of his gloved hand. It was unlocked. He pulled the rear doors open and stepped back, motioning Elder forward. It was damp underfoot.

A single mattress, old and soiled, lay across the floor, edged upwards where it butted up against the front seats. Mattress aside, the interior was bare; there were no

discarded items of clothing, no obvious clues, no – Elder held his breath – evident signs of blood.

Elder turned towards Maureen and shook his head.

Other vehicles could be heard arriving on the road below. Briefly, Maureen touched Elder's arm. Loake had moved a few paces off and was talking into his mobile phone. Soon, the track would be cordoned off at both ends and Scene of Crime would set to work on the van; the inhabitants of several large houses, set back behind high walls along the track, would be woken with questions and the focus of the search would shift. The immediate area first, then spreading out along the course of the river, west towards Grosmont and the moor, east to where the estuary opened out into the sea.

Come on in. The water's fine!

Elder walked a short way up the track and looked back down across the rough grass of open fields towards the river bottom. The map, he remembered, showed the Esk meandering through a series of curves and bends, passing between pasture, woodland and high moor, farm buildings dotted in between.

Was that where Katherine was, somewhere there?

When he walked back down, officers in protective clothing were nearing the van.

◆

By mid-morning they had found nothing. The interior of the van had been wiped clean; no hair or fragments of clothing seemed to have been left behind, no prints. The mattress had been wrapped in plastic and removed for further forensic examination. Statements from residents

in the area had established that the lane had been empty as late as one thirty; one elderly woman recalled the sound of a vehicle breaking her sleep at close to four. Two hours before the runner had made his discovery: two hours for Keach to move Katherine how far? And how? Could she still be forced to walk or would she have to be carried? Dragged?

The terrain was difficult in places, uneven and overgrown, thick with trees. Going east, back along the river towards the estuary, sudden patches of mist still made visibility limited.

Dispirited, Elder headed back to the town on foot, following both river and railway line to Ruswarp and from there a footpath that brought him close to the centre.

The young officer who had taken the call that morning was standing outside the communications room, finishing a cigarette. Seeing Elder, he stubbed it out and went back inside. Aside from two civilian clerks, one seated at the computer, the other at the phones, they had the place to themselves.

'Couple on lunch,' the officer said, feeling the need to explain. 'Everyone else, you know, out searching.'

Elder nodded: he knew well enough.

He sat on a stiff-backed school chair at the side of the room, listening to the soft clicking of the computer keyboard, while three pairs of eyes avoided his as best they could.

The sound of the telephone made them jump.

The clerk listened briefly and turned, the receiver in her hand. 'Mr Elder. It's for you.'

They've found her, Elder thought, and the blood drained from his face. It was impossible to move.

'Should I take a message?' the woman said.

'No.' With difficulty, he got to his feet.

'Frank Elder.'

'Everyone busy, I hope. Chasing shadows.' It was a voice, a man's voice he didn't recognise.

'Who is this?'

He laughed and then Elder knew who it was. 'I'd've sent a card from Port Mulgrave, only there weren't any.'

And the connection was broken.

'Port Mulgrave,' Elder said. 'Where is it?'

'Up the coast. By Staithes.'

'Show me. Show me on the map.'

The officer pointed to a small indentation in the coast, north of Runswick Bay and close to the main A174 road.

'What's there?'

'Just a few houses. Not a lot more.'

Elder nodded and moved towards the door. 'I think that was him, Keach, on the phone. Tell your boss. Port Mulgrave. Tell Maureen.'

The Ford was in the corner of the car park and it took him two attempts to engage reverse. He could feel the blood pumping back into his veins, a pulse alive at the side of his head. Far too fast into the roundabout that would take him across the back of town and out towards the coast road, he forced himself to slow down, but on the straight stretch past the golf course he pushed the accelerator to the floor. The slow gradient twisting up from Sandsend into Lythe seemed to take an age. The smell of his sweat filled the car. Runswick Bay. Hinderwell. The road to Port Mulgrave turned off just before a church. A pub and then a telephone box some little way along. The phone from which Keach had made his call?

If it had been Keach and not a hoax.

If he had not lied.

Elder drove on to where the road stopped, petered out into a footpath leading off across ploughed fields. The last of the mist had cleared and in its place dark cloud was bulking to the west. Slowly he reversed back, then turned. On the coast side of the road a deep saucer of land had been scooped out or fallen away and it lay there thick with bracken and patched with mud, criss-crossed by broken tracks. Beyond that the tide had rolled back to reveal slabs of grey-black rock and, pushing out above a mesh of sand and shale, the remains of two short piers that seemed to be crumbling into the sea. Huddled close by them, fast in against the cliff, was a ramshackle collection of huts.

Cautious, Elder began to make his way down.

Gulls careened raucously overhead.

Ten metres from the bottom, a flurry of small stones spun out from under his foot and he slithered, balance gone, his left ankle turning painfully beneath him as he fell.

For several moments he stayed crouched down, massaging his ankle, listening. Gulls aside, there was nothing but the shuffling fall and rise of water and his own jagged breath.

Backed up against the cliff, the huts leaned precariously against each other like an ill-assorted deck of cards. Raw planks and sheets of treated timber, patched and covered here and there with heavy plastic and tarpaulin, held with nails and rope. The walls of some were painted weathered reds and blues but most were bare. A jerry-built tin chimney poking from the roof of

one; a rusted hasp hanging down from the door of another, the hinges having given way when the padlock held.

A fire had been lit on the beach close by, its embers faintly warm.

Slowly, Elder eased the door back, waited for his eyes to adjust, and stepped inside.

There were more ashes, soft shades of grey close against the corners. Drawings, crude and simplistic, fading on the walls. His ankle felt better now, no more than a twinge of pain when it took his weight.

Standing there, shadowed, quite still, he heard, or thought he heard, a sound from beyond the wall where two broad lengths of wood seemed to have been levered slightly apart. He leaned his weight against one and it gave a couple of centimetres, then refused to budge. Again, the slightest scuffling sound and now a rank smell, feral and damp. He pushed again with no response.

Stepping back, he raised his right foot and drove the sole of his shoe fast and hard against the wood.

It gave and the cats leapt past him, hissing, a mass of moving fur, and as he stumbled back, one jumped at his face, its claws scratching deep into his cheek.

When he touched the side of his face, his fingers came away smeared with blood.

I know this, Elder thought: I know where I am. Like the pulse of an engine, his brain was beginning to misfire and throb.

Ducking his head, he stepped through the space he had made.

An old cupboard stood close, a nest of ageing news-

papers on top. Through gaps in the roof, light spilled, weak, across the floor. The bed was where it should be, pushed up against the furthest wall. So much else was right but wrong.

Elder walked slowly forward.

The blanket was not grey but the colour of weeviled flour. The air was thick with the salt-sweet stink of rotting fish and drying blood.

Elder stood by the bed, staring at the shape that lay covered and curled inwards, fearing what he would find. Steeling himself, he gripped the blanket's edge and slowly pulled it back.

Katherine lay turned in upon herself, naked, blood blisters on her arms and legs, bruises discolouring her shoulders and her back.

Elder's heart stopped.

Face close to hers he could hear the rattle of her breath.

'Katherine,' he said softly. 'Kate, it's me.'

When he touched her gently she whimpered and pulled her knees still closer to her chest. Her eyes flickered and then closed.

'Kate.'

He bent his head to kiss her hair. 'You'll be all right. I'll get help.'

Straightening, Elder had half-turned before he was aware of someone else.

The iron bar swung for his head and at the last moment he threw up an arm and blocked its path. Pain jarred deep and keen from his elbow to his wrist, so severe he was sure the bone was broken.

Adam Keach wore a black T-shirt, work boots and black jeans; the muscles of his arms well-defined. His

hair was thick and dark, his eyes, even in that dull space, bright blue. A smile scarred his face.

'Beautiful, isn't she?' he said. 'At least she was.' And he laughed. 'Sleeping Beauty. That what you were thinking? Waking her with a kiss?'

Elder moved fast, reaching for the bar, but not fast enough.

Keach swayed back, lifted both arms high, then brought them down. This time he struck Elder across the top of his left shoulder and forced him to his knees.

'Not bad for an old man.'

Keach kicked him in the chest and Elder fell back; a second kick, the toe of the boot hard against the breast-bone and Elder's head jerked forward, choking.

Keach side-swiped him and pushed him flat, kneeling over him with the bar tight across his neck, knees holding it down leaving his hands free. Vomit caught in Elder's throat.

The knife that Keach drew from the sheath at his back had a slender, slightly curving blade. A skinning knife, Elder thought.

'Quite a catch,' Keach said. 'You here. You and her.' He laughed again and when Elder tried to raise himself from the floor he increased the pressure with his knees and rested the knife above the bridge of Elder's nose.

'Alan'd like that. The one who locked him up, put him inside. And of course he'll read about it now, everyone will. How I fucked the daughter half to death and then finished the pair of them, side by side. Famous, eh? Fuckin' famous!'

The tip of the blade slid beneath the skin and pushed against the bone.

Elder roared and rocked backwards, grabbing the underside of the bar with both hands. Blood flooded one of his eyes.

Pushing the bar up, he rolled sideways, swinging his elbow full force into Keach's face even as Keach's knee drove down into his side.

Adrenaline brought Elder to his feet first.

The knife on the floor between them.

Keach cursing, tasting blood.

From outside, unmistakable, the sound of a helicopter approaching, police sirens.

As Keach glanced down, reaching for the knife, Elder aimed a kick between his legs which Keach partly parried, turning now, the knife forgotten, heading for the open door.

The helicopter hovered low overhead, the updraft from its blades tugging at Keach's hair and clothes. From inside its cabin, an armed officer in dark overalls aimed a semi-automatic rifle at his chest.

'Jesus!' Keach exclaimed. 'Jesus fucking Christ!' His words all but lost. And he started to laugh.

Officers, Loake amongst them, were scrambling down the bank.

Staunching the flow of blood from his head with his sleeve, Elder stood outside the hut and watched as Keach, still laughing, raised his hands above his head.

'Crazy, that's what they'll say,' Keach was shouting above the noise. 'Stark raving, got to be. Unfit to plead.'

Rob Loake punched him in the face and when he fell, pulled his arms up high behind his back and cuffed him and still Keach laughed.

Elder turned away, Maureen hurrying to his side.

'Katherine . . .?'

'She's alive.'

'Thank God!'

He winced when she touched his arm. The ambulance had arrived on the road above, paramedics with stretchers running.

'Frank, you've lost a lot of blood.'

'I'll be fine.'

As they stood over Katherine, Elder swayed and Maureen steadied him.

'Kate,' he said. 'It's going to be okay. I promise.'

He kissed her then, but she didn't wake, not till they were in the ambulance and he was sitting beside her, holding her hand.

'Daddy,' she said, opening her eyes. 'Dad.' Then closed her eyes again while Elder cried.

51

They took them, Elder and Katherine, to Leeds Infirmary. Keach, under tight guard, was taken to York. Maureen informed Joanne the first moment she had and Martyn drove her north.

Katherine lay pale beneath white covers, amidst the quiet humming of machinery and muted light, a nurse watchful at her side.

Joanne found Elder in a side room of A & E, a temporary dressing taped to the front of his head.

'Don't worry,' Elder said. 'She's okay.'

Joanne looked at him, incredulous, anger firing the dark shadows around her eyes. 'Okay, Frank? Is that what you call okay?'

'You know what I mean. She's . . .'

'I know what you mean. You saved her. She's alive. She's alive and you're some great hero, your picture all over the papers, all over the screen every time you turn on the bloody TV.'

'Joanne . . .'

'And what happened to her, Frank? You know what. It's your fault.'

'That's not . . .'

415

'Why do you think he went for her, Frank? Why Katherine?'

Elder turned his face away.

'You nearly killed her, Frank. You. Not him. Because you had to get involved, you couldn't let things be. You always knew better than anybody else, that's why.'

'Joanne . . .'

'And you know what, Frank, you'll get over this. You'll come to terms, find a way. But Katherine, she never will.'

Elder remained there, not moving, long after the door had closed and the sound of Joanne's footsteps had faded to silence along the corridor, her words reverberating loud inside his head.

◆

They kept Elder in overnight: despite careful work by the doctor on duty, his forehead would always bear a scar some seven centimetres long. The longer of the two bones in the forearm was chipped but not broken and he was given a sling and paracetamol for the pain.

Katherine would stay for ten days in intensive care, after which she would be transferred to the Queen's Medical Centre in Nottingham and begin a course of physiotherapy before being allowed home. She was young and fit and given time her body would mend; even her internal injuries would heal. As for the rest . . .

When Elder came to see her she found it difficult to look him in the eye: whether, like her mother, this was because she held him to blame, or because, in some way, she was embarrassed by his knowledge of what had happened to her, he was never sure.

He couldn't ask; she couldn't say.

When they talked, if they talked at all, they stuck to safer things – though for Katherine, who had been snatched off the street and put through days of purgatory and hell, what could be safe again?

'What's happened to him?' Katherine asked one day.

'Who?' Elder asked, though of course he knew.

Both he and Joanne had tried to keep the papers from her, but this was an open ward.

'He's in Rampton.'

'The mental hospital?'

'Secure, yes.'

'They're saying he's insane.'

'He'll be given tests, to see if he's fit to plead.'

'To stand trial, you mean?'

'Yes.'

'And if he's not?'

'They'll keep him there, I suppose. Rampton. Broadmoor.'

'He'll get off.'

'Not exactly.'

'That other poor girl he killed.'

Elder sought and held her hand. He knew all too well what it would be like for her if Keach were brought to trial; one way or another she would have to give evidence, face cross-examination, he did this and then he did that.

'When are you going back to Cornwall?' Katherine asked.

'Not yet.'

'But you will go?'

'I expect so.'

Katherine smiled. 'What about this girlfriend of yours?'

'What girlfriend's this?'

'Mum told me about her.'

'Past fifty,' Elder said, 'there's got to be a better word.'

'Lover,' Katherine suggested. 'Floozy. Bit of stuff.'

'Helen,' Elder said. 'Her name's Helen.'

'And is it serious?'

'I don't know.'

Elder and Helen had spent a day in Sheffield, another in York, anonymous places and convenient, easy enough to pass the time in each other's company, drink coffee, eat lunch, take in the sights. Sometimes she took his arm, less frequently he held her hand. Neither broached what had come between them: the daughter he had found and saved had been his own, not hers.

'You can't still be reading that book,' Katherine said, looking at the thick and curling copy of *David Copperfield*.

'I've had other things on my mind.'

'Like me.'

'Like you. Plus I keep forgetting what's happened and having to go back.'

'Why don't you just give it up? Find something shorter?'

'I hate doing that once I've started. Besides, I want to know what happened.'

'Who did it.'

'Not exactly.'

'I should hate him, shouldn't I?'

'I don't know. Probably. No one'd blame you if you did.'

'Do you?'

'Hate him?'

418

'Mm.'

'Oh, yes. With every bone of my body,' Elder said.

'Even the injured one?'

'Especially that.'

As she smiled, tears flooded her eyes.

◆

At first, Katherine had refused to see the psychotherapist at all. Then, when she did, she would deny her flashbacks and her dreams and say, when pushed, that she remembered nothing, nothing: she had shut it out.

'Why do you want to make me think about it?' she all but screamed. 'Why make me go through it all again?'

At home, she spent much of her time in her room. A few friends visited, brought flowers, selections of chocolates from Thornton's, boxed and tied with ribbon, magazines. But conversation was awkward, what to ask, what to avoid, and after a while they came less often. Katherine didn't seem to mind. Martyn bought her a new television and a DVD player for her room and she watched movies endlessly, back to back. *Spider-Man*. The new *Star Wars*. Anything with Johnny Depp. Ethan Hawke.

One evening Elder sat with her and watched *Hamlet*, a modern version set in New York, Ethan Hawke as the young prince feigning madness, a schoolgirl Ophelia driven to take her own life by circumstances she could not control.

Knowing what happened, he found it compulsive nonetheless, sitting in a chair alongside Katherine's bed, his eyes drawn to her almost as much as the screen, the action played out in images reflected on her face.

419

As the denouement approached, Joanne quietly opened the door, looked in, and quietly went away.

Some half an hour later, order restored and Katherine sleeping, Elder rose and just went downstairs; Joanne was in the kitchen, mixing a gin and tonic.

'You want one, Frank?'

'No, thanks.'

'You're being careful, aren't you?'

'I hope so.'

He watched her as she sliced a lemon and forked one segment into a tall glass.

'This Helen woman,' Joanne said, 'she still just a friend?'

'She's a friend, yes.'

'A friend you fuck, Frank?'

'Aren't they the best kind?' he might have said, smiling, trying for some lightness of tone, or, more caustically, 'You'd know more about that than me.' Instead he said none of these things.

'Cat got your tongue, Frank?'

'It's time,' he said, 'I was leaving.'

Joanne tasted her drink, allowing it to linger a moment on the back of her tongue. 'I'm sorry about what I said. That first day at the hospital. I was upset.'

'I know. And it's all right.'

'Even so.' She touched his arm, his hand. 'We should be friends, Frank. Especially now.'

'We are.'

She kissed him close alongside the mouth and he could smell the gin, this glass not her first.

'He's leaving me, Frank. Just as soon as Katherine's over the worst. Leaving me just like I left you.'

'I'm sorry.'

'Are you? I'd have thought you might be pleased.'

'No.'

'No more than I deserve.' She laughed. 'He's running off to London for some model with no hips and no tits and a mouth like the London drain.'

Elder took a pace away.

'Generous though. Letting me stay here in the house as long as I want. Half the proceeds when it goes up for sale.'

'I'd better go,' Elder said.

'Why don't you stay?'

'No.'

'We were a family,' Joanne said, as he reached the door.

'Yes,' Elder said. 'I remember.'

With barely a hesitation he carried on through, closing the door at his back.

◆

It was one of those strange and sudden days when the beginnings of winter seem to fall away and everything is blue and clear. Sunlight sparkled off the water of the canal and made the brickwork glow. The new Nottingham magistrates court building, glass and steel, shone like a palace in a fairy tale. Adam Keach had already been formally charged and remanded into custody. Some time in the next few weeks, after exhaustive tests, two out of three psychiatrists would find him fit to plead, the date of his trial in the Crown Court still some months in the future.

Before that, however, it was Shane Donald's turn to stand before the magistrate, scrawny in grey, face pale, a plaster over his eye from some incident or other, forever picking at the shredded skin raw around his nails. He had seen Angel when he was led into the court and refused to look in her direction since. His licence already revoked, he was remanded on one charge of robbery and one of assault occasioning actual bodily harm. Aside from confirming his name and that he understood the charges, there was little more for him to say.

Angel stood as he was taken down and his name came faint from her lips but if he heard or cared Shane gave no sign. Watching, Elder wanted to go to her and apologise, explain, tell her that it would all turn out for the best, but he thought one betrayal was enough.

52

The Air Malaysia flight left Heathrow Airport, terminal three, at ten-thirty in the evening; at five-thirty the following evening it touched down in Kuala Lumpur and took off again two hours later, finally arriving in Auckland at eleven-fifteen the next morning.

Plenty of time, between surprisingly tasty meals and gobbets of God-awful films, to finish *David Copperfield*. Established as a successful writer and, after an overlong and ill-judged marriage, together with a good woman, Dickens's hero finally enjoyed his quiet triumph. His happiness. Yet Elder couldn't help but wonder if a man whose reading of character had been so woefully wrong and whose choices had been so palpably foolish, could be said to deserve happiness at all.

He wondered about himself.

He set the book aside but found his attention being pulled back to chapter thirty-one, 'A Greater Loss', and the letter young Emily wrote when she fled with her lover, her seducer – *'When you, who love me so much better than I have ever deserved, even when my mind was innocent, see this, I shall be far away.'*

The letter Susan Blacklock perhaps wrote but never sent.

At Auckland, Elder checked his baggage, such as it was, through customs, showed his passport to the officer at immigration.

'Business or pleasure?'

Elder wasn't sure: he suspected the truth might be neither.

Karori, Helen Blacklock had told him, when he'd asked if she knew where Susan's father was living. Wherever that is. It was a suburb of Wellington, Elder had discovered, west of the city. The likelihood that Ulney was still at the same address was not great, but tracking people down was one of the things Elder was trained to do.

The road from the airport soon gave way to narrow streets that rose through a series of sharp twists and turns as they skirted the centre of the city. The taxi let him down beside a small parade of shops, a garage, banks, a library. Elder checked the map he had bought to get his bearings.

The wooden exteriors of the houses were mostly painted white or cream beneath terracotta tiles, with patches of lawn shielded by shrubs and small trees from the wind. The people he spoke to were friendly, not over-suspicious, happy to talk. David Ulney had moved on but not far, exchanged one address in Karori for another, before moving out of the city altogether.

The man sat in front of a partly demolished garage, chipping mortar from one of a haphazard pile of bricks, white dust thick on his shirt and arms and streaked across his face and hair. 'Paekakariki they moved to. Less than an hour's drive up Highway 1. Or you could take the train. We used to have an address for them but not any

more. You'll not find it difficult to find them, though. I doubt there's more than a hundred or so places all told and most of them holiday homes. Not too many live there all year round.'

Elder thanked him. 'If you do see him,' the man said, 'ask him why he built this garage the wrong side of the house, the daft bugger, blocking out the light.'

◆

He was woken by rain slashing against the window. The clock at his bedside read 4:27. He pummelled his pillow a little, pulled up the covers and closed his eyes. When they next opened it was 9:23 and the rain had ceased. A quick shower, coffee and toast and he was on his way to the railway station. By the time the train drew into Paekakariki, most of the clouds had dispersed leaving sun and blue sky.

As the train pulled away, the crossing gates swung high and traffic coming off the highway, two dusty trucks and a shiny black four-by-four, rolled along the broad road that led from the rail tracks towards the beach.

Elder asked a woman clearing tables outside a small café if she knew where the Ulneys lived.

Balancing plates and cups, she shook her head. 'Ask Michael over at the book store. He knows everybody.'

Michael O'Leary was a bearded man with long grey hair, wearing a black T-shirt with the words *'Which Way?'* in white across his chest.

Elder introduced himself and held out his hand.

'Ulney,' O'Leary said in response to Elder's question. 'Yes, I might.'

425

'I'm a friend of the family,' Elder said. 'Lost touch, you know how it can be.'

'And you're visiting?'

'That's right.'

O'Leary took his time, no call to rush. 'You'll find them along the coast road, the Parade. The far corner of Ocean Drive. Small place set back. The woman there, she stops by once in a while, likes to read.'

'That'd be Susan,' Elder said.

The bookseller nodded. 'Susan Ulney, that's right.'

By the door, Elder noticed, amongst a stack of paperbacks, several by Katherine Mansfield, slightly dog-eared and well-thumbed. *D. H. Lawrence, you know, he lived there with Frieda, his wife. One of the cottages. Katherine Mansfield, too, for a while.* His landlady's words when he first rented the house in Cornwall. The one he chose, more or less at random, had a faded picture on the front, a woman seated at a mirror, muted blues and greys. *Bliss and Other Stories.* Six New Zealand dollars.

When he left the shop Michael O'Leary was singing contentedly to himself, something slow and old by the Rolling Stones.

Pocketing the book, Elder followed the road up a slight incline and around to the sea. On one side a mismatch of beach houses stretched as far as the eye could see; along the other ran a promenade, tapering into the distance above a narrowing strip of sand. Black-and-white birds with red legs and long red beaks jittered along the tideline. A handful of children ran, shrieking, in and out of the slow, rolling waves.

The house was small and single-storeyed, raised up on

426

stilts at the front and reached by wooden steps which climbed through a garden that was largely overgrown, small yellow and white flowers growing wild.

At the right, a broad, three-paned window looked out towards the beach; alongside, shaded, a deep porch ran back beneath the roof. The white boards were cracked and weathered and in need of fresh paint; the blue-green guttering sagged and lacked attention.

As Elder watched a woman came out through the door alongside the porch and shook crumbs from the cutting board in her hands. A check shirt, loose over a pale T-shirt, hung outside her blue jeans. Her fair hair had darkened and her figure had thickened but Elder was certain she was the same person who had stood on the cliff path near Saltwick Nab, that Tuesday fourteen years before, buffeted a little by the wind.

She paused for several seconds, staring out over his head, her gaze fastened on something beyond where he stood. And then she turned and was lost to sight.

Blood pulsing faster than it should, Elder pushed open the small gate and walked towards the steps.

'Yes?' She opened the door almost immediately in response to Elder's knock.

Matched against the photographs he had seen, her mouth seemed to have shrunk a little, become turned in; lines of tiredness lightly etched her face and the lustre had gone from her eyes. Life had made her older than her thirty years.

'Susan?'

'Yes.'

'Susan Blacklock?'

For a moment he thought she might run, jump back

inside and bolt the door; all the times she had imagined this happening, her one nightmare, her recurring dream.

Close her eyes and he would disappear: open them and he would be gone.

He was still there.

'Who are you?' she said, her voice pitched low.

'Frank Elder. I was one of the detectives looking into your disappearance.'

'Oh, God!'

Mouth open, the air punched through her and as she swayed forward Elder reached out towards her, but she steadied herself, one hand against the frame of the door.

'How did you . . . No, no, I mean . . . I mean why? Why after all this time?'

'I wanted to be certain.'

'And you came all this way?'

'Yes.'

Tears welled in her eyes and she turned her head aside. Behind her, on the kitchen table, Elder could see a Thermos, slices of freshly buttered bread, the crusts of some removed, cheese and thin slices of ham.

Susan fished a tissue from her jeans pocket and wiped it across her face, blew her nose, apologised.

Elder shook his head.

'You know then,' Susan said, 'what happened?'

'I think so, yes.'

She nodded, sniffed and took half a pace back inside. 'We usually go for a walk about this time. Take sandwiches, a flask. For lunch.' Even after all that time, the more she spoke the more clearly the East Midlands accent showed through. 'If you'd like to wait, we'll not be long.'

428

Minutes later, rucksack on her back and wearing a fleece against the wind, Susan manoeuvred the wheelchair through the door.

Dave Ulney no longer cut a dash, a ladies' man with kiss-curl quiff, suede shoes and full drape suit. His head lolled to one side, face pale and gaunt, hair sparse and white, his eyes a distant watery blue. Inside his carefully buttoned clothes, blanket wrapped around his legs, his body was shrivelled and old. Sixty-five, Elder thought, seventy at best, he could be a dozen more.

'Dad,' Susan said, 'this is the man I told you about. From England.'

The eyes flickered a little; the hand that rested on the blanket, fingers knotted, lifted and was still.

'He's going to walk with us. So we can talk.'

Saliva dribbled colourless from one corner of her father's mouth and, practised, she dabbed it away.

'Okay, Dad?'

She reversed the wheelchair on the porch and backed towards the steps. When Elder offered to help she shook her head.

'It's all right. I'm used to it now.'

◆

There were a few more clouds, coming in high from the west but not yet threatening. Despite the sun, the chill in the wind was real and Elder was glad to slip his hands into his pockets as they walked. No need to ask questions, he knew she would talk now, in her own time.

On the beach a small, terrier-like dog raced after a ball.

'When I found out,' Susan said, 'you know, who my real dad was . . .' She paused and started again. 'Kids, you're always thinking: your parents, they're not your real parents, they can't be, like in fairy stories or *Superman*, and then when . . . when it happens . . . when I found that picture of my dad, that photo . . . I was like, this is all wrong, it isn't me. And Mum, she wouldn't talk about it, tell me anything, where he was or where he'd gone and I suppose I made up this person, this version of who he was. How he'd be different from Trevor, my stepfather, not always getting on at me, and he'd do exciting things, we'd do them together, him and me, and then one day he got in touch with me . . . Dave . . . my real dad. He gave this note to one of the girls in my school. I was fifteen. Just fifteen. Said he'd meet me. And he did. He was waiting . . . he was so . . . he was so . . .'

She stopped and turned away, head down, letting the tears fall, and Elder stood there, awkward, to one side, not knowing what to do or say.

Eventually, she wiped her face and tucked the blanket tighter round her father's legs, pushing on into the wind.

'You met your father,' Elder prompted.

'Yes. We went to this café, he said he didn't have long – Mum'd have killed me if she'd known – he talked to me about where he lived, wonderful he made it seem, the other side of the world. There was this photo booth round the corner, he said he wanted a picture of me to carry with him. And then he said he'd come back for me. He promised. Our secret, he said, our secret. And he did. That summer we were in Whitby. Here, he said, I've got the tickets, yours and mine. A passport, everything. It's all arranged. I didn't know what to do. I thought: I can't

just go. But no, now, he said. You must come now. Or not at all. Don't tell your mum. Don't tell a soul.'

She looked at Elder for a moment, then away.

'I know I should have written, left a note, phoned, something. Mum, what she must have been going through. But when I read about all the fuss – it was in the papers, even here – I just couldn't. I don't know if I was embarrassed or ashamed, but the longer I left it, the more impossible it became. And Dad said that was how she'd treated him all those years, as if he was dead. She'll get over it, he said.'

Lightly, she touched his arm. 'She hasn't, has she?'

'Not really, no.'

Elder was thinking about Helen, her marriage falling apart, the pilgrimages she made to lay flowers at what was never quite a grave.

'We usually go just as far as the park,' Susan said, pointing ahead. 'There's a place we can be out of the wind and have our lunch. There's usually a sandwich going spare.'

'Thanks.'

'Better you than the gulls.' In mock anger, she shook her fist towards them as they wheeled over their heads. 'Varmints. Scavenging varmints.' She smiled and when she did her whole face changed. 'A book I had when I was a kid. They were always stealing the lighthouse keeper's lunch. That's what he called them, varmints.'

Still smiling a little, she unscrewed the top of the Thermos and Elder held the cup while she poured.

She helped her father first, tilting back his head a little and catching the liquid that ran back from his mouth with a paper towel.

431

They sat beside the wheelchair, eating their sandwiches, staring out to sea.

'When I first came it was fine. I finished school, got on really well. And Dad was great, like a friend, a pal. The other girls, they were all jealous: I wish I had a dad like yours. Then after college I got this job with a children's theatre company, doing a bit of everything. It was great. The sort of thing I'd always wanted. We used to go off sometimes, little tours. It was when we were down in Christchurch Dad had his first stroke. He was in hospital when I got back. Not too serious, the doctor said. He'd have to be careful, you know, but most of the use of his limbs had come back. And he could talk, there wasn't anything wrong with his mind, he . . .'

She set down the cup and for a moment closed her eyes.

'He couldn't really work, not any more, but that didn't matter, we managed. And then three years ago he had another massive stroke. After that he needed someone to look after him all the time and it was easier for me just to pack up work. He can't . . . he can't really do anything for himself. Not now.'

Reaching across, she squeezed her father's hand.

'It would have made more sense if we'd stayed in Karori where we were, but he'd always loved it out here. It was one of the first places he brought me when I first arrived. There weren't so many houses back then. It was wild. When I'm dead, he'd say, this is where I want my ashes scattered, here along the beach.'

Standing, she threw the remains of a sandwich down towards one of the gulls and watched the others swarm and call around it.

432

'We ought to be setting off back, I don't want Dad to catch a chill.'

Outside the house they shook hands.

'You won't mind if I don't ask you in?'

Elder shook his head.

'Will you see my mother when you get back?'

'I expect so, yes.'

'Tell her I'm sorry.'

'Yes.'

'Tell her she should have told the truth.'

Elder thought he might not tell her that.

'If things change,' he said, 'do you think you might come back to England?'

'No. I don't think so.'

'Okay.' Elder turned and, hands in pockets, set off back the way he'd come. With any luck he wouldn't have to wait too long for a train. He was trying to imagine what Susan Blacklock's life was like now, knowing without fully understanding why she'd come, why she'd stayed. He saw her patiently unfastening her father's clothes and easing them past his feet and hands, beginning to sponge his sallow skin . . .

In the event one train was cancelled, another delayed. Back outside the café, he opened the book of stories, half a mind to pass it on to Katherine when he was home. She and the writer, namesakes after all. But the stories were too depressing, he realised, too many lives left unful-filled. He would buy her something at the airport instead. When he got up to go he left the book beside his empty cup.

53

On the seventh day of Christmas and still on remand, Shane Donald gouged a piece out of his arm with a rusted edge of razor blade. After a visit to the hospital and two sessions with the prison psychologist, he was transferred to the secure wing under Rule 43. Vulnerable prisoners like himself.

In Association, free to mill around under the officers' eyes before being locked down, one of the prisoners pushed a scrap of paper into Donald's hand and walked on.

The writing was scribbled and fast.

'Merry Christmas, sweetheart! I'll make sure to give your love to Alan next time he calls. Though what he saw in you fuck knows!'

The paper nearly slipped between Donald's fingers. He read the note again and then once more.

It didn't take him long to pick out Adam Keach through the slow back and forth of other prisoners, alone near the far wall, mocking smile on his face.

Donald shivered, screwed up the piece of paper tight and put it in his mouth, chewed it up and spat it out.

'You all right, son?' one of the officers said.

Donald nodded and moved on.

When he looked again, Keach smiled and blew him a kiss.

◆

Winter became spring. This time Katherine took the train, no argument, and Elder met her at the station in Penzance, driving back across the peninsula by the narrowest of lanes. The following day she felt strong enough to walk along the coast path into St Ives and then back across the fields. If everything went according to plan, she would start some light training when she returned to Nottingham.

That evening Elder suggested dinner in the pub where they had eaten before, but Katherine had wanted to cook. She had shopped in St. Ives for that purpose. Happily, Elder opened a bottle of wine while the kitchen filled with the sweet, sharp smell of onions and garlic softening in the pan, music playing from the radio in another room. Elder laid the table and they sat down to pasta with spinach and blue cheese, some good bread, a salad of cos lettuce and rocket and small tomatoes.

Katherine watched her father take one mouthful, winding the spaghetti on to his fork with care, and then a second.

'Well?'

'Well what?'

'You know damn well.'

'It's lovely.' Laughing. 'Really tasty.'

'You're sure?'

'Sure.'

435

They had agreed not to talk about what had happened and, in truth, Elder was relieved. I can do all that with my shrink, Katherine had said, it's what she's paid for after all. Since Christmas the sessions had been pulled back to once a week.

Katherine collected up the plates. 'Is it warm enough to sit outside?'

'Just.'

There was a violet light in the sky, the last vestiges of sun leaking into the far edge of sea. They sat with collars up, glasses of wine in their hands.

'Can I ask you something?' Katherine said.

'Ask away.' He thought it would be about her mother, but he was wrong.

'That woman you were seeing, Helen – you don't see her any more.'

'No.'

'Why not?'

The taste of wine was ripe in his mouth, blackcurranty. He had driven up to Whitby almost as soon as he'd arrived back in England. Promises to keep and at last that promise could be fulfilled. Helen's daughter, he had found her. Wasn't that what he'd sworn to do?

Sitting there in that small, cluttered room, he had watched Helen's face as he described what he had found, skin tightening over bone. Watched her expression as she unfolded the sheet of paper on which he had written Susan's address. What had he expected? Tears of joy? Relief? Instead she had stared at the floor and whatever she had felt she had clutched it to herself.

When, later, he had tried to hold her, she had pulled back from his touch.

436

Her daughter's desertion building a wall between them, brick by brick.

'I don't know,' he said now. 'One of those things.'

Katherine nodded. 'A shame. That time she came to the hospital, I thought she was nice.'

Helen still walked out from time to time, Elder knew, along the cliff path to Saltwick Nab and left flowers at the spot where Susan had disappeared. As if she had not been found; as if she'd died. He didn't know if she had written to her daughter, if she ever would.

'The trial,' Katherine began.

'There's still a chance it might not come to that.'

'What do you mean?'

'He could still plead guilty.'

'Why would he do that?'

'A lighter sentence. If he pleads not guilty and the verdict goes against him, the judge will come down hard.'

'And do you think that's what he'll do?'

'I should think that's what his brief will be telling him to do.'

Katherine fiddled with a strand of hair. 'If he doesn't, though; if I do have to give evidence, promise me you won't be there. In court.'

'Kate . . .'

'Promise me.'

'All right.'

That night, Elder was awoken by the sound of his daughter's screams and when he pushed open the door to her room, she was sitting up in bed, the covers strewn around her, sweat like beads of marble on her cheeks and brow. Her eyes were closed tight as if something sharp was slicing deep into her skull.

437

'Katie . . . Kate . . .'

When she opened her eyes she saw nothing: blinded by the memory of the pain.

'Katherine . . .'

Carefully, Elder took hold of both her hands and spoke her name again and then she saw him and let herself fall back against the pillows. He fetched a towel and wiped her face and sat with her a while longer, not speaking, then when he thought it was all right to do so, went downstairs and made tea while she changed her clothes, sweat pants and a clean T-shirt.

'How long have you been having them?' Elder asked. 'The dreams.'

'Ever since it happened. Since you found me.'

The same moment, Elder thought, that my dream was broken. Disappeared.

'How often?' he asked.

She looked back at him with a wan smile. 'Often enough.'

He poured more tea into her cup, added milk and sugar, stirred.

'Those huts,' Katherine said, 'on the beach – were there cats?'

'Yes. A few. Wild, I suppose.'

'I wasn't sure if they were real or part, you know, of the dream.'

'No, they were real enough.'

'You remember when I was a kid I always wanted one, a kitten?'

'I remember.'

'I must have driven you and Mum crazy.'

'Your mother was allergic.'

'I thought that was just to you.'

'Very funny.'

Katherine laughed, then shook her head. 'She's miserable, you know.'

'She'll get over it. Find someone else, I'd not be surprised.'

'You think so.'

'I don't see why not.'

'Or Martyn will come crawling back.'

'Probably.'

'You don't care, do you?'

'I don't want her to be unhappy.'

'I think,' Katherine said, 'I'll go back up to bed.'

'Okay. I'll just rinse these cups.'

Near the top of the stairs, Katherine stopped and called back down. 'These dreams, they will go, won't they? I mean, with time.'

'Yes.' He looked up at her from below. 'Yes, I'm sure they will.'

'Yours did, after all.'

'Yes, mine did.'

She smiled. 'Good-night, Dad.'

'Good-night, love. Sleep well.'

'You too.'

He waited till he heard the door click before going back into the kitchen. There was an almost new bottle of Jameson's in the cupboard and he poured generously into a glass. It was not so far short of four by the clock. Outside it was still dark and he had to stand there for some while before he could make out the edge of stone wall, the shapes of cattle in the field. If he stood there long enough it would begin to get light.

Acknowledgements

Everyone needs a helping hand and in the writing of this novel I've gratefully grasped more than a few.

My special thanks are due to my agent, Sarah Lutyens, and to Andy McKillop, Susan Sandon and Justine Taylor at Random House (UK); to Detective Superintendent Peter Coles (retired) and Caroline Smith, Senior Development Co-ordinator for UK Athletics; to Michael O'Leary, proprietor of the Pukapuka Bookshop in Paekakariki and other friends in New Zealand; to Sarah Boiling and, most especially, to my friend and adviser, Graham Nicholls.

*Available soon in William Heinemann
John Harvey's stunning new novel featuring retired
Detective Inspector Frank Elder*

Ash and Bone

Detective Sergeant Maddy Birch will never see thirty again. Nor forty. A lifetime on the force and all she has to show for it is a few hundred pounds in the bank and a mortgaged flat in Highgate Borders. When the take down of a violent criminal goes badly wrong leaving both the target and a young constable dead, something doesn't feel right to Maddy. And her uneasiness is only compounded when she starts to believe someone is following her home.

In Cornwall retired Detective Inspector Elder's solitary life is disturbed by a phone call from his estranged wife Joanne. Seventeen-year-old Katherine is running wild. Elder's fears for his daughter are underscored by remorse and guilt for it was his involvement that led directly to the abduction and rape that has so unbalanced Katherine's' life.

Maddy and Elder have a connection. A brief, clumsy encounter sixteen years earlier. Just a quick grope and a cuddle, leading to nothing, but leaving a trace of lingering regret.

In *Ash and Bone* the unsettled, unhappy Elder is once again persuaded out of retirement. A cold, cold case has a devastating present day impact with sinister implications for the crime squad itself. Elder's investigation takes place against the backdrop of his increasing concern for his daughter and he must battle his own demons before he can uncover the truth.

Read on for an exclusive extract . . .

1

Maddy Birch would never see thirty again. Nor forty either. Stepping back from the mirror, she scowled at the wrinkles that were beginning to show at the edges of her mouth and the corners of her eyes; the grey infiltrating her otherwise dark brown, almost chestnut hair. Next birthday she would be forty-four. Forty-four and a detective sergeant attached to SO7, Serious and Organised Crime. A few hundred in the bank and a mortgaged flat in the part of Upper Holloway that North London estate agents got away with calling Highgate Borders. Not a lot to show for half a lifetime on the force. Wrinkles aside.

Slipping a scarlet band from her pocket, she pulled her hair sharply back and twisted the band into place. Taking a step away, she glanced quickly down at her boots and the front of her jeans, secured the velcro straps of her bullet-proof vest, gave the pony tail a final tug and walked back into the main room.

To accommodate all the personnel involved, the briefing had been held in the hall of an abandoned school, Detective Superintendent George Mallory, in charge of the operation, addressing the troops from the small stage

on which head teachers since Victorian times had, each autumn, admonished generations of small children to plough the fields and scatter. The fields, that would be, of Green Lanes and Finsbury Park.

Climbing frames, worn and filmed with grey dust, were still attached to the walls. New flip charts, freshly marked in bright colours, stood at either side of a now blank screen. Officers from the tactical firearms unit, SO19, stood in clusters of three or four, heads down, or sat at trestle tables, mostly silent, with Maddy's new colleagues from Serious Crime. She had been with her particular unit three weeks and two days.

Moving alongside Maddy, Paul Draper gestured towards the watch on his wrist. Ten minutes shy of half-five. 'Waiting. Worst bloody time.'

Maddy nodded.

Draper was a young DC who'd moved down from Manchester a month before, a wife and kid and still not twenty five; he and Maddy had reported for duty at Hendon on the same day.

'Why the hell can't we get on with it?'

Maddy nodded again.

The hall was thick with the smell of sweat and after-shave and the oil that clung to recently cleaned 9mm Brownings, Glock semi-automatic pistols, Heckler and Koch MP5 carbines. Though she'd taken the firearms training course at Lippetts Hill, Maddy herself, like roughly half the officers present, was unarmed.

'All this for one bloke,' Draper said.

This time Maddy didn't even bother to nod. She could sense the fear coming off Draper's body, read it in his eyes.

444

From his position near the door, the superintendent cast an eye across the hall then spoke to Maurice Repton, his DCI.

Repton smiled and checked his watch. 'All right, gentlemen,' he said. 'And ladies. Let's nail the bastard.'

Outside, the light was just beginning to clear.

Maddy found herself sitting across from Draper inside the transit, their knees almost touching. To her right sat an officer from SO19, ginger moustache curling round his reddish mouth; whenever she looked away, Maddy could feel his eyes following her. When the van went too fast over a speed bump and he jolted against her, his hand, for an instant, rested on her thigh. 'Sorry,' he said and grinned.

Maddy stared straight ahead and for several minutes closed her eyes, willing the image of their target to reappear as it had on the screen. James William Grant. Born, Hainault, Essex, October twentieth, 1952. Not so far then, Maddy thought, off his fifty-second birthday. Birthdays were on her mind.

Armed robbery, money laundering, drug dealing, extortion, conspiracy to murder, more than a dozen arrests and only one conviction: Grant had been a target for years. Phone taps, surveillance, the meticulous unravelling of his financial dealings, here and abroad. The closer they got, the more likely it was that Grant would catch wind and flee somewhere the extradition laws rendered him virtually untouchable.

'It's time we took this one down,' Mallory had said at the end of his briefing. 'Way past time.'

Five years before, an associate of Grant's, ambitious

enough to try and freelance some Colombian cocaine conveniently mislaid between Amsterdam and the Sussex coast, had been shot dead at the traffic lights midway along Pentonville Road, smack in the middle of the London rush hour. After a trial lasting seven weeks and costing three quarters of a million pounds, one of Grant's lieutenants had eventually been convicted of the killing, while Grant himself had slipped away scott free.

'What d'you think?' Paul Draper asked, leaning forward. 'You think he'll be there? Grant?'

Maddy shrugged her head.

'He fuckin' better be,' the Firearms officer said, touching the barrel of his carbine much as earlier he had touched Maddy's leg. 'Feather in our fuckin' cap, landing a bastard like him.' He grinned. 'All I hope is he don't bottle out and give it up, come walking out with his hands behind his fuckin' head.'

As the transit veered left off Liverpool Road, someone towards the rear of the van started humming tunelessly; heads turned sharply in his direction and he ceased as abruptly as he'd begun. Sweat gathered in the palms of Maddy's hands.

'There pretty soon,' Draper said to nobody in particular. 'Got to be.'

Conscious that the man next to her was staring more openly, Maddy turned to face him. 'What?' she said. 'What?'

The man looked away.

Once, after a successful operation in Lincoln, her old patch, a good result, she and this officer who'd been eyeing her all evening had ended up with a quick grope and cuddle in a doorway. His hand on her breast. What in

446

God's name had made her think about that now?

'We're getting close,' the driver said over his shoulder.

One side of York Way was derelict, half-hidden behind blackened walls and wire fencing; on the other, old warehouses and small factories were in the process of being converted into loft apartments. Underground parking, twenty-four hour portering, fifteen-year-old prostitutes with festering sores down their legs and arms a convenient ten minute stroll away.

From the front the building seemed little changed, a high-arched wooden door held fast with double padlock and chain, its paint work blistered and chipped. Small windows whose cobwebbed glass was barred across. Maddy knew from the briefing the guts of the place had already been torn out and restoration was well in hand. A light showed dimly behind one of the windows on the upper floor.

Either side of her, armed officers in black overalls, the single word *Police* picked out in white at the front of their vests, were moving silently into position.

No sweat in her palms now and her throat was dry.

'You bastard!' Laughing.

'What?'

'You know.'

'No. What?'

Wary, Vicki walked over to where Grant was stretched out on the bed, cotton sheet folded back below his waist. For a man of his years, she thought, and not for the first time, he was in good shape. Trim. Lithe. He worked out. And when he'd grabbed her just now, fingers tightening about her wrist, it had been like being locked into a vice.

'C'mere a minute,' he said. 'Come on.' A smile snaking across his face. 'Not gonna do anythin' am I? So soon after the last time. My age.'

She knew he was lying, of course, but complied. Vicki standing there in a tight white t-shirt and silver thong, the t-shirt finishing well above the platinum ring in her navel. What else was it about but this?

When she'd first met him, a month or so before, it had been at the Motor Show, Birmingham. Vicki not wearing a whole lot more than she was now, truth be told, a couple of hundred quid a day to draw attention to the virtues of a 3.2 litre direct injection diesel engine, climate control and all-leather interior.

He'd practically bought the vehicle out from under her and later screwed her on the back seat in a lay-by off the A6. 'Christen the upholstery,' he'd said with a wink, tucking a couple of fifty pound notes down inside her dress. She'd balled them up and thrown them back in his face. He'd paid more attention to her after that.

'I've got this place in London,' he'd said. 'Why don't you come and stay for a bit.'

'A bit of what?'

The first time he'd seen her naked it had stopped him in his tracks: he'd had more beautiful women before but none with buttocks so round and tight and high.

'Jesus!' he'd said.

'What?'

'You've got a gorgeous arse.'

She'd laughed. 'Just don't think you're getting any of it, that's all.'

'We'll see about that,' he'd said.

Fingers resting lightly just below her hips, he'd planted

a careful kiss in the small of her back. 'Who was it?' he'd said, hands sliding down. 'Pushed in his thumb and pulled out a plum? Little Jack Horner? Little Tommy Tucker?'

After that he took her face down on the polished wood floor, bruises on her knees and breasts that smelled of linseed oil.

'Will, don't,' she said now, shaking herself free. 'Not now. I have to go and pee.'

'What's wrong with here?' Pointing at his chest.

'Over you, you mean?'

'Why not? Wouldn't be the first time.'

'You're disgusting.'

'You don't know the half of it.' He reached for her but she skipped away.

'Don't be long,' he said, leaning back against the pillows and watching her as she walked towards the door.

There was access from a courtyard at the rear, stairs leading past three balconies to the upper floor. The loft apartment where Grant lived was entered through double doors, a single emergency exit leading to a fire escape at the furthest end.

Draper close behind her, Maddy turned a corner into the courtyard and flattened herself against the wall. Weapons angled upwards, armed officers were in position at the corners of the square, others scurrying towards the first and second balconies, and she waited for the signal to proceed. When it came, moments later, she sprinted for the stairs.

The walls were exposed brick, furnishings tasteful and sparse. Shifting his position, Grant poured himself

another glass of wine. Dusty was still in the CD player and he clicked the remote.

'Why do you listen to that old stuff?' Vicki asked from the far end of the room.

'Greatest white soul singer ever was,' Grant said.

'History,' Vicki replied.

Grant grinned. 'Like me you mean?'

'If you like.'

One knee on the bed, she ran her fingers up through the greying hairs on his chest and, reaching up, he kissed her on the mouth.

At the head of the stairs, Maddy waited, catching her breath, Draper on the landing below. The outer door to Grant's apartment was in clear sight. Mallory appeared level with Draper and then went on past. There was armament everywhere.

'After a little glory?' the superintendent whispered in Maddy's ear.

'No, sir.'

He smiled and there were mint and garlic on his breath. 'Second fiddle this time, Birch. Sweeping up the odds and ends.'

'Yes, sir.'

'You and your pal Draper. Down a floor. Just in case.'

Mallory moved on towards the door, Repton at his back, two officers wielding sledgehammers in their wake.

Volume high, the interior of the loft pulsated with sound: french horn, strings, piano, and then the voice. Unmistakable.

Vicki reached down and touched Grant's face, straddling him. Arching his back, eyes closed, Grant found her nipples with his finger tips.

Dusty swooped and soared and swooped again.

At the first crash, Grant swung Vicki on to her side and sprang clear, one hand clawing at a pair of chinos alongside the bed, the other reaching past Vicki's head.

The outer door splintered inwards off its hinges.

Fear flooded Vicki's face and she began to scream.

The pistol was tight in Grant's grasp as he turned away.

From the landing below, Maddy heard music, shouts, feet moving fast across bare boards, the slamming of doors.

'What the fuck?' Draper said.

'Move,' Maddy said, pushing him aside. 'Now.'

Positioned on the balcony opposite, one of the police marksmen had Grant in his sights for several seconds, a clear shot through plate glass as he raced down the emergency stairs, but without the order to fire the moment passed and Grant was lost to sight.

'In here,' Maddy said, kicking open the door and ducking low.

Draper followed, swerving left.

Maddy could feel the blood jolting through her veins, her heart pumping fast against her ribs. The room they were in ran the length of the building, iron supports strategically placed floor to ceiling. Some of the floor boards had been removed prior to being replaced. Building materials were stacked against the back wall, work begun and then abandoned. Low level light seeped through windows smeared with grease and dust.

Maddy reached for the switch to her left with no result.

451

Voices from the stairs, urgent and loud, descending; more shouts, muffled, from the courtyard outside.

'Come on,' Draper said. 'Let's go.'

Maddy was almost through the door when she stopped, alerted by the smallest of sounds. She swung back into the room as Grant eased open the door at the far end and stepped through. Bare-chested, barefoot, pistol held down at his side.

Maddy's voice wedged, immovable, in her throat.

'Police,' Draper shouted. 'Put your weapon on the ground now.'

She would wonder afterwards if Grant had truly smiled as he raised his gun and fired.

Draper collapsed back through the doorway, clutching his neck. Instinctively, Maddy turned towards him and, as she did so, Grant ran forward, jumping through a gap in the boards to the floor below. With barely a moment's hesitation she raced after him; when she braced herself, legs hanging through a gap a metre wide, the boards on either side gave way and she was down.

Grant had landed badly, twisting his ankle, and was scrabbling, crab-like, across the floor, seeking the pistol that had been jarred from his grasp. A 9mm Beretta, hard up against the wall. As he pushed himself up and hopped towards it, Maddy launched herself at him, one hand seizing his ankle and bringing him down. Flailing, his hand struck the squared-off butt of the pistol and sent it spinning beyond reach.

'Bitch!'

He kicked out at her and she stumbled back.

'Fucking bitch!'

452

Grant was on his feet and moving towards her. No smiling now.

Maddy heard movement behind and then the sound of a weapon being discharged close to her ear. Once and then once again. As she watched, Grant skidded backwards then crumpled to his knees, his face all but disappeared in a welter of blood.

'Text book,' Mallory said softly. 'Head and heart.'

Maddy's skin was cold; her body shook.

'You or him, of course. Didn't give me any choice.'

Vomit caught in the back of Maddy's throat. Her eyes fastened on Grant's pistol, still some metres away across the floor.

The superintendent bent low towards the body. 'Ambulance, I dare say. Not that it'll do a scrap of good. He's bleeding out.'

When he stood up, a second weapon, a .22 Derringer, was close by Grant's inturned leg, small enough to hide inside a fist. Now you see it, now you don't. No matter how many times Maddy would run it through in her mind, she would never be sure.

'Trouser pocket,' Mallory was saying conversationally. 'Small of the back.' He shrugged. 'There'll be an enquiry, routine.' His hand on her shoulder was light, almost no pressure at all. 'You'll be a good witness, I know.'

Armed officers were standing at both doors, weapons angled towards the ground.

Lonely Hearts

John Harvey

'Harvey reminds me of Graham Greene – a stylist who tells you everything you need to know while keeping the prose clean and simple'
Elmore Leonard

Shirley Peters is dead. Murdered. Her body is found twelve hours later in her own home. Just one of the many sordid domestic crimes hitting the city.

Tony Macliesch, her rejected boyfriend, is the obvious prime suspect and he's just been picked off the Aberdeen train and put straight into custody.

But then another woman is sexually abused and throttled to death. And suddenly there seems to be one too many connections between these seemingly unrelated crimes.

Because Detective Inspector Resnick is sure that the two murders are the work of one sadistic killer – two lonely hearts broken by one maniac. And it's up to Resnick to put the record straight – and put the bastard where he belongs.

'Crime fiction that . . . gets at something deeper – the sometimes rancid, always pungent smell of real life'
Booklist

arrow books

"Yes, Mr. Brandon-Dumaine?"

"She told me to trust and believe."

"And did you?"

He nodded.

"We'll cherish this forever," Haley said fingering the quilt.

"Not nearly as much as I cherish you."

And then he kissed her.

* * * * *

Dear Reader,

Thank you for reading *Sweet Accord*. I hope you were in some way blessed by Matt and Haley's story. I've wanted to write it for some time.

This is my first Love Inspired novel. It's set in Oregon because I fell in love with that part of the country during several trips there. If I've made any errors, blame it on my head and not my heart. The town of Wayside and its history are fictional, but the details about the settlers who came to the Northwest following the Lewis and Clarke Expedition are true.

I hope to return to Wayside, and I hope you'll take the trip with me. In the meantime, the next time you listen to Christian radio or a CD, I hope Matt and Haley will come to mind.

If you'd like to write, I'd love to hear from you. I can be reached at P.O. Box 1438, Dept. LI, Yorktown, VA 23692.

Blessings to you,